D1053010

Celestina

Celestina

FERNANDO DE ROJAS

TRANSLATED FROM THE SPANISH BY

MARGARET SAYERS PEDEN

EDITED AND WITH AN INTRODUCTION BY

ROBERTO GONZÁLEZ ECHEVARRÍA

YALE UNIVERSITY PRESS ■ NEW HAVEN & LONDON

A MARGELLOS
WORLD REPUBLIC OF LETTERS BOOK

Published with assistance from the Mary Cady Tew Memorial Fund.

The Margellos World Republic of Letters is dedicated to making literary works from around the globe available in English through translation. It brings to the English-speaking world the work of leading poets, novelists, essayists, philosophers, and playwrights from Europe, Latin America, Africa, Asia, and the Middle East to stimulate international discourse and creative exchange.

Copyright © 2009 by Yale University.
All rights reserved.
This book may not be reproduced, in whole or in part, including illustrations, in any form (beyond that copying permitted by Sections 107 and 108 of the U.S. Copyright Law and except by reviewers for the public press), without written permission from the publishers.

Set in Electra and Nobel types by Keystone Typesetting, Inc.
Printed in the United States of America.

Woodcuts reproduced from *Celestina* printing in 1534 by Venetian master printer Estephano da Sabio (Beinecke Rare Book and Manuscript Library, Yale University)

p. 248: Spain postage stamp from 1998 depicting "La Celestina" (Reproduced with permission of Correos)

Library of Congress Cataloging-in-Publication Data
Rojas, Fernando de, d. 1541.
[Celestina. English]
Celestina / Fernando de Rojas; translated from the Spanish by Margaret Sayers Peden; edited and with an introduction by Roberto González Echevarría.
p. cm.—(Margellos world republic of letters)
Includes bibliographical references.
ISBN 978-0-300-14198-6 (hardcover: alk. paper)
1. Tragicomedy. I. Peden, Margaret Sayers. II. González Echevarría, Roberto. III. Title.
PQ6427.E56 2009
862'.2—dc22   2009008381

A catalogue record for this book is available from the British Library.

This paper meets the requirements of ANSI/NISO Z39.48-1992 (Permanence of Paper).

10 9 8 7 6 5 4 3 2 1

CONTENTS

The *Celestina*. For me the ultimate challenge. Years ago, when I was still teaching, I formulated a "wheel of difficulty," a pie chart with labeled sections progressing from least to most troublesome. One of the most difficult sectors was that of period. Period in the sense of time, elapsed time. How can one enter the atmosphere of 1500, the ambiance of Fernando de Rojas's early sixteenth century Salamanca, how to set this in an English that will evoke the era? How can one penetrate the mind and feelings and fears and ecstasies of an individual who lived then? How closely did words reflect those realities? One's first thought might be that words had not as yet endured the assaults of additional centuries. But with more thought we might consider two words crucial to Celestina's world: honor and love. The codes of that time are very clear. Honor is central to the society. A man must challenge and resolve offenses to his honor. Women must retain their purity, which is their honor— fortunately for Celestina, a great part of whose livelihood derived from stitching up rent maidenheads. Yet conversations among Celestina's "daughters" remind us that honor had little import to them. And as for love, we find among that class the infatuations, deceits, and calculations that are familiar to us today. Areúsa and Elicia complain of their inability to pursue their emotions openly; they are jealous of the aristocratic Melibea's privileges and that she is gifted with a fine suitor who "honors" her being and showers her with "love." Even in a period that seems so remote to us today, words had, like an amoeba, already spread out from their central core, their true meaning diffused in a surrounding nebulous cloud of interpretations and perceptions. Though the composition of Rojas's society differs greatly from many of the world's societies today, we are familiar with its class prejudices and struggles. When reading of the wide divisions in financial status among the classes, as mentioned by González Echevarría in his introduction, we cannot but be reminded of the similarity to the divisions that permeated the political rhetoric of the second presidential race of this new century in the United States. So the translator is faced with the differences and similarities between that society and ours, just as we recognize the range of definitions and perceptions in lexicon between the two periods.

So if we decide that some aspects of the *Celestina* are relatively modern while some remain markedly sixteenth century, how does that affect the rhetorical level of the translation? Is it best presented in contemporary language? That is something I considered carefully. The advantage would be a much more accessible text, a book that sounds familiar to the ear of a contemporary reader. I decided, however, that I did not want to take that approach, that I wanted what appears on the English language page to be as close as possible to the original Spanish, whether the content be unique to that period or applicable to the course of human history. That cannot, of course, be achieved, but I wanted to change as little as possible the tone of the original, which would be the inevitable effect in creating a more readable version. Despite some apprehension, I chose, for instance, to maintain all the series of laments—"O dear Melibea!" "O such a wretch am I!"—as annoying as they may sound today, and despite that other translators chose to eliminate them. My argument is that one would not take a surrealist work and pull out the figures and features that allow us to tag it for what it is. The people in Celestina's world felt, thought, and spoke as they did. In the same vein I did not transpose curses to present-day equivalents. Our common four-letter, excremental, animal, genital curses did not exist in that period. Curses were largely blasphemous, or addressed to intelligence and character. So that was my choice. I consciously changed—I regret any changes I made *un*knowingly—very little, but one was the indication of laughter: "Ha! Ha! Ha!" and "Hee! Hee! Hee!" Apologies for this, but those are sounds I dislike and so substituted "He laughs." In some places I bypassed maxims or proverbs for which we have a good equivalent in order to enjoy the jolt of a new sound to an old saying. For example, I left "Zamora was not built in a day," the literal translation. And I did not yield to contractions. I know that this lends a kind of formality to the text, even possible awkwardness at times, but it is my feeling that contractions and elisions pull the translation toward modern times. These are the sorts of conclusions one reaches every day, choices one must make. How to? How to? We weigh and choose, consider, reject, and hope for a uniform result.

I am very grateful for previous translations of the *Celestina*. They are *The Celestina*, translated by Lesley Byrd Simpson and published by University of California Press, 1955; *Celestina*, Mack Hendricks Singleton, University of Wisconsin Press, 1958; and *The Spanish Bawd*, J. M. Cohen, Penguin Classics, 1964. I appreciate their work greatly even though I did not always agree with their translations. Not surprising, for the *Celestina* is a difficult book. It is always extremely interesting to compare translations. There are usually a few scattered lines that the translators have "read" in exactly the same way. (Those are very reassuring to the translator comparing her version with earlier ones.) More frequently, however, one discovers parts where versions vary greatly. That will always be the case. In placing a number of monkeys (not the infinite simian) in a room, each with a computer (not the more limited typewriter), might one emerge with the perfect translation? That is doubtful. Having taught translation over the years, I have, as an example, found that students, and friends who made the experiment, have never produced identical translations of the opening paragraph of Jorge Luis Borges's "Las ruinas circulares," "The Circular Ruins." In fact, the incredible variety within a single sentence can reach astounding degrees. And certainly that is true of the *Celestina*. We who have attempted a translation often disagree in both meaning and expression. I believe nevertheless that there *is* a perfect translation, and that it lies among the lines of all the versions produced by diligent and sincere "readers."

I also want to give warmest thanks to Roberto González Echevarría, who invited me to undertake a translation of *La Celestina*, and without whose help and encouragement this one would not exist.

Margaret Sayers Peden

ACKNOWLEDGMENTS

Working with Margaret Sayers Peden has been a pleasure and an honor. She is today the most accomplished active translator of Spanish-language literature into English. There is something magical about how "Petch," as she is known to her friends, turns herself into writers as diverse as Sor Juana Inés de la Cruz and Isabel Allende, and, in this case, Fernando de Rojas. I cannot presume to know the secret, but I believe that at least part of it is her rich and resonant Southern English, which has something Faulknerian about it. But, deeply, the strength of her work is due to a love of literature that shows through her compelling renderings of Spanish texts. Petch had done some translations for my *Oxford Book of Latin American Short Stories*, but working with her on *Celestina* has been a more sustained, intimate, and thrilling experience. I hope that the aesthetic delight that we have shared will be conveyed to the reader of this book.

I want to thank those absent or distant friends whom I heard with my eyes, to echo Quevedo; the distinguished scholars and critics from whose published works I have profited more than I myself probably know: Marcel Bataillon, A. D. Deyermond, Peter N. Dunn, Otis H. Green, Javier Herrero, Ian Michael, Peter E. Russell, Stephen Gilman, and Dorothy S. Severin. My current doctoral student William H. Hinrichs was kind enough to share with me his exciting work-in-progress. I have also learned much from the students in my graduate seminar on "The Picaresque and the Spanish Origins of Realism and the Novel."

I have as usual had the scholarly and affectionate assistance of my esteemed and distinguished colleague Rolena Adorno, whose unwavering high standards and rigorous editing improve my work in more ways than I can say. Charlotte Rogers, research assistant, student, and treasured friend, has assisted me in many ways, from tracking down elusive bibliographical items to easing my relationship with the labyrinthine electronic world. Isabel, my devoted wife, read my introduction with an eye for traces of my native Spanish and turgid turns of phrase. Jonathan Brent, my editor and friend, kept a loose leash on me as I labored and dawdled.

RGE

INTRODUCTION

Published in 1499, *Celestina* is as fresh and relevant a work of fiction as if it had been written today. Its most scandalous innovation is that its protagonist is an old whore and procuress who runs a brothel, restores virgins, arranges for clandestine sexual encounters, and corrupts young men and women. Yet, for all these unsavory characteristics and immoral activities, Celestina is a self-possessed, willful, and courageous character whom the reader cannot but admire. She is a modern tragic heroine, perhaps the first, and surely the only one whose misfortunes are not the result of a love affair of her own. Though Celestina often says and does humorous things, she is not a comical character, as could be expected of such a figure in the period, and the work has none of the farcical elements typical of the portrayal of lower-class people in the classical, medieval, and early modern periods. *Celestina* is a serious, somber work, blending tragic and comic elements in ways never achieved before, and hardly accomplished ever since. The work anticipates Cervantes and Shakespeare, and it picks up the legacies of Dante, Boccaccio, and Chaucer as renovators of the classics in the transition from the Middle Ages to the Renaissance. With the possible exception of *King Lear*, in none of the works by those giants of Western literature is there a more pessimistic yet compelling picture of humankind. It was Cervantes who most clearly saw this, and he expressed it in a lapidary phrase that says it all: "*Celestina*, would be a divine work, had it only concealed a bit more the human."

Celestina is a masterpiece of Spanish literature that appeared during the reign of the Catholic Kings, Ferdinand and Isabella. It is recognized by scholars and critics as being second only to the *Quijote* as a work of prose fiction in the Spanish language. Written in dialogue form and divided into acts as if it had been intended for the stage, which it was not, *Celestina* is pitiless in its depiction of human weaknesses, particularly those related to love. It is so explicit in this respect that it sometimes strays into outright obscenity and even pornography. For this reason it is the most repressed classic in Spanish, and its circulation abroad has been limited. Like most masterworks in Spanish, *Celestina* hardly figures in what is now commonly called the Western Canon, following Harold Bloom's popular book. It is too disturbing, lacks a noteworthy author to exalt, adheres to no known genre, and has not been promoted by Spain as a national treasure, as has the *Quijote*, whose two famous protagonists have merited statues at the Plaza de España, in Madrid. There are "Cervantes Institutes" all over the world, but one could hardly conceive of a Celestina Institute, or imagine the likeness of the old bawd gracing a square in the Spanish capital.

The story begins with a conventional courtly love situation: Calisto is struck sick with amorous passion for Melibea, whom he idealizes and who appears unreachable to him. A young nobleman, he falls frenetically in love after meeting her by chance in her garden, which he happened to enter while chasing his falcon. Calisto pines madly for Melibea in the courtly fashion, as if she were completely inaccessible, though they are both from the upper classes and no ostensible impediment to their marriage stands between them. He acts as if insane, or as if playing a literary role: that of the mad courtly lover. But this hackneyed beginning is quickly left behind when Calisto's servant Sempronio tells him to quit moaning and seek the services of Celestina, a well-known procuress. She is an old prostitute and madam who propitiates amorous encounters, sews up rent hymens to pass off women who have transgressed as virgins fit for marriage, or young whores as innocent maidens for the delight of well-paying customers (often powerful men, including those in the church).

Celestina, who quickly becomes the protagonist of the work, accepts the commission and makes an alliance with Sempronio and Pármeno, Calisto's other servant, whom she convinces to betray his master and help her fleece him for the benefit of all three. Her plan is to make as much material gain as possible from the affair, tactically putting off its resolution to extract the most profit. Celestina leads Calisto on, playing up the difficulties in gaining access to Melibea's household, which she does aided by Lucrecia, the young woman's maid. A secret meeting is set up in Melibea's garden, where Calisto enjoys her much sooner than he expected. Celestina, who ultimately refuses to live up to the bargain and share the rewards she received from Calisto, is stabbed to death by Sempronio and Pármeno, who are apprehended after they jump to the street from a high window, critically injuring themselves in the process, and summarily executed. Scared by ruffians in the employ of Areúsa and Elicia, two whores bent on avenging their lovers, Sempronio and Pármeno, Calisto leaps over the wall of Melibea's garden and falls to his death. Melibea, defiant in her passion for Calisto, confesses her misconduct to Pleberio, her father, and leaps off a tower to her death, leaving him to pronounce a bitter lament with which the work ends. A story that began as a typical courtly love tale ends with the violent death of all the protagonists. Indeed, a work that started as a comedy—its first title was *Comedia de Calisto y Melibea*—winds up as tragedy; in 1514 it was renamed *Tragicomedia de Calisto y Melibea*, and by 1518 its title was transformed into *La Celestina*, in recognition of its true protagonist.

Celestina is, indeed, an odd work, bristling with complicated problems concerning its genesis, textual evolution, genre, and author. More important, it is a work whose richness of detail in the development of the characters, the crisp unfolding of its plot, and the sublimity of its themes are the stuff of a masterpiece. Its protagonist deserves to be elevated to a literary myth like those of Don Quijote and especially Don Juan, which also emerged in the Spain of the Golden Age. But how can an old whore and procuress become a myth? How can her perverted sense of mission, her perseverance in immorality, and her will to live be deemed heroic enough to raise her to the realm of myth? Besides, serendipity and improvisation are the hallmarks of the origin and evolution of *Celestina*, promoted by the author himself who, in an offhand remark, said that he wrote the work during a fifteen-day vacation from law school. But who was that author and what sort of work did he intend to write? And how was *Celestina* received by the reading public? The answers to those questions fill volumes of criticism and scholarship, though the yield is meager and mixed, perhaps reflecting the work's intrinsic elusiveness.

In 1499, *Celestina* was published anonymously. In a 1500 edition, which contained expanded front matter, the author identified himself in an acrostic as Fernando de Rojas. He also stated in a "Letter to a Friend," which served as prologue, that he had found the first act already written, and simply continued the work to the end. The poem and prologue declare *Celestina* to be a *reprobatio amoris*, or warning against reckless love in the medieval tradition: an example of reprehensible behavior written to caution young lovers. In a later edition, dated 1502, the author added, besides numerous word changes as well as whole paragraphs, five new acts to the original sixteen. He inserted these between Calisto and Melibea's first meeting and the fatal one at the end—that is, between just before the end of act 14 to well into what is now act 19. This addition contains the plot against Calisto organized by Elicia and Areúsa, the lovers of the executed Sempronio and Pármeno, designed to take revenge for their demise on the young aristocrat. They engage Centurio, a thug and pimp, whom they entice to provoke a ruckus in the street outside Melibea's garden to expose her and Calisto, thus creating a scandal that would bring them dishonor. Centurio, a boastful coward, has other unsavory characters perform the deed, which tragically results in Calisto's death and Melibea's suicide.

Painstaking research revealed that Rojas, who never published another work, was, at the time *Celestina* appeared, a law student at the University of Salamanca. He was from the nearby township of Montalbán, where he was born probably in 1475 or 1476, and in around 1507 he moved to Talavera de la Reina, where he worked as a lawyer for almost forty years, rising to the position of Lord Mayor. He died in 1541. It has also been ascertained that Rojas descended from *conversos*, or new Christians who had converted from Judaism. Although much was made of this by biographical critics such as Stephen Gilman, others like Otis H. Green maintain that Rojas led a fairly humdrum life, unhindered by the authorities, adding that *Celestina* was untouched by the Inquisition until 1640, when a few lines were suppressed. But one need not attribute the bitter criticism in the work to the presumed resentment of a barely known author, when the same outlook prevailed among humanists of diverse backgrounds. The questioning of medieval certainties both in Spain and elsewhere was a general trend with implications far broader than religious strife within the Spanish Peninsula. The anguish that Gilman, who was steeped in the existentialism he absorbed from his teacher Américo Castro, projects upon Rojas is nothing but the restlessness that led to the Reformation and to a change in the intellectual climate of Europe. It owed much to major historical ruptures such as those caused by the discovery of the New World and to the scientific theories of Copernicus and, later, Galileo, as well as to socioeconomic conditions following the collapse of feudalism.

The multiple classical allusions in *Celestina*, its very form as a dialogue, its tragic turn, and the obvious Roman-comedy tone clearly show that the author was a humanist with the typical Renaissance reverence for Greek and Latin authors. His indebtedness to Petrarch also reveals the same tendency. Humanism was a strong movement during the reign of Ferdinand and Isabella, who promoted it at their court. The importance of matters of crime and punishment in *Celestina* as well as the frequent legal terms and rhetorical turns of phrase clearly show the hand of someone steeped in the law. The thin moralistic clothing of the work after the first edition has swayed only religiously committed scholars, or others blinded by an abundance of pious literature that can be construed as a relevant context, and by the predictable absence of any recognition of the allure of immorality, except for literary works such as Rojas's. In its day, *Celestina* was a best-seller, with over one hundred editions in the sixteenth century as well as second, third, and even fourth "parts" published before 1550 (which gave rise to the trend of writing sequels, as William Hinrichs demonstrates). These books were not distributed gratis by the church, but sold by lay publishers seeking profit. It is difficult to believe that the buying public took home *Celestina* and its sequels for piously edifying purposes. Rojas, who stood at the threshold between the Middle Ages and the Renaissance, dressed his work in medieval garb half in jest, half to comply with the conventional pieties of the times. But *Celestina* was hardly medieval in form or content.

A remarkable modern feature of *Celestina* is the characters' development, particularly, but not exclusively, that of its protagonist. These characters are not flat, unchanging, and lacking a past that weighs upon the present action. In the course of the work the reader learns that Celestina was once married and lived near Melibea's family, that she was widowed and had to move to a dilapidated house by the river near some tanneries (with their awful smell), that up to ten prostitutes worked for her at some point, that she was twice punished by being honeyed and feathered for witchery, and that she controlled the city from her brothel by catering to powerful men and safeguarding the secrets of the deflowered women she "fixed." There is even the faint suggestion that Celestina's fortunes declined after her husband died and that she had to make a living by developing her various skills and opening up a whorehouse, giving a socioeconomic reason for her conduct. Once in business, which she practices because she cannot "live off of air," she perseveres by dint of her will to live, to survive at any cost, in an unjust society in which the rich and powerful take advantage of the poor, as she tells Pármeno to convince him to betray his master and become her accomplice. In her dealings, Celestina has no friends; she fools or tries to fool all, which brings about her murder by Sempronio and Pármeno. She is keenly aware of the dangers present, and when about to start her approach to Melibea she hesitates, fearful that she might be killed for it. But in a dramatic soliloquy Celestina tells herself that she must persist, even at the risk of her life, not only to obtain the rewards promised by Calisto, but more poignantly to be true to herself. This is the decision of a tragic figure, willing to bring about her own downfall, to meet her fate head on.

Celestina tricks others by appealing to their weakness, mostly lust but also greed. She toys with Calisto, a willing dupe prepared to give her anything in exchange for Melibea. But her most elaborate seduction is that of Pármeno, who at first is reluctant to let Celestina ruin his master. She convinces Pármeno first by using the argument already mentioned about class injustices, but more importantly by reminding him of his past. Like the old bawd, Pármeno is a character with temporal density. Celestina recalls that Claudina, the young servant's mother, now dead, was her associate, almost a sister, that she was also a witch who had been publicly shamed; that she too was, in short, a whore and procuress. Celestina also tells Pármeno that his father, before dying, entrusted him, then a mere child, to her as well as a substantial sum that she would turn over to him at the appropriate moment. Celestina not only whets his appetite for money, but hints that he is in debt to her, and also to the legacies of his forebears. As if this were not enough, she promises him Areúsa, a whore after whom Pármeno lusts. In a magnificent scene, Celestina convinces Areúsa to receive Pármeno as she massages her belly because she has a pain in her womb that the old bawd says can be cured by more lovemaking. (This is one of the pornographic moments in the work.) Celestina does all this while the drooling Pármeno waits outside, presumably hearing the whole thing. Celestina succeeds. Areúsa, who was at first squeamish about being unfaithful to another lover, lets Pármeno in, they spend the night together, and the pact between Celestina and the young man is sealed. Pármeno, in short, is a character who changes and develops during the action of the work. He too, like Celestina, has a few moments of Hamlet-like hesitation, but decides to go forward.

Sempronio is a pedant who backs up his opinions with allusions to the classics, the Bible, and philosophy (he could have acquired this erudition by attending class with his master, but such realistic consistency was not required yet). He is also a cynic, an Iago type, full of class resentments against his master and reluctant to accept Celestina's authority. Like her, he does not trust anyone. Areúsa and Elicia are exceptional because they protest that their immorality and profession are due to need; they sell their bodies to keep from starving and to benefit from the protection of men. In the added five acts they express a touching sense of loss, abandonment, and vulnerability, now that their lovers are dead, even as they plot their ruthless revenge against Calisto. Neither is Centurio, a braggart, merely a stock character whose hilarious actions are predictable. After much boasting about his erotic feats and menacing violent actions, out of cowardice he contracts out the job the women give him. Lucrecia, Melibea's maid and accomplice, reveals compelling female jealousy for her mistress when she regales the assembled company at Celestina's house with an explicit, disparaging description of Melibea's body. She is also a reluctant voyeur when Calisto invites her to witness his deflowering of Melibea.

Calisto is the less developed of the two lovers. He acts irascibly throughout. His most telling moment comes when he learns of the dishonorable deaths of Sempronio and Pármeno and chooses to go on with his plans to see Melibea. He justifies his inaction by telling himself that, given their impetuousness, one way or another they would have eventually brought upon themselves such an end. He reveals a perverse indifference fueled by his uncontrollable desire to lie again with his beloved—they have seen each other eight times in a month, the reader learns in this most explicit of works, as he learns that they make love three times on Calisto's cape, which they have presumably spread on the ground, the night of their final and fatal encounter. Melibea surprisingly turns out to be a more complex character than Calisto. At first she appears to be an innocent young beauty corrupted by Celestina, but, during her second encounter with the bawd, Melibea discloses a burning passion for Calisto that she expresses with as much vehemence as she had when first rejecting Celestina's pleas. She is no passive courtly damsel with an ardent suitor, but a woman lusting for her lover and willing to go to any lengths to meet with him. Her best moment, however, comes at the end, when she learns of Calisto's catastrophic fall. Instead of swooning or going mad, she faces her fate with unflinching courage and determination, proclaiming her passion for him in explicit terms and telling her father the reason for her decision to jump off the tower she has climbed. Like Celestina, Melibea perseveres in her depravity, and this makes her a modern tragic heroine, even if not as developed a literary personality as the procuress.

Pleberio and Alisa, her aggrieved parents, though sketchily outlined, likewise have distinct characteristics; Pleberio in particular has a great closing moment when he delivers his moving lament over the death of Melibea. Alisa appears distracted with her anodyne affairs and does not react at first when she discovers Celestina at her house, though she eventually remembers her from when they were neighbors, and warns Melibea about her probable evil intentions. Pleberio's *planctus*, for all its clichés and conventional rhetorical flourishes, has a touching immediacy, provided by the details he furnishes about his business transactions and his efforts to provide for his family, particularly Melibea. There is also a hint of remorse as well as an element of temporal depth when he avows that he too had something of a debauched youth, but reformed to enjoy forty years of matrimonial bliss with Alisa. These are masterful brush-strokes that fill out the figure.

But the principal characters in *Celestina* are the bawd and what Marcel Bataillon once called the "whorehouse gallery" surrounding her. What is truly extraordinary about them is that they and their actions, which would traditionally be the stuff of comedy, are serious and even tragic, as we have seen. The obscenities in *Celestina* are not new or remarkable in themselves, for such raunchiness existed earlier in Roman comedy, Petronius's *Satyricon*, the fabliaux, Chaucer, the *Libro de buen amor*, Boccaccio, and other authors and works. What is truly original and modern, however, is that they do not appear in a farcical context. There is comedy but no farce in *Celestina*. The mixture of styles, the high and the low, or the high applied to the low classes, is part of the trend brought about by the advent of Christianity, as Erich Auerbach proposed in his influential *Mimesis*. Because the Judeo-Christian stories involved people from the low classes—indeed the Son of God as a mere carpenter engaged in activities of the most sublime nature—the separation of styles inherited from classical antiquity broke down. With the rediscovery of the classics in the Renaissance the separation might have reacquired some authority, but not in *Celestina*, where Calisto can move from the high-blown rhetoric of courtly love to telling Melibea that he is undressing her because he who wants to eat fowl has to pluck the feathers. As a result of the social leveling and combination of styles, *Celestina* is, following Auerbach's scheme, a profoundly Christian work, exhibiting the anticlericalism rampant in its time.

In addition, the desperate economic and social conditions of these characters are due not to their inherent evil and penchant for crime, but to the unjust class structure of the society in which they live. *Celestina* is a work in which there is a bitter and radical critique of class stratification, as well as a ruthless satire of the aristocracy and the clergy. As already mentioned, Celestina complains that she cannot live "off of air," while the young whores are painfully aware of why they need to work and seek the protection of men, and the whole plot to swindle Calisto is concocted by Sempronio and later Celestina and Pármeno with resentful deliberation. They gleefully steal his food to enjoy a raucous banquet at Celestina's house, planning to extract as much as possible from him before the Melibea affair is ended. Celestina, Sempronio, and Pármeno have no illusions about Calisto's sense of obligation to them or his willingness to discharge his duties as master in protecting them; they are proven right by his inaction. Pleberio and Alisa seem negligent in caring for their daughter and in preparing her for marriage within the conventions of the time. Pleberio appears to have devoted most of his attention to becoming rich, even if he claims in his lament that it had all been for the purpose of making Melibea an attractive marriage match. Men from the upper classes, clergymen among them, hover around Celestina's brothel, showering gifts on the old whore. One priest cannot keep his mind on celebrating the mass when he sees her at church. Uncontrolled sexual passions run the city, with Celestina as the agent who uncovers the submission to them by prominent members of the nobility and the church.

Such a critique in *Celestina* is a reaction to the dire social conditions created by the crowding of cities as the result of centralization, as suggested by Javier Herrero in his masterful essay on Renaissance poverty and the birth of the picaresque. I would add that, in more general terms, this situation followed the breakup of the feudal system, which brought about misery to many. Peasants previously fed and protected within the feudal estates flocked to the cities without means or skills to make a living. Minor aristocrats displaced from their families' domains also gathered in them, unprepared and unwilling to work for a living. This process was intensified in Spain by the Catholic Kings' unification of the Peninsula and their efforts to undermine the aristocracy's power, which they wished to concentrate in their own hands. Rojas's critique of the nobility possibly reflected such policies issuing from the Crown. It is more likely, however, that the portrayal of an unjust social structure in *Celestina* is due to the increasing awareness on the part of humanists and theologians of the inherently abusive distribution of wealth, which ran counter to the basic tenets of Christianity. The poor are poor not because God made them so, but because the rich make them so with their greed. Erasmus, who was Rojas's contemporary, wrote about this and influenced such disciples as Thomas More and Juan Luis Vives. There followed a whole movement of reformist thinking in Spain during the sixteenth century, according to Herrero, whose beginning may be glimpsed in *Celestina* itself.

Reflecting these socioeconomic conditions, the city is a powerful presence in *Celestina*, yet because its name is not given it lacks a specific historical dimension. The characters live hemmed in by walls and doors, they visit markets and churches, and there are rich and poor houses, a river, and tanneries. There are also streets through which the protagonist ambles, sometimes surrounded by her entourage, encumbered by her voluminous skirts and avoiding the ankle-twisting paving stones. These are streets that also have civic and judicial functions; they are the sites of Celestina's and Claudina's public shaming and the beheading of Sempronio and Pármeno. And then there are priests, diplomats, and the ever-threatening police and night watch, which, though mentioned only in passing, complete the human urban landscape. *Celestina*'s is not an idealized Renaissance setting fit for pastoral or chivalric romances. Nature appears in the work only in Melibea's garden, into which Calisto's falcon strays, and on whose ground he and Melibea make love, watched by Lucrecia. It is a walled garden surrounded by streets filled with disturbing noises and paved with the hard stones that will shatter the bodies of all the protagonists. This is no *locus amoenus*. It is, in fact, the urban context in which social strife is predominant—and will prevail in the modern novel that *Celestina* seems to announce.

The critique of social stratification in *Celestina* reflects the breakdown of the medieval cosmology within which the division of classes obeyed the same structuring system that governed the universe from top to bottom. This disintegration is manifested in the constant bickering among the characters, and, most importantly, through the prevailing irony in the work. This ironic perspective is conveyed mostly through the subtle use of language that reveals the disconnection between words, feelings, beliefs, and things, and between words and their traditionally assigned meanings: Celestina is hardly "celestial." She who is the mistress of eros and of language is at the center of this collapse of meaning. She profits from it until the end, when it turns on her and she becomes its victim. Celestina may be said to stand for Logos-turned-textuality, and to have in her background the mythic Pharmakon that Jacques Derrida so masterfully analyzed in his "Plato's Pharmacy." She is the Socratic figure presiding over the banquet in her brothel as she and her disciples discuss love in a scene that appears to be a parody of the *Symposium* and, sacrilegiously, of the Last Supper, which would make her a grotesque Christ figure. Like the Pharmakon, Celestina wounds and cures by stitching hymens, and in the end, she dies a violent death as the scapegoat of the story.

The product of Celestina's work is wholly artificial and secondary—she passes off the broken as new—and it is dependent on her pharmaceutical skills, by which she makes use of potions, unguents, pomades, and the paraphernalia of witchcraft. This could be the myth that has eluded *Celestina* in the reception of the work throughout the centuries and that is embedded in language itself. Her control of the malleability of words allows her to confuse Melibea when she asks for her belt as an amulet to cure Calisto's toothache, and also to dupe Calisto, who in a fetishistic fit adores the object and has to be reminded by both Sempronio and Celestina herself that he should not take it as a substitute for Melibea herself. Language is both wound and cure, and it assumes in Celestina's tongue the nature of writing, of text. Its emblem is the ugly scar across Celestina's face, which is the mark that identifies her like a signature carved on her flesh; it is a tangible, readable sign of her lewd and violent past. As speech, language courses through the air and serves to communicate but also to dissemble and delay, to differ and defer; these contrasting and concomitant functions are dramatized in *Celestina* by the multiple asides and the harangues that the characters, particularly the protagonist, address to themselves as soliloquies that others cannot hear or understand.

The air occupied by speech, presumably present as spirit in the characters' very breathing, is also their enemy. Though insubstantial and transparent, air is the medium through which their vulnerable bodies drop to the stones where they will be shattered, becoming different from them as their spirits vanish, and from themselves by their formlessness, which supplants the shape that identified them when whole. They are an array of spilled differences, a mass of scars like Celestina's, texts inscribed upon the streets. In Calisto's case his most hidden gray matter—the seat of his soul and origin of language—spills out and has to be gathered and returned to his skull. The broken bodies are like pieces of a puzzle, or like fragmented human figures in a Picasso painting. Air and gravity are physical elements and forces that become the instruments of fate in *Celestina*.

Although it is no longer fashionable to speak of national characteristics in reference to art, it seems to me that *Celestina*, with its sarcasm, sacrilegiousness, crudeness, unmitigated mocking of humanity, and disregard for generic conventions, could not be but Spanish. It has all these features in common with other prominent Spanish works throughout history, literary and otherwise. In Spanish-language literature its legacy is manifest in *Lazarillo de Tormes* and the Picaresque novel in general, in Lope de Vega's *La Dorotea*, in some of Cervantes's *Exemplary Novels* (though he did know how to conceal some human foibles), and in Quevedo's *El buscón*. In Latin America her figure is present in the colonial *El Carnero*, by Juan Rodríguez Freyle, and in modern works like *Terra Nostra*, by Carlos Fuentes, Gabriel García Márquez's story about Eréndira's grandmother, and Severo Sarduy's *Cobra*. But I can also imagine *Celestina* illustrated by Velázquez, Goya, or Picasso, or as a film by Luis Buñuel or Pedro Almodóvar. And are there not echoes of *Celestina* in some of Lorca's plays, like *Yerma* and *Blood Wedding?* I cannot conceive that *Celestina* could have been written by a Frenchman or an Italian, much less by an Englishman or a German. Perhaps there is something, after all, essentially Spanish in Rojas's masterpiece.

Roberto González Echevarría

Celestina

There follows here the Tragicomedy of Calisto and Melibea, composed as a caution to crazed lovers who, overcome by their immoderate appetites, call and declare that their lady friends are their gods. It is also intended to serve as warning of the deceptions and tricks of procuresses and of bad and fawning servants.

THE FULL PLOT

Calisto was of noble blood, obvious intelligence, gentle disposition; he was well brought up, endowed with many graces, and well fixed in the world. He was a prisoner of his love for Melibea, a young woman of noble and most serene blood, and prosperous estate, the sole heir of her father, Pleberio, and much loved by her mother, Alisa. Besieged by the love-struck Calisto, her chaste intentions were overcome by the intervention of Celestina, an evil, astute woman, who, with the two servants of this stricken Calisto—deceived by Celestina and for that reason become disloyal to him, their loyalty impaled upon the hook of greed and pleasure—drove the lovers and those who served them to a bitter and disastrous end. As the beginning of all this, adverse fortune provided an opportune time for the desired Melibea to come into the presence of Calisto.

ACT ONE

(Calisto, Melibea, Sempronio, Celestina, Elicia, Crito, Pármeno)

PLOT

Calisto enters a garden in pursuit of his falcon and there finds Melibea, of whose love he becomes prisoner; he begins to speak to her. Roundly dispatched from the garden, he returns to his house, deeply anguished. There he speaks with a servant named Sempronio, who, after much discussion, directs him to an old woman named Celestina, in whose house this same servant has a lover named Elicia. She in turn, as Sempronio approaches the house of Celestina to conduct his master's business, has with her another lover, named Crito, whom she and Celestina hide. All the while Sempronio is negotiating with Celestina, Calisto, at his home, is speaking to yet another of his servants, Pármeno by name; their conversation lasts until Sempronio and Celestina return to the home of Calisto. Pármeno was known to Celestina, who has much to say regarding his mother's accomplishments and knowledge, and she encourages him to work in harmony with Sempronio.

CALISTO. In this, Melibea, I see the greatness of God.

MELIBEA. In what, Calisto?

CALISTO. In giving nature the power to have endowed you with such perfect beauty, and to have granted me, undeserving as I am, the grace of seeing you, and in an appropriate surrounding that allows my secret malady to be manifest. There is no doubt that such a reward is incomparably greater than the service, sacrifice, devotion, and pious works I have offered to God in order to come to this place. And no other power could have fulfilled my human wishes. Who in this life below has seen a man as blessed as I am now? The glorious saints who are gifted with divine vision draw no contentment greater than I from my reverence for you. But, alas! In this we differ; being pure they rejoice in their glory without fear of falling from such a blessed state, but I, both human and immortal, will joyfully suffer the brutal torment that not seeing you will cause me.

MELIBEA. You take this as a reward, Calisto?

CALISTO. In all truth, I hold it as such, for if God should offer me a seat in heaven higher than those of his saints, it would not bring me such bliss as this.

MELIBEA. Then if you persevere, I can promise you an even greater reward.

CALISTO. O most blessed ears that so unworthily have heard these happy words!

MELIBEA. *Un*blessed, alas, what you have just heard, because the payment will be as savage as your daring deserves. The intent of your words, Calisto, has been what would be expected from the wit of a man like you, but your words will be wasted against the virtue of a woman like me. Be gone, fool, for my patience cannot tolerate that the illicit love I perceive in your heart should sing out its delight!

CALISTO. I will go as one against whom adverse Fortune directs her fervor with cruel hatred.

CALISTO. Sempronio! Sempronio! Sempronio! Where is this accursed rogue?

SEMPRONIO. Here I am, Señor, tending the horses.

CALISTO. Well, why have you left the drawing room?

SEMPRONIO. The falcon broke free and I came to capture it and return it to its perch.

CALISTO. Devil take you! May you perish from some sudden calamity, or be visited by an eternal, unbearable torment that immeasurably surpasses the painful and disastrous death that awaits me. Insolent pup. Go, go. Go to my chamber and prepare my bed!

SEMPRONIO. Señor, it is soon done.

CALISTO. Close the window and let darkness accompany my sorrow, and blindness my misery. My sorrowful thoughts are not worthy of light. How blessed the death welcomed by the afflicted! O Eristratus, exalted physician, were you but living today, you would sense my malady. O silent pity of the stars, breathe within her Pleberian heart that my spirit not be sent, with no hope of health, to join that unfortunate Pyramus and ill-fated Thisbe.

SEMPRONIO. And what might that mean?

CALISTO. Go! Not another word or it may pass that before I am overtaken by raging death my hands will deal you a violent demise.

SEMPRONIO. I will go, then, for you want only to suffer your affliction.

CALISTO. Go with the Devil!

SEMPRONIO. I do not see how I can go with the one who stays so close by your side. Such misfortune! How suddenly he fell ill! What was it that so abruptly stole this man's happiness, and, what is worse, his wits? Shall I leave him alone, or shall I go in to him? If I leave him, he will kill himself; if I go in, he will kill me. Let him be, it will not help me; better that he who finds life burdensome die, and not I, who celebrate it. And for another thing, I want to live in order to see my Elicia, and must guard myself from danger. But if he kills himself without another witness, I will be called to give an account of his life. I will go in. But once I do, he will not want consolation or counsel. Which is a lethal sign of not wanting to be well. Withal, I would like to leave him time to grow calm and ripen a little; I have heard it said that it is dangerous to open or to squeeze a green boil, for it becomes more inflamed. Yes, stay a bit; let the sorrowful weep, for tears and sighs greatly ease the grieving heart. And yet, if he has me before him, he will grow the angrier with me, for the sun blazes hottest where it can reverberate; the eyes of someone who has nothing before him grow weary, but when someone is near they sharpen. Therefore, I will bear with it a bit. If in the meantime he kills himself, then let him die. Perhaps I will end up with something that no one knows about, with which I may better my condition, even though it is not seemly to await a benefit from the death of another, and it may be that the Devil is playing tricks on me and if my master dies they will kill me and I will be the rope that follows the cauldron down the well. In addition, wise men say that it is a great comfort for the afflicted to have someone with whom to weep their cares, and that it is the inner wound that does most harm. Well, considering the extreme perplexity with which I now find myself, it is the sanest course to go in, and to suffer him and console him, because if it is possible to heal without skill or instrument, then it is even easier to heal with art and medicines.

CALISTO. Sempronio!

SEMPRONIO. Señor?

CALISTO. Bring me my lute.

SEMPRONIO. Here it is, Señor.

CALISTO (*singing*). What pain can ever be so great
as that dealt me by my fate?

SEMPRONIO. This lute is out of tune.

CALISTO. And how may one who is out-of-tune tune? How may he who is himself so discordant know harmony, he whose will does not obey reason, who holds within his heart barbs, peace, war, truce, love, enmity, injuries, sins, suspicions, all from one cause? But take it up and sing the saddest song you know.

SEMPRONIO (*singing*). Nero of Tarpei looks down
upon a Rome aflame;
screams from young and old alike
but that man feels no pain.

CALISTO. Greater is my fire, and far less the mercy of the person I speak of.

SEMPRONIO (*apart*). I do not deceive myself, this master of mine is mad.

CALISTO. What are you muttering, Sempronio?

SEMPRONIO. I said nothing.

CALISTO. Say aloud what you are saying; have no fear.

SEMPRONIO. I am saying how can the fire that torments a living being be greater than one that burned an entire city, and such a multitude of people?

CALISTO. How? I will tell you how. Greater is the flame that lasts eighty years than the one that passes in a day, and greater the one that kills a soul than one that burns a hundred thousand bodies. As different as appearance from reality, as the real from the painted, as the shadow from the physical, that great the difference between the fire you speak of and the one that is burning me. But truly, if the fire of purgatory rages like this, I would rather my spirit be one with the brute beasts than suffer this torment to attain the glory of the saints.

SEMPRONIO (*apart*). I was not far wrong; this is not the end of this business. Mad does not say enough, he is a heretic.

CALISTO. Have I not told you to speak aloud when you speak? What are you saying?

SEMPRONIO. I was saying that God would not want to hear such a thing! That what you just spoke is a kind of heresy.

CALISTO. Why so?

SEMPRONIO. Because what you say contradicts the Christian religion.

CALISTO. And what does that mean to me?

SEMPRONIO. You are not a Christian?

CALISTO. I am a Melibean, and I worship Melibea and I put my faith in Melibea and I adore Melibea.

SEMPRONIO (*apart*). It is you who say it. As Melibea is so great, the heart of my master is not large enough to contain her, she must spew forth from between his lips. (*To Calisto*) But enough of this. I know which foot you limp on. I will heal you.

CALISTO. It is an incredible thing you promise.

SEMPRONIO. Easy enough: for the beginning of good health is to identify the disorder of the one who suffers.

CALISTO. But what logic can prevail in what has neither order nor logic?

SEMPRONIO (*apart; he laughs*). This then is Calisto's fire? These are his anxieties? As if love aimed its shots only against him! All-powerful God, how imponderable are your mysteries! What power You placed in love to create such agitation in the lover! How rarely You set limits. It seems to the lover that he is left behind. All break past him like raging bulls poked and pricked by the goad stick. Uncurbed, they leap the barriers. You have commanded man to leave his father and his mother and cleave to his wife; now they do more than obey your will, they forsake You and Your law as well, as Calisto does now. I do not marvel at that, for wise men, saints, prophets have all forgotten You for love.

CALISTO. Sempronio!

SEMPRONIO. Señor?

CALISTO. Do not leave me.

SEMPRONIO (*apart*). This bagpipe now plays a gentler tune.

CALISTO. What do you make of my ailment?

SEMPRONIO. That you love Melibea.

CALISTO. And nothing more?

SEMPRONIO. It is bad enough to have one's will captive in a single place.

CALISTO. How little you know of constancy.

SEMPRONIO. To continue on a bad course is not constancy; in my land it is called stubbornness, or obstinacy. You, Cupid's philosophers, may call it as you wish.

CALISTO. It is foul to lie when instructing another, for you yourself take pride in praising your friend Elicia.

SEMPRONIO. Do what I say well, and not what I do badly.

CALISTO. Why are you reproaching me?

SEMPRONIO. You subject man's dignity to the imperfection of a weak woman.

CALISTO. Woman? You oaf! She is a goddess! A goddess!

SEMPRONIO. And that is what you believe, or are you jesting?

CALISTO. Jesting? God knows I believe it. God knows I confess it. And I believe there is no other sovereign in heaven . . . though Melibea dwells among us.

SEMPRONIO (*apart; he laughs*). Was ever such blasphemy heard? Was there ever such blindness?

CALISTO. Why are you laughing?

SEMPRONIO. I laugh because I did not think there could be a graver sin than those practiced in Sodom.

CALISTO. And how so?

SEMPRONIO. Because they strove for abominable congress with unknown angels, but you with one you hold to be a goddess.

CALISTO. You antic ass! You've made me laugh, which I did not intend to do again this year.

SEMPRONIO. No? You were going to weep away your life?

CALISTO. Yes.

SEMPRONIO. And why?

CALISTO. Because I love one before whom I find myself so unworthy that I cannot hope to have her.

SEMPRONIO (*apart*). O weakling! O whoreson! Think of Nimrod! Of an Alexander the Great! They judged themselves worthy to rule not only the world, but the heavens as well.

CALISTO. I did not hear clearly what you said. Come back. Say it again before you go.

SEMPRONIO. I said that you, you who have more heart than Nimrod or Alexander, despair of having a woman, though many of them, of high estate, have given themselves to the embrace and foul breath of lowly muleteers, and others even to beasts. Have you never read of Pasiphae and the bull? Of Minerva and a dog?

CALISTO. I do not believe that; pure prattle.

SEMPRONIO. And what about your grandmother and the simian? That was prattle? Proof are the horns she placed on your grandfather.

CALISTO. Curse this nitwit servant of mine, what drivel he speaks!

SEMPRONIO. Did that sting you? Read the historians, study the philosophers, consult the poets. Books are filled with vile and foul examples of women, and of falls suffered by men who like you esteemed them. Hear Solomon, where he says that women and wine make men deny God. Consult Seneca and you will see in what state he holds them. Listen to Aristotle, look at Bernard. Gentiles, Jews, Christians, and Moors, are all in agreement. But despite what is said, and what women may say, do not commit the error of supposing all women are like that, for they are many, and some are saintly, virtuous, and noble, and their shining crowns exempt them from vituperation. But of these others, who could tell you of their lies, their tiring busyness, their moods, their fickleness, their whimpering, their arguments, their daring to do anything that occurs to them without a thought, their dissembling, their sharp tongues, their deceit, their forgetfulness, their indifference, their ingratitude, their inconstancy, their false testimony, their denial, their trouble-making, their presumption, their vainglory, their depression, their madness, their disdain, their pride, their subjection, their chatter, their gluttony, their carnality, their fear, their boldness, their sorcery, their wrath, their derision, their coarseness, their lack of shame, their procuring? Consider the miniscule brain hidden beneath those tall and elegant toques! The thoughts beneath those gorgets, beneath that ostentation, beneath those long impressive robes! What imperfection, what cesspools beneath painted temples. Of them it is said: "Weapon of Satan, head of sin, destroyer of Paradise." Have you not prayed during the festival of Saint John, where it says: "Women and wine make men renounce their faith"; where it says: "This is woman, ancient evil who drove Adam from the delights of Paradise. This is she who condemned the human race to Hell. This is she who was rebuked by the prophet Elijah." And on and on.

CALISTO. Tell me, then, this Adam, this Solomon, this David, this Aristotle, this Virgil, all these you speak of, why did they succumb to women? Am I more than they?

SEMPRONIO. I would refer you to those who conquered women, and not to those conquered by them. Flee their traps and deceits. You know they do things it is difficult to comprehend. They have no method, no reason, no plan. With meticulous care they prepare the offering they want to make of themselves. Those they slip into their houses they scorn in the street. They invite and disinvite, they beckon and then drive away, they signal love then declare enmity, they display their cruelty then they calm down. They want men to divine their wishes. What a plague! What a vexation! How trying to talk with them more than the brief time we need in making love to them!

CALISTO. You see? The more you tell me and the more obstacles you pose, the more I love her. I do not know why that is.

SEMPRONIO. As I see it, this is not advice for boys, for they do not know as yet how to submit to reason, they do not know how to govern themselves. It is despicable for a man who has never been a disciple to consider himself a master.

CALISTO. And you, what do you know? Who taught you these things?

SEMPRONIO. Who? Why women, of course. From the moment they let down their guard they lose all shame and reveal all these things, and more. So measure yourself, then, on the scale of honor; strive to be more worthy than you are reputed to be, for certainly it is a worse extreme for a man to fall from what he deserves than to place himself higher than he merits.

CALISTO. Well, what has all this to do with me?

SEMPRONIO. What? First, you are a man, and a man of obvious intelligence. And more, a man on whom nature bestowed her best gifts, as you must know: you are handsome, you have grace, you are well built, strong, and agile. And beyond these things, Fortune has shared her wealth with you so generously that your inner gifts, along with those that are external, shine resplendently. For without those worldly goods, those of which Fortune is mistress, no one in this life may be blessed. And finally, by the design of the stars, you are loved by all.

CALISTO. But not by Melibea. And in every way you have glorified me, Sempronio, Melibea is disproportionately, immeasurably, above me. Look upon the nobility and antiquity of her lineage, her vast patrimony, her most excellent wit, her resplendent virtues, her sublime soul, her ineffable grace, her sovereign beauty, of which I entreat you to allow me to speak further, for it will comfort me. And I shall tell you of her outer beauty only, for if I knew how to tell you of what is hidden, there would be no cause for us to have this wretched exchange.

SEMPRONIO (apart). What lies and what madness will this love captive, my master, speak now?

CALISTO. What is it you are saying?

SEMPRONIO. I said speak, so I may find pleasure in hearing it. (Apart) And if God allows you to prosper, I will take pleasure from this sermon.

CALISTO. What?

SEMPRONIO. I said, if God allows me to prosper, what pleasure I will have in listening!

CALISTO. Well, seeing it is for your enjoyment, I will paint her portrait in several parts.

SEMPRONIO (*apart*). Ay! Calamity ahead! This will be more than I wanted. I will have to find a way to get through it.

CALISTO. I will begin with her hair. Have you seen the skeins of fine gold they spin in Arabia? More beautiful are the threads of hers, and they gleam no less brightly. Their ripples fall to her heels; then, combed and bound with a fine ribbon, as she wears it, it takes no more to turn men to stone.

SEMPRONIO (*apart*). To asses, you mean!

CALISTO. What do you say?

SEMPRONIO. I said that her locks are very different from an ass's tail.

CALISTO. What an idiot you are, and what a comparison!

SEMPRONIO (*apart*). And you are not?

CALISTO. The eyes, green, and wide; eyebrows, fine and arched; nose, moderate; mouth, modest; teeth, small and white; lips, red and full; the outline of the face, slightly longer than round; bosom, high; the roundness and form of the small breasts, who could describe to you? How it rouses the man who looks upon them! Her skin is smooth and glowing, and her body makes snow seem shadow; the tint, shaded, as if chosen by her.

SEMPRONIO (*apart*). This fool cannot be reined in!

CALISTO. Her hands are small, but not too small, the flesh like silk, the fingers long, tapering to rosy nails that shine like rubies among pearls. The more intimate proportions that I am unable to describe, hidden as they are by her outer clothing, I judge incomparably better than those of the three goddesses Paris chose among.

SEMPRONIO. Have you finished?

CALISTO. As briefly as I could.

SEMPRONIO. And even if this is true, as a man you are the worthier.

CALISTO. How so?

SEMPRONIO. In that she is the imperfect copy, and for that defect she desires and lusts after you, even one lesser than you. Have you not read the philosopher who says, "As matter yearns for form, so woman for man"?

CALISTO. How sad! And when will I see Melibea yearn for me?

SEMPRONIO. It can happen. And it might even be that you will abhor her as much as you love her now, once you possess her and see her with different eyes, eyes free of the deception now in them.

CALISTO. With *what* eyes?

SEMPRONIO. With clear eyes.

CALISTO. And how do I see her now?

SEMPRONIO. With eyes that magnify what is little to seem a lot and what is small to appear large. And so you do not despair, I would like to assume responsibility for fulfilling your desire.

CALISTO. May God grant your wish! How glorious to hear these words, although I cannot hope you will accomplish it!

SEMPRONIO. I will do it, I am certain.

CALISTO. God comfort you. The brocaded waistcoat I wore yesterday, Sempronio, it is yours.

SEMPRONIO (*apart*). May God favor you for it, and for many more you will be giving me. I mock him yet go away with the best.

And if he prods me a few more times, I will bring her to his bed. So, I'm off! I will do this because of what my master gave me; for nothing is done well without reward.

CALISTO. Be diligent about it.

SEMPRONIO. And you as well; it is impossible for a negligent master to turn out a diligent servant.

CALISTO. How do you plan to go about this act of mercy?

SEMPRONIO. I will tell you. For some time now I have known a bearded old crone who lives at no great distance from here. A witch, astute, wise in every wickedness that exists, she calls herself Celestina. I understand that in this city over five thousand maidenheads have been restored and undone by her hand. If she puts her mind to it she can move rocks and stones to lust.

CALISTO. May I speak with her?

SEMPRONIO. I will bring her to you. Be ready to greet her; be cordial, be openhanded. Think hard while I am gone so that you can describe your pain to her so well that she can provide you the remedy.

CALISTO. And will that be soon?

SEMPRONIO. I am leaving now. May God be with you.

CALISTO. And go with you. (*Alone*) O omnipotent and eternal God! You who guide lost souls and led the kings of the East by way of the star, proceeding to Bethlehem and then back to their land. I humbly pray Thee to guide my Sempronio in such a way that my pain and sadness may be converted into pleasure, and I, unworthy as I am, may reach the desired goal.

SCENE 5

CELESTINA. Good news! Good news, Elicia! It is Sempronio. Sempronio!

ELICIA (*apart*). Sh, sh, sh.

CELESTINA (*apart*). Why *sh*?

ELICIA (*apart*). Because Crito is here with me.

CELESTINA (*apart*). Put him in the little closet for the brooms. Hurry! Tell him your cousin, a relative of mine, is coming.

ELICIA (*apart*). Crito! Come here! My cousin is coming! I am lost!

CRITO. I will hide. Do not be distressed.

SEMPRONIO. Most blessed mother! I come with a great wish! Thanks be to God that He has let me see you!

CELESTINA. My son, my king! You have worried me greatly. I cannot speak. Come, give me another hug! Three days, is it not, that you have endured without seeing us? Elicia! Elicia! Come see who is here!

ELICIA. Who is it, Mother?

CELESTINA. Sempronio.

ELICIA (*apart*). Ay woe! How my heart is leaping. And what does he want?

CELESTINA. Come here, come look. But I will have his embrace, not you.

ELICIA. Ay! A curse upon you, traitor! May boils and tumors eat you, or may you die at the hands of your enemies; may you find yourself in the hands of a severe justice for crimes deserving a cruel death! Ay! Ay!

SEMPRONIO (*laughs*). O, ho! What is it, my Elicia? What is your complaint?

ELICIA. Three days since you have seen me. May God never see *you*! May God never comfort you or visit you! Have pity on the sad girl who put her hope in you, and the goal for all her well-being!

SEMPRONIO. Hush, dear girl! Do you believe that distance is powerful enough to quench my deep affection for you, the fire that is in my heart? Where I go, you go with me, you are there. Do not be upset, or torment me more than I have already suffered. But tell me, whose are the steps I hear up there?

ELICIA. Who? Why one of my lovers.

SEMPRONIO. Of course, just believe that.

ELICIA. On my faith, it is true! Go up and see for yourself.

SEMPRONIO. I am going.

CELESTINA. Here now. Ignore this silly girl, for she is flighty and upset by your absence; she cannot think straight. She will say anything. Come, you and I will talk; we do not want to waste time.

SEMPRONIO. But who is it up there?

CELESTINA. You want to know?

SEMPRONIO. I do.

CELESTINA. A girl a priest entrusted to me.

SEMPRONIO. What priest?

CELESTINA. Do not ask.

SEMPRONIO. On my life, Mother, what priest?

CELESTINA. You persist? The abbot, the fat one.

SEMPRONIO. Poor girl, what a burden awaits her!

CELESTINA. We all carry one. You have not, though, seen much saddle gall on any belly.

SEMPRONIO. Saddle gall, maybe not, but more than a few girth burns.

CELESTINA. Ay, you are a japer!

SEMPRONIO. Japer or jester, just show her to me.

ELICIA. Aha, you wicked man! You want to see her? I hope your eyes leap out of your head! One is not enough! Go, get a good look, but do not ever come back to me!

SEMPRONIO. Hush. God's bones. You are angry? I do not want to see her or any woman born. I want to speak with my mother here, and leave you with God.

ELICIA. Go on, go! Be a stranger, and this time let it be three *years* that you do not see me!

SEMPRONIO. Mother mine, you will do well to trust me, believe that I am not playing a trick. Get your cloak, and we will go, and along the way you will learn what will go against your good fortune and mine if I linger here to tell you.

CELESTINA. We are going, Elicia. Be with God. Close the door. Adios, my blessed walls!

SCENE 6

SEMPRONIO. Now, Mother dear, put other things aside, be attentive and think on what I am telling you and do not scatter your thoughts in many directions, for she who sends them to many places has none, and only by chance learns the truth. I want you to know what you have not heard from me before. And that is that I have never, from the time I put my faith in you, wanted any benefit you do not share.

CELESTINA. May God, Son, share with you half of all that is His; and He would not be without reason to do so, perhaps because you have taken pity on this aged sinner. But speak, do not hold back; with the friendship we have there is no need for preambles or corollaries or preliminaries to earn my goodwill. Be brief and come to the point, for it is wasteful to tell in many words what can be understood in a few.

SEMPRONIO. And it will be so. Calisto is burning with love for Melibea. He has need of you and of me. And since he needs both of us, we will profit together. Recognizing an opportunity and seizing it is how men prosper.

CELESTINA. You put it well; I hear you. A wink is enough for me to catch it. I am most happy with this news, as much as a surgeon brought a patient with a cracked head. And as they first dabble around in the wound, and with the promise of health make the treatment more dear, so I will do with Calisto. I will postpone assurance of a cure, for, as is said, a long wait afflicts the heart, and the longer Calisto waits, the more I will promise. You get my meaning.

SEMPRONIO. Hush now, we have come to the door, and you know the saying: the walls have ears.

CELESTINA. Knock!

SEMPRONIO. (*He knocks loudly.*)

SCENE 7

CALISTO. Pármeno!

PÁRMENO. Señor?

CALISTO. Are you deaf, you dolt?

PÁRMENO. What is it you want, Señor?

CALISTO. There is someone at the door. Hurry!

PÁRMENO. Who is it?

SEMPRONIO. Open to me and this fine mistress.

PÁRMENO. Señor, it is Sempronio and a painted bawd doing all that banging.

CALISTO. Hush, hush, villain, it is my aunt! Hurry, hurry and open up. (*Apart*) I have always seen that when a man flees a danger, he falls into one greater. Because I did not inform Pármeno, who out of love or fidelity or fear has tried to curb my desire, I have stirred the wrath of Celestina, who has no less power in my life than God.

PÁRMENO. Why, Señor, such haste? Why, Señor, this distress? And do you think that she takes as vituperation the name I called her? Do not believe that; she is as glorified to hear it as you when they say, "What a fine horseman that Calisto is." And further, that is what she is called and by that name she is known. If she is walking among a hundred women and someone calls out, "Auld hoor!" without a flicker of embarrassment she turns her head and responds with a happy face. At celebrations, festivals, weddings, guilds, funerals, everywhere people gather, it is with her they pass time. If she walks among dogs, they bark and howl; if she passes birds, they sing no other tune; if it is sheep, they proclaim it with their bleating; donkeys bray out, "Old trull!" Frogs in the pond know no other thing to call her. If she walks into a smithy, hammers ring out those words. Carpenters and armorers, farriers, tinkers, wool beaters, every trade with a tool sounds out her name. Joiners sing it, hairdressers comb it, weavers weave it, laborers in gardens, in plowed fields, in vineyards, at harvest time, with her ease their daily labors. Losers at the tables sing her praise. All things that are created, wherever she may be, repeat that name. What a cuckold her husband was, his nuts were well roasted. Do you want more? Why, when one rock touches another, the sound will be, "Old whore!"

CALISTO. And you, how do you know this and know her?

PÁRMENO. You will know how. Many days have passed since my mother, poor soul, lived in Celestina's neighborhood and, at her entreaty, gave me to her as a servant. She does not recognize me because of the brief time I served her and the changes age has wrought.

CALISTO. How did you serve her?

PÁRMENO. Señor, I went to the plaza and brought her back food, I stayed at her side, and I performed those duties my youthful strength would allow. But of that time I served her, my memory collected things that years have not erased. This fine mistress lives at the edge of the city, out by the tanneries, on the slope of the river-bank; it is an isolated house, half fallen down, poorly constructed and even more poorly furnished. She had six trades, that is helpful to know: seamstress, perfumer, wondrous concocter of paints and pow-ders, and restorer of maidenheads, procuress, and, on occasion, witch. The first office was cover for the others, under which pretense many girls, among them servants, came to her house to be stitched and to stitch neck coverings and many other things. None came without a rasher of bacon, wheat, flour, a jug of wine, and other provisions they stole from their mistresses. And other thefts of even greater worth were hidden there. Celestina was friend to many stu-dents, and stewards, and servants of clerics, and to these she sold the innocent blood of the hapless young girls who foolishly took risks on the basis of the restitution she promised them. And she aimed even higher, for through these girls she communicated with others more closely guarded, and thus carried out her intent. And on honorable occasions, such as Stations of the Cross, night processions, dawn and midnight masses, and other secluded devotions, I saw many cloaked women enter her house. Following them came barefoot men, peni-tent, faces muffled, breeches unlaced, who went in there to weep their sins. What a commerce, when you think on it, she engaged in! She physicked babies, took yarn from one house to be woven in another, all excuses for entering. Some would call, "Here, Mother!," others, "Over there, Mother!," "Come see the old woman!," and "Here comes the mistress." O, she was well known. With all these tasks, she never missed a mass or vespers, or a monastery for priests or nuns, for that was where she offered her hallelujahs and her contracts. And in her house she distilled perfumes; she perfected storax, benzoin, resins, ambergris, civet, powders, musk, blackberry blossoms. She had a room filled with alambics, small retorts, little pots of clay, glass, copper, and tin in a thousand shapes and sizes. She made corrosive sublimate, a variety of face paints, waxes, little paddles for smoothing them on, lotions, polishers, smoothers, cleansers, whiteners, and enhancing waters from root of asphodel, bark of sienna, dragontea, gall, grape pits, and wine, distilled and sweetened. She made skin smooth with lemon juice, with urvino, with deer and heron marrow, and similar compounds. She brewed toilet waters from roses, orange blossoms, jasmine, clover, honeysuckle, carnations, and grape hyacinth, pulverized and soaked in wine. She made hair lightener from vine shoots, holly oak, rye, and horehound, with saltpeter, with alum, with yarrow, and other diverse ingredients. And the ointments and salves she assembled are tedious to recount: from cows, bears, horses, and camels, from snakes and rabbits, from whales, from herons, and from curlews and fallow deer and wild cats and badgers, from squirrels, hedgehogs, and otters. As for appointments for baths, she had a marvel of herbs and roots hanging from the rafters of her house: chamomile, rosemary, mallow, maidenhair fern, sweet clover, elderberry flower and mustard, lavender and white laurel, rose, wildflower and castor plant, gold bill and red leaf. The facial embellishments she created are not to be believed: from storax and jasmine, from lemon, fruit pips, violets, benzoin, pistachio, and pine nuts, from fine grain, field fennel, lupine, vetch and from carillas and herbs. She carried a small vial of balm that she applied to that scratch on her nose. As for maidenheads, she contrived some from small animal bladders and others she repaired with stitching. On a little shelf she kept fine needles and threads of waxed silk, and hanging there roots of St. John's wort and blood bloom, squill and cardoon. With these she worked marvels, for when the French ambassador was here, she three times sold him one of her servants as a virgin.

CALISTO. I wish she had done a hundred!

PÁRMENO. Yes, God a-mercy! And out of charity she repaired many orphaned and wayward girls who had been entrusted to her. And in another room she had remedies for invigorating passion and for mesmerizing objects of affection. She had hearts of deer, tongue of viper, pheasant heads, asses' brains, camel skin, birth sacs, Moorish bean, lodestones, hangman's rope, ivy flower, sea urchin spine, badger's foot, lettuce seed, geodes, and another thousand items. There came to her many men and women, some demanding magical dead-man's-bread, others, her garments, some, her hair, and there were some on whose palms she painted letters with saffron or vermillion; to others she gave wax hearts filled with broken needles, and to others objects of clay and lead frightening to behold. She painted figures, scratched words in the dirt. Who could tell you what this old crone did? And all of it was mockery and lies.

CALISTO. So be it, Pármeno. Leave it for another occasion. I am sufficiently advised, and I am obliged. Let us move along, for necessity takes precedence over dawdling. Listen well: this woman comes invited. She has waited too long already. Do not irritate her. I am afraid, and fear diminishes memory and wakens divine guidance. Zounds! Come, let us be about it. But I beg you, Pármeno, not to allow your envy of Sempronio, who is serving and assisting me in this, to be an impediment to remedying my life; if for him there was a doublet, you shall have a waistcoat. Do not think that I hold your counsel and advice in any less esteem than his work and efforts. I know that the spiritual goes before the corporal, and that though beasts work harder than men and for that are fed and cared for, they are never considered a friend; such will be the difference between my relations with you and Sempronio, and under secret agreement, I will forgo a master's dominance and call you my friend.

PÁRMENO. It is distressing, Calisto, that you doubted my loyalty and service, and offered me promises and counsel. When, Señor, have you seen envy in me, or seen me place my self-interest or displeasure before your well-being?

CALISTO. Do not be offended, there is no doubt that in my eyes your behavior and good breeding stand above all who serve me. But in such a difficult situation, one on which my well-being and life depend, we must look ahead. I want you to know that I believe that your good conduct blossoms from nature, as nature is the origin of excellence. But enough; let us see to my healing.

SCENE 8

CELESTINA (*apart*; *outside*). I hear footsteps coming downstairs. Pretend, Sempronio, that you do not hear them. Listen, and let me speak to the plan that will benefit us both.

SEMPRONIO (*outside*). Speak then.

CALISTO. Pármeno, stop! Sh! Listen to what they are saying. Let us see where we stand.

CELESTINA (*outside*). Now, do not berate or importune me; to place too great a weight on caution is to prod the already exhausted ox. You so feel the pain of your master Calisto that it seems that you are he and he you, and that his torments are one for both. But understand that I have come here to resolve this plight or die in the attempt.

CALISTO. What a remarkable woman! Worldly wealth is unfit to be possessed by such a noble heart! And faithful and true Sempronio! Have you seen, Pármeno? Did you hear? Am I right? What say you, dear keeper of my secret, my counsel and my soul?

PÁRMENO. Protesting my innocence of your first suspicion and acting with loyalty, I will, because you conceded it to me, speak. Hear me, and do not let affection deafen you or hope of delight blind you. Calm yourself and do not act in haste; for many who are too eager to score in the bull's eye miss the target. Although I am young, I have seen many such things, and good sense and a sharp eye illuminate experience. On seeing you or hearing you come down the stairs, these two have been crafting the deceit, the false words, on which you place the satisfaction of your desire.

SEMPRONIO (*apart; outside*). Celestina, what Pármeno is saying seems to signal my ruin.

CELESTINA (*apart; outside*). Hush, for on my faith where the ass comes, so too will come the packsaddle. Leave Pármeno to me, for I will make him one of us, and of what we gain we will give him part, for worldly wealth, if not shared, is not wealth. We will all gain, we will all share, we will all be happy. I will bring him to you so calm and affable that he will eat out of your hand, and we will be partners, and as they say in the game, we will be three against the master.

SCENE 9

CALISTO. Pármeno!

PÁRMENO. Señor?

CALISTO. What are you doing, key to my life? Open the door! Ah, Pármeno, I see her now. I am well, I am alive! Look how dignified she is, such reverence! Usually, inner virtue shows itself in the physiognomy. O virtuous old age. O aged virtue. O glorious hope for my desired prize! O here the end of my delighting hope! O health of my passion, cure to my torment, regeneration and enlivenment of my life, resurrection from death! I want to rush to you and fervently kiss those healing hands. But I am unworthy. Instead I will worship the ground you walk on, kiss it with reverence.

CELESTINA (*apart*). Ha, Sempronio, do I live on those words? This idiot master of yours is planning to give me bones I have already chewed. I dream of more; he will see that as things develop. Tell him to close his mouth and open his purse, and that I trust his actions even less than his words. Ho, I will bring you up short, you lame ass! You will have to get up much earlier to get ahead of me!

PÁRMENO (*apart*). O that my poor ears should hear such things! Lost is he who follows one already lost. Ah, Calisto, wretched, crushed, blind man! And on earth you are worshiping the oldest and most whorish bawd whose shoulders have rubbed the slats of every brothel in town! You are undone, vanquished, fallen! You are beyond redemption, or counsel, or effort.

CALISTO. What was my dear mother saying? It seems to me she thought that I was offering her words in place of reward.

SEMPRONIO. So I heard it.

CALISTO. Well, come with me; bring the keys, and I will cure her doubts.

SEMPRONIO. It is well to do so, and then we will go; for we cannot allow weeds to grow among the grain, or suspicion in the hearts of friends; rather, with the hoe of good works, we will clear them out.

CALISTO. You speak wisely. Let us go, and not tarry.

SCENE 10

CELESTINA. It pleases me, Pármeno, that we have this opportunity for you to learn of the love I have for you, and for the place that you, though unworthy, have in my heart. And I say unworthy because of the things I heard you say, things to which I give no attention, because virtue counsels us to suffer temptations and not repay a wrong with another, especially when we are tempted by youths not well instructed in the ways of the world, in which with foolish loyalty they ruin themselves and their masters, as you are doing to Calisto. I heard everything you said; you must not think that in my old age I have lost my hearing, or any other of my senses. For not only do I see and hear and know you, but with the eyes of my intellect I penetrate even your inner being. You must know, Pármeno, that Calisto is suffering a pathetic love, but you must not for that judge him weak, for invincible love conquers all. And he knows, if you do not, that two conclusions may be drawn: the first, that it is inevitable that man will love woman, and woman, man. Second, that he who truly loves will necessarily be perturbed by the sweet taste of sovereign delight, which was put there by our Maker so that mankind be perpetuated, and without which it would vanish from the earth. And this is true not only in the human species but also in fish, beasts, birds, and reptiles; and in the green kingdom, some plants have this relation, if they are set close without the interference of anything between them; and herbalists and agriculturists have determined that there are male and female plants. What do you say to that, Pármeno? Clay-brain, wild thing, angel mine, pearl of my heart, simpleton! What, you screw up your face at me? Come here to me, little whoreson, for you know nothing of the world and its pleasures. But may I die of a raging fever if I let you near me, even if I am an old woman! Your voice is changing, you show signs of a beard, and what you have at the tip of your belly must sting!

PÁRMENO. Like a scorpion's tail!

CELESTINA. Even worse; its bite does not cause swelling, while yours leaves its results for nine months.

PÁRMENO. (*He laughs.*)

CELESTINA. That made you laugh, little pimple?

PÁRMENO. Hush, Mother, do not blame me or, even though I am a boy, think I am stupid. I love Calisto because I owe him loyalty: because I am his servant; because of the good he has done me; because I am respected and well treated by him, which is the best shackle to bind a servant to serving his señor, as much as being ill treated is just the opposite. I see he is lost, and there is nothing worse than to follow a desire without hope of a good end, and especially when planning to remedy such an arduous and difficult struggle through the vain counsel and dimwitted reasoning of that ass Sempronio, which is like digging out mites with a pick and hoe. I cannot let him suffer. I say it and I weep.

CELESTINA. Pármeno, can you not see that it is foolish and simpleminded to weep over what cannot be remedied with weeping?

PÁRMENO. That is *why* I am weeping. For if my tears were able to provide my master a remedy, my pleasure at such hope would be so great that my joy would not allow tears. But as it is, with all hope already lost, my happiness evaporates, and I weep.

CELESTINA. You will weep to no advantage for what weeping cannot prevent or presume to heal. So you think, Pármeno, that this has not happened to others?

PÁRMENO. Yes, but I would not want my master to suffer.

CELESTINA. He does not; but even if he did, he could be cured.

PÁRMENO. I find no cure in what you say, because in good things the fulfillment is better than the potential, and in bad ones the potential better than fulfillment. Thus it is better to be healthy than to be able to be, and better to be able to have pain than to be ill, and therefore, the being able to be ill is better than being it.

CELESTINA. O wicked boy! Why is it I cannot make you understand? Do you not feel his illness? What have you said till now? What is your complaint? Well, deceive him, or say that what is false is true and believe whatever you wish, for he is ill with loving, and the power to be well is in the hands of this scrawny old woman.

PÁRMENO. No, of this scrawny old whore!

CELESTINA. You live perilously, young pillicock! How dare you say such a thing?

PÁRMENO. I dare because I know you.

CELESTINA. Who are you!

PÁRMENO. Who? Pármeno, son of Alberto, your old friend. I lived with you a month. My mother gave me to you when you dwelled near the tanneries, on the bank of the river.

CELESTINA. Jesú, Jesú! And you are Pármeno, son of Claudina?

PÁRMENO. I am. None other.

CELESTINA. Well may you roast in consuming fire, your mother was as much an old whore as I! Why have you come looking for me, little Parmenico? It is he, it *is* he, by all of God's saints! Come here to me, come here; I gave you a thousand lashes and punches in this world, and another thousand kisses. Do you remember when you slept at my feet, little scatterbrain?

PÁRMENO. Yes, in good faith I do. And sometimes, though I was but a boy, you pulled me up to the head of the bed and held me tight, and I pushed away because you smelled like an old woman.

CELESTINA. May you die of oozing sores! And what does this impudent boy have to say? Leave your mocking and dilly-dallying behind; hear me now, Son, listen: for although I was called here for one purpose, I have come for another, and although I have pretended I did not know you, you are the reason I am here. Son, you know that your father was still alive when your mother, who is with God, gave you to me. Since you had fled from me, he died with only one anxiety, uncertainty about your life and person. Because you were gone, the years of his old age were passed in anguish and worry. And at the time he was departing this world, he sent for me, and in secret, with no other witness present but He who is witness to all works and thoughts, He who scrutinizes hearts and souls, your father and I arranged between us that I would go out to look for you and take you in and give you shelter. And when you reached a certain age, a time when you knew to give shape and form to your life, I was to reveal to you the place where he had left buried a treasure of gold and silver that is worth more than the wealth of your master Calisto. And because I promised him, and with my promise he found rest—and a promise made to the dead is more to be kept than one to the living, for they cannot act for themselves—I have till this day spent so much time and goods in searching for you that finally it has pleased He who cares for us and answers our pleas and directs our pious works, and that is why I am come here, only three days after I learned where you were living. I have been melancholy because you have wandered so many places and roamed so far that you have not gained wealth or made a friend. As Seneca tells us, pilgrims have many inns and few friends because in such brief encounters they cannot establish friendship with anyone, and he who is in many places is in none. Nor can a body profit from food that is thrown up once eaten, nor is there anything that more greatly impedes good health than diversity and change and variety of diet; and never does the wound heal on which many treatments are tried, nor the plant recover that many times is transplanted; nor is there anything so profitable that it yields profit from the beginning. Therefore, my son, put apart the impulses of youth and return, with the guidance of your elders, to reason. Settle somewhere. And where better than in my care, with the guidance of my spirit, with my counsel, with me to whom your parents gave you. And thus, as I am your true mother, I tell you—and bear in mind the curses that your parents placed on you should you disobey!—to serve and suffer this master you have chosen for the present, until you have further counsel from me; but do not do it out of foolish loyalty, proposing to establish a firm footing upon a shifting base, for that is how the masters of today can be. Win friends, for a friend is lasting, and be steadfast with them. Do not live flitting from flower to flower. Do not trust the vain promises of masters, they drain the substance of their servants with hollow promises the way the leech sucks blood; they offer no thanks, they insult, they forget services, they refuse compensation. Woe to him who grows old in a palace! As is written of the Pool of Bethesda, of the hundred who entered, one was cured. These masters today love themselves more than their servants, and they are not hurt by it; their servants should do the same. Gone now are favors, magnanimity, noble acts. Each of these señores selfishly uses his servants for selfish interests; his servants, though subordinate, should do no less, and live by their masters' law. I tell you this, Pármeno my son, because it seems to me that this master of yours will walk over you roughshod. He wants to be served by everyone. Look around, believe me. While in his household, make new friends, for a friend has the greatest value in the world, but do not attempt to be a friend to him, because substantial differences in status and condition seldom allow a friendship. We have an opportunity, as you know, in which we all may profit and in which you may remedy your situation. The other matter, what I told you I had hidden away, will wait to a later time. And you will benefit greatly by being Sempronio's friend.

PÁRMENO. Celestina, I tremble when I hear what you say. I do not know what to do. This is confusing. On the one hand, I have you as a mother. On the other, I have Calisto for a master. I wish for riches, but he who is dishonest in his climb is likely to fall farther than he climbed. I would not want wealth gained through deceit.

CELESTINA. I would. By foul means or fair, we take our share!

PÁRMENO. Well, I would not be happy living on ill-gotten

gains; I hold contented poverty to be the decent thing. And I want to say even more: it is not those who have very little who are poor, but those who want very much. And for this reason, no matter what you can add, I do not believe this part of what you say. I would like to spend my life free of envy, cross deserts and rugged lands without fear, sleep without sudden fright, speak without insults, be strong without abuse, be compensated without opposition.

CELESTINA. Ah, my son, it is said that only the old may be prudent, and you are still very much a boy!

PÁRMENO. Genteel poverty is very secure.

CELESTINA. Say instead, like Virgil, that Fortune favors the bold. And, beyond this, who in the republic has wealth and chooses to live without friends? Well, praise God that you have wealth, but do you not know that you need friends to keep it? And do not believe that favor with this master makes you safe; when you have great Fortune, little is safe. And therefore, in difficult times the remedy is friends. And where can you better win them than where the three modes of friendship come together: betterment, profit, and pleasure. For betterment, see Sempronio's will conforming to yours, and how the two of you have similar virtues. For profit, it is at hand, if you come to an agreement. For pleasure, the same, as you are at an age ready for all manner of pleasure, in which youths indulge more than the old, as they do in the game, dress, sport, eating and drinking, negotiating affairs, together, in company. If you choose, Pármeno, what a life we would enjoy! Sempronio loves Elicia, the cousin of Areúsa.

PÁRMENO. Of Areúsa?

CELESTINA. Of Areúsa.

PÁRMENO. Of Areúsa, daughter of Elisa?

CELESTINA. Of Areúsa, daughter of Elisa.

PÁRMENO. You are sure?

CELESTINA. I am sure.

PÁRMENO. What a wondrous thing.

CELESTINA. You think it seems good?

PÁRMENO. Nothing better.

CELESTINA. Well, your good fortune wishes that, for here is the one who will give her to you.

PÁRMENO. 'Pon my faith, Mother, I cannot believe anyone!

CELESTINA. It is excessive to believe everyone, but a mistake not to believe anyone.

PÁRMENO. I mean, I believe *you*! But I do not dare. Please go.

CELESTINA. O sick of soul! It is not possible for a faint heart to accept good! God, after all, gives nuts to a man who has no teeth. How simpleminded you are! You say that where there is greater understanding there is less Fortune, and where greater sagacity, there too less Fortune. Old sayings.

PÁRMENO. Ah Celestina! I have heard my elders say that an example of lust or avarice does great harm, and that a man should confine his dealings to those who make him better, and not those he plans to improve. And Sempronio as example will not make me better, nor will I cure him of his vices. And though I am inclined toward what you tell me, I would like to be the only one to know, so at least my sin be hidden. And if man gives in to pleasure and acts against virtue, he will not dare to be honest.

CELESTINA. There is no wisdom in what you say, for there is no pleasure without company. Do not hold back or be bitter, for nature flees sadness and hungers for what is delectable. Pleasure in sensual matters comes with friends, and especially in telling every detail: I did this, She told me that, We trifled like this, I took her in this way, This is how I kissed her, This is how she bit me, This is how I embraced her, This is how she yielded, What talk! What pleasure! What games! What kisses! Let us go there! Let us come back here, Bring some music, Let us make riddles, sing songs, make things up, joust. What crest will be our signal, what writing? She is on her way to mass. She will be out tomorrow. Let us stroll down her street. Look, here is her note! We are going tonight. You hold the ladder! Watch the door! How did it go? Watch for the cuckold, he leaves her alone! Go again! Let us go back there! And in all this, Pármeno, can you find pleasure without company? On my faith, ask one who knows how the tune goes. This is pleasure . . . as for the other, asses do it better in the pasture.

PÁRMENO. I would not, Mother, want to be persuaded with promises of pleasure the way those who, lacking a rational basis, formed sects enveloped in sweet poison to capture the wills of the weak, and with sweet powders of affection blinded the eyes of reason.

CELESTINA. Tell me, fool, what is reason? What is affection, little donkey? It is knowledge, which you do not have, that defines them. And greater than knowledge is prudence, and prudence comes only with experience, and only the old can know experience. And we elders are called mothers and fathers, and good parents counsel their children, as I especially you, whose life and honor I value more than my own. And when will you repay me for this? Never! For parents and teachers may not be given equal service.

PÁRMENO. It frightens me, Mother, that I may be receiving questionable counsel.

CELESTINA. You do not want it? Well, I will tell you what Solomon says: to the man who is so stiff-necked that he scorns the one who chastises him will come a quick and violent end and never have good health. And so, Pármeno, I take my leave of you and of this business.

PÁRMENO (*apart*). My mother is very angry. I have questioned her counsel. It is a mistake not to believe, and a fault to believe everything. Yet it is more human to have faith, most of all in this woman who promises profit for us, and in addition love. I have heard that man must believe his elders. Then what does this one advise me? Peace with Sempronio. Peace should not be denied, for blessed are the peacemakers, who will be called children of God. Love should not be refused, nor charity to brothers. Few turn away profit. I want to please her and will listen. (*Aloud*) Mother, a teacher should not be angered by the ignorance of the disciple. If that were not so, knowledge would rarely, and in few places, be transmitted, though it is by its nature teachable. For that reason, forgive me, talk to me; not only do I want to hear you and believe you, I will consider your counsel a rare favor. And do not thank me, for it is more virtuous to do good than to be recipient of it. Therefore, command, and I will humble myself to consent.

CELESTINA. It is human to make mistakes, but only a beast is stubborn. Therefore, I am pleased, Pármeno, that you have swept away the dark veils from before your eyes and responded to the protection, knowledge, and ingenuity of your father, whom I can now see in my memory, making the pious eyes from which you see such copious tears spilling grow tender. At times, like you, he defended problematical propositions, but then returned to what is certain. In God and in my heart, watching how stubborn you were but how you changed to truth, it seems that I see him alive before me. What a man! What a full life! What a venerable face! But we must end our discussion, for here come Calisto and your new friend Sempronio! I leave to give you a better opportunity to talk with him: two living in one heart are more powerful in acting and in understanding.

CALISTO. I came doubting, Mother, because of my misfortunes, that I would find you alive. But even more a marvel, considering my wish, is that I have arrived alive. Receive the poor gift of one who along with it offers you his life.

CELESTINA. As in very fine gold worked by a hand of subtle artifice, the work outweighs the material, so is your magnificent gift surpassed by the grace and form of your generosity. And without doubt, the swiftness of the gift has doubled the effect, because he who drags his feet shows sign of rescinding the promise and repenting of the gift.

PÁRMENO (*apart*). What did he give her, Sempronio?

SEMPRONIO (*apart*). A hundred pieces of gold.

PÁRMENO. (A*part; he laughs.*)

SEMPRONIO (*apart*). Did Mother speak with you?

PÁRMENO (*apart*). Shh, she did.

SEMPRONIO (*apart*). Well, how are we?

PÁRMENO (*apart*). As you wished, though I am frightened.

SEMPRONIO (*apart*). Then quiet, else I will make you twice as frightened.

PÁRMENO (*apart*). O God! There is no pestilence more deadly than an enemy in one's own house.

CALISTO. Go now, Mother, and reassure your house. And then come back and bring cheer to mine.

CELESTINA. May God be with you.

CALISTO. And may He guard you for me.

ACT TWO

(Calisto, Sempronio, Pármeno)

PLOT

Celestina has left Calisto to return home; Calisto stays talking with Sempronio, his servant. Calisto, now that his hopes have been raised, is agitated by inaction; he sends Sempronio to spur Celestina to move more quickly with their business. In the meantime, Calisto and Pármeno remain behind in conversation.

SCENE 1

CALISTO. My brothers, I gave Mother a hundred coins. Did I do well?

SEMPRONIO. By my oath, yes, you did well! In addition to improving your life, you won great honor. And what are the favors and prosperity of Fortune for if not to serve honor, which is the greatest of earthly rewards. That is why we offer honor to God, because we have no greater thing to give Him, the greatest part of which consists of liberality and generosity. Treasures that do not know charity blacken and damage honor, while magnanimity and liberality win and exalt it. What advantage is there in having what brings no profit? There is no doubt that using riches is better than possessing them. How glorious it is to give! How wretched to receive! How much better, more noble to give! As much better giving is than possessing, that much nobler the giver than the receiver. Among the elements, fire, for being the most active, is the most noble, and in the spheres is placed in the most noble location. And some say that nobility is glory shed on us because of the merit and antiquity of our line; I say that light reflected from another will not shine brightly unless you radiate a light of your own. And therefore, do not judge your value in the reflection from your father, who was so magnificent, but in your own. That is how one wins honor, which is the greatest wealth man possesses. And in that regard, it is not the evil man but, rather, the good man like you who is worthy of attaining perfect virtue. And I will say more: perfect virtue does not have to be practiced to display honor. Therefore, take pleasure from having been so munificent, and take my counsel; go to your chamber and rest, for your business is in good hands. And of this be certain: since the beginning has gone well, the end will be even better.

CALISTO. Let us go, then, because I want to speak with you at greater length about this business.

SCENE 2

CALISTO. Sempronio, it does not seem good counsel for me to be here in company and the woman who seeks the remedy to my malady to go alone. It will be better if you go with her and encourage her, for you know that my health depends on her diligence, and from her delay and forgetting comes my despair. You are well informed, I feel that you are loyal and I hold you to be a good servant. Act so that in merely seeing you, she will recall the pain I am left with, and the fire that torments me, whose ardor is so great that I could not describe to her the third part of my secret illness, which occupies my tongue and all my feelings. You, as a man free of such passion, must speak to her and not hold back.

SEMPRONIO. Señor, I would like to go out to obey your order, and I would also like to stay to alleviate your concerns. Your fear troubles me, your being here alone holds me here. I want to listen and do your bidding, which is to go and hurry the old woman along. But how shall I do it? For if you are alone, you rave and rant like a man who has lost his senses, sighing, moaning, making bad verses, lying about in the dark, seeking solitude, looking for new modes of deep thought, which, if you persevere, will lead either to death or to madness you will be unable to escape unless you have always with you someone to provide entertainment and light humor, to play happy songs and sing ballads, make little riddles, tell stories and spin tales, play at cards and chess; finally, one who knows every kind of sweet pastime that will keep your thoughts from following the cruel byways that lady sent you down in the first stages of your love.

CALISTO. How, simpleton? Do you not know that it eases pain to weep over the cause? How sweet it is to those who are sad to bemoan their passion, what calm those heavy sighs bring, how greatly tearful moaning relieves sorrow. Those who have written on such matters say nothing else.

SEMPRONIO. Read further, turn the page. You will find they say that to put your faith in what may quickly change and to seek out reasons to be sad is a kind of madness. And that well-known Macías, the idol of lovers, complained of forgetting because he did *not* forget. The pain of love lies in reflecting; rest, in forgetting. Do not keep kicking at what goads you. Pretend to be happy and that is how you will be; for often what we think carries us where it wishes, not in order to change truth, but to moderate our feelings and control our judgment.

CALISTO. Sempronio, my friend, since you so clearly feel my loneliness, summon Pármeno. He will stay with me. And from here forward be, as you are accustomed, loyal: in the service of the servant is the master's reward.

SCENE 3

PÁRMENO. I am here, Señor.

CALISTO. Not I, for I did not see you. Do not leave her side, Sempronio, nor forget me. Go with God. You, Pármeno, what do you think of what has happened today? My pain is great, Melibea high above me, and Celestina a wise and good mistress in these matters. We cannot go wrong. You have given me approval despite your animosity. I believe you: for such is the force of truth that it draws the tongues of enemies back to it. So, since she is as she is, I would rather give this woman a hundred coins than five to another.

PÁRMENO (*apart*). And you are already weeping over them? Calamity ahead. Here in the household we will have to do without such generosity.

CALISTO. Well I ask your sense of it. Be agreeable, Pármeno; do not hang your head when you answer. But, as envy is sad, sadness without tongue, your will may have more power than your fear of me. What did you say, you noxious flea?

PÁRMENO. I say, Señor, that your generosity would be better employed in presents and services for Melibea, and not in giving money to that old bawd I know; and what is even worse, in making yourself her captive.

CALISTO. Are you mad? And how her captive?

PÁRMENO. Because the one to whom you tell a secret you give your freedom.

CALISTO. So, the muddlehead says something! But I want you to know that when there is a great distance between he who beseeches and the one beseeched, either from obligation of obedience or from superiority of state or elusiveness of type, as there is between this my fine mistress and me, an intermediary or go-between is needed to see that my message is passed from hand to hand until it reaches the ear of the one to whom I cannot hope to speak a second time. And that being the way it is, tell me if you approve what I have done.

PÁRMENO (*apart*). Devil approve it!

CALISTO. What do you say?

PÁRMENO. I say, Señor, that no error comes unaccompanied, and that one misadventure opens the door to many more.

CALISTO. I approve what you have said, but I do not understand the premise.

PÁRMENO. Señor, because the other day your fine falcon broke free and looking for it was the cause of your going into Melibea's garden; your going in, the reason you saw and spoke to her. The talking engendered love; love gave birth to your pain; pain will cause you to lose your body and soul and estate. Yet what I regret even more is that you have fallen into the hands of that old conventtrotter, who has been honeyed and feathered three times.

CALISTO. And so, Pármeno, tell me more of this, for it pleases me; the more you belittle her, the better she seems. Let her do my bidding and they can feather her a fourth time. You are a fool and you speak with a light heart; you do not hurt as I do, Pármeno.

PÁRMENO. Señor, I would rather you reproach me in anger for annoying you than with repentance curse me because I did not give you good counsel; for when your will was captured you lost your freedom.

CALISTO (*apart*). This rascal is asking for a beating! (*To Pár-meno*) Tell me, pissmire, why do you speak ill of the one I adore? And you, what do you know of honor? Tell me, what is love? Since you present yourself to me as having good sense, what constitutes good upbringing? Do you not know that the first step toward madness is to believe oneself wise? If you felt my sorrow, you would use a different water to sprinkle on the burning wound Cupid's cruel arrow inflicted on me. Any remedy Sempronio has brought closer with his feet you undo with your tongue, with your vain words. Pretending to be loyal, you are a gob of fawning, a pot of malice, the very inn and lodging of envy. In defaming the old woman, you question my love. Well, know this: my pain and turbulent sorrow cannot be ruled by reason, does not welcome advice, does not heed counsel. And if I could teach you anything, it would be not to separate or upset something I cannot part with. Sempronio feared his going and your staying. I wanted it all, and thus I am suffering his absence and your presence. I am far better alone than consorting with bad company.

PÁRMENO. Señor, weak indeed is the loyalty that fear of pain converts into flattery, and even more with a master whom sorrow or affliction have deprived of, or driven away, his natural good judgment. He must tear off the veil of blindness. These short-lived fires will fade. You will know my bitter words to be better for killing this vicious cancer than the bland ones of Sempronio, for they feed it; they stir the fire, they enliven your love, they light the flame, and add fuel that will burn until you are put into your tomb.

CALISTO. Quiet, blaggard! No more! I am suffering and you are philosophizing. I will not wait any longer. Have them get a horse, curry it, cinch the girth tight, because I want to ride by the house of my fine mistress and my God.

PÁRMENO (*apart, outside*). Boy! Are there no grooms in this household? I will have to do it, and worse will come to me than acting as a stable boy! Here, here. "No one loves to hear the truth . . ." You are whinnying, Don Caballo? Is one stud not enough in this house? Or do you, too, sniff Melibea?

CALISTO. Are they bringing my horse? What are you doing, Pármeno?

PÁRMENO. Señor, here you are; Sosia is not around.

CALISTO. Well, hold this stirrup. Open that door wider. If Sempronio should come with that old woman, tell them to wait, that I will be back very soon.

PÁRMENO (*alone*). May that never happen! Ride on with the Devil. Tell these madmen what you do for them and they will not see you. 'Pon my soul, if they would drive a lance into my master's heel he would lose more brains from it than from his head. So go, go on. It is my bet that Celestina and Sempronio will fleece you. Woe is me! I suffer for being loyal; others win by being evil, I lose by being good. The way of the world. It would be best to follow along with other people, for they call traitors knowledgeable and those who are loyal stupid. If I believed Celestina with her six dozen years on her back, Calisto would not mistreat me. But this will serve as a warning to me from now on. If he says "Let us eat," I will eat too; if he wants to tear down the house, I will approve; burn his belongings, I will go for fire. Destroy, tear down, break, damage, give everything he has to procuresses, I will get my part. As they say, "River running wild, fisherman's gain." Never lick someone's boots again.

ACT THREE

(Sempronio, Celestina, Elicia)

PLOT

Sempronio goes to the house of Celestina, whom he reprimands for taking so long. They set about searching for the path to take in the matter of Calisto's pursuit of Melibea. Elicia happens by. Celestina goes to the house of Pleberius. Sempronio and Elicia stay at the house of Celestina.

SCENE 1

SEMPRONIO (*apart*). What a lot of time the bearded old hag is taking. Her feet were more lively on the way here. You pay in advance, you get no romance. Ho! Señora Celestina, we have not seen any hustle from you.

CELESTINA. What are you doing here, Son?

SEMPRONIO. Our love-stricken Calisto does not know what to ask of you. He is like a baker with no dough, he does not know what to do with his hands. He is afraid that you are not tending to his problem, and he is cursing himself for being so tightfisted and miserly with you.

CELESTINA. Nothing is more normal for the lover than impatience. Every delay is torment for them, they take no pleasure from procrastination. They want to put their proposals into effect in no time at all, and would rather see them concluded than begun. These novice lovers fly off after any bait without a thought, not considering the harm that feeding their desire might bring to themselves and their servants.

SEMPRONIO. What is that you are saying about servants? By your reasoning it seems that harm may come to us from this business, and that we could be burned by sparks that shoot from Calisto's fire. (*Apart*) I would give his loves to the Devil! At the first sign of crisis I see in this business, I will not be eating his bread any longer. I would do better to lose pay I've earned than give my life to collect it. Time will tell me what to do, for before everything collapses there will be a sign, like a house tilting before it collapses. (*Aloud*) If it is seemly to you, Mother, let us guard ourselves from danger, from whatever lies ahead. If he gets her now, fine; if not, another year, or if not that, never. He will be the one to suffer. There is nothing so difficult to endure in its beginnings that time does not soften and make bearable. No wound is felt so deeply that the passing days do not ease its torment, nor pleasure so sublime that it is not dimmed by time. Evil and good, prosperity and adversity, glory and pain: over time all things lose the force of accelerated beginnings. Things we have admired and attained with great desire are forgotten as quickly as they have passed. Every day we see and hear new things, and we pass them by and leave them behind. Time diminishes them; makes them contingent. Would you not marvel if someone told you, "The earth shook," or something of the sort that you would not later forget. The same is true of "The river has frozen over," "The blind man can see," "Your father has died," "Lightning struck," "Granada has fallen," "The King rides in today," "The Turks are defeated," "There is an eclipse tomorrow," "The bridge has washed out," "He has been made a Bishop," "Pedro was robbed," "Inés hanged herself." What will you tell me other than after three days, or a second look, no one marvels at such news? It is all like that, everything happens that way, everything is forgotten, everything is left behind. And so too my master's love: the faster it moves the sooner it wanes. For habit soothes sorrows, diminishes and wears down pleasure, dims marvels. Let us take our gain while the battle is being waged. And if we keep our feet dry we can help him, that's the best of it; and if not, little by little we will let him know of Melibea's reproaches and scorn. If we do not succeed it is better that the master suffer than the servant run a risk.

CELESTINA. You have spoken well. I am with you, and I am grateful to you. We cannot go wrong. But yet, Son, we need to have a lawyer put work into this case, concoct some false arguments, complete some sophist transactions, come and go to court, even if reprimanded by the judge. He would not want those who witness it to say he is doing nothing to earn his fees. And afterward everyone will come to him with their legal problems and to Celestina with their affairs of the heart.

SEMPRONIO. Do as you will, for this is not the first business you have taken on.

CELESTINA. The first, Son? Few virgins, praise God, have you seen open up shop in this city for whom I have not been the agent of their first sale. When a girl child is born I enter her name in my register in order to know how many escape my net. What were you thinking? Do you think I live on air? That I inherited an estate? Do I have another house or vineyard? Do you know of any wealth other than what this profession provides me, my food and drink, my gowns and shoes? I was born in this city, brought up in it, maintaining my honor as all the world knows. Am I, then, not known? The man who does not know my name and my house I hold to be a stranger.

SEMPRONIO. Tell me, Mother, what did you say to my companion Pármeno during the time I went up with Calisto for the money?

CELESTINA. I told him what had happened and gave him the lay of the land, and how he would gain more from our company than he would fawning over his master; how he would live forever poor and insulted if he did not take new counsel, and not to play the saint with an old bitch like me. I reminded him who his mother was so he would not denigrate my profession, because anything foul he says of me would strike her first.

SEMPRONIO. How long have you known him, Mother?

CELESTINA. This Celestina saw him born and helped bring him up. His mother and I were flesh and bone. From her I learned the best I know of my office. We ate together, we slept together, we had our good times together, and we counseled and planned together. In the house and out in the world we were like two sisters; I never earned a coin that she did not have half. If my fortune had wanted her to be with me I would never have known disillusion. O death, death! How many you deprive of agreeable company! How many are left disconsolate by your dread visitation! For every one you devour at their time, you cut off a thousand prematurely. For when she was alive, I was never without company. May she rest in peace, for she was a loyal friend and good companion. She never let me do anything on my own if she was there. If I had the bread, she brought the meat; if I set the table, she had the cloth. Not silly, not filled with fantasies or presumption, like girls today. On my soul, she would walk bareheaded to the end of the city with her jug in her hand, and all the way she never heard worse than, "Ho, Señora Claudina!" And I can tell you that there was no one who knew wine and other merchandise better. When I thought she had not had time to get there, she was already on her way back. She was always invited in because of the love they all had for her. She never came back without eight or ten tasty treats, good measures in the jug and one in her body. Merchants poured her two or three weights of wine as freely as if she'd offered a silver cup. Her word was a gift of gold in every wine cellar in the city. When we went down the street, anywhere we were thirsty we would go in the first tavern and ask for a cup to be poured to wet our lips. And I assure you that they did not take her bonnet in pay, but merely marked the board and we went on our way. If her son were like that now, I can promise you that your master would be plucked clean, he without a feather and we without a complaint. But if I am still alive, he will be made over in my pattern. I will count him one of my own.

SEMPRONIO. How have you thought to do it, he being so treacherous?

CELESTINA. That will simply be one backstabber against two of the same cloth. I will give him Areúsa. She will be one of us. She will clear away obstacles and make us room to lay out our nets for Calisto's coins.

SEMPRONIO. Do you think that you will be able to get to Melibea? Do you have some sign to put out, the way wine sellers do?

CELESTINA. There is no surgeon who can cure an injury with the first treatment. I will tell you what I see at this moment: Melibea is beautiful. Calisto is mad but he is also openhanded. It will not bother him to spend, or me to trot around. Money will flow and may the contest be long-lasting! Money can do everything; it breaks down cliffs and crosses dry through rivers. There is no place so high that an ass laden with gold cannot climb it. Calisto's stupidity and ardor are enough to ruin him and award us gain. I have felt this, I have calculated this, I know about him and about her, and this is something we will take advantage of. I will go see Pleberius. You go with God. For even if Melibea is a fierce opponent, she is not, may it please God, the first I have choked the cackle out of. They are all a bit skittish in the beginning, but after they have once been saddled they never want a rest. The course is open to them; kill them, yes, weary them, no. If they run by night, they will never want it to dawn; they curse the roosters because they announce the day and the clock because it turns so fast. They seek the Pleiades and the North Star, turning into stargazers. Now when they see the morning star their soul wants to leave their body, and its brightness darkens their heart. This is a road, Son, that I never grew tired of walking; no, I never found myself weary. And even as old as I am, God knows my longings. How much more these girls who boil without fire! They are captivated from the first embrace, they entreat the one who entreated them, they feel pain for the one who is in pain, they make themselves servants to the one they once gave orders to, they give up command and are themselves commanded, they destroy walls, they fling open windows, they feign illnesses, they apply oils to the squeaking hinges of doors so that they can carry out their duties. I do not know how to tell you how much the sweetness from the first kisses lingers. They are all enemies of the middle; they are always poised at the extremes.

SEMPRONIO. I do not understand your terms, Mother.

CELESTINA. I am saying that either a woman loves the one who is wooing her or she loathes him; so it is that if she says goodbye to love, she cannot rein in her cruel words against the one she loved. And with this, which I know to be true, I am going to Melibea's house as confidently as if I had her in the palm of my hand, because I know that although first I will be begging her, in the end it will be she who begs me; although at first she threatens me, in the end she will flatter me. I have here in my pouch a little thread, along with other items I always carry with me in order, on my first visit, to have reason to go in where I am not well known: things like ruffs, hair netting, shoulder rolls, pluckers, kohl, and assorted potions and lotions, even needles and pins. I have everything anyone might want.

Because wherever my voice is heard, I want to be prepared to set out my bait and set things in motion on my first visit.

SEMPRONIO. Mother, look carefully to what you are doing, because if something goes wrong at the beginning, a good ending cannot follow. Think about her father, who is noble and stern, her strict and jealous mother, and you, suspicion itself. Melibea is their only child, without her they have no blessing. I tremble to think of that. Do not go for wool and come back with feathers.

CELESTINA. Feathers, Son?

SEMPRONIO. Or honey and feathers, Mother, which is what they do to convent-trotting go-betweens.

CELESTINA. Here now. This is no time to have *you* as a companion! You may even think you want to advise Celestina on how to tend to her trade. But when you were born, I had all my teeth to eat a hard loaf. Some fine conspirator you make, loaded down with omens and distrust!

SEMPRONIO. Do not marvel, Mother, at my fear, for it is a common human condition to fret that you will never see concluded the thing you most desire; and even more, in this case I fear for you and for me. True, I want to profit from this, and I would like for this business to come to a good end—not in order that my master be relieved of his pain, but for me to make my way out of penury. And so I, with my limited experience, see problems that you, who have mastered your trade, cannot see.

SCENE 2

ELICIA. Well bless me, if it is not Sempronio! I want to see this line drawn on water before it disappears! Is this something new, to come two times today?

CELESTINA. Hush, silly girl; drop it; we have more important things to think about. Tell me, is the house empty? Did the girl leave who was waiting for the judge?

ELICIA. Yes, and then another came and she's gone too.

CELESTINA. But she did not come for nothing, I hope?

ELICIA. O, by my faith, no; nor would God have that, for although she was not the early bird, she got the . . . and you know the rest.

CELESTINA. Run up to the room off the gallery and bring down the bottle of snake oil you will find hanging on that length of hangman's noose I brought back the other night when it was raining and very dark. And open the coffer where I keep the strong thread; to your right you will find a paper covered with signs written in the blood of a bat, and underneath that the claws we pulled yesterday from its dragon wings. And do not spill the May night dew I was brought to use in my preparations.

ELICIA. Mother, it is not where you say. You never remember where you keep things.

CELESTINA. God's bones! Do not chastise me in my old age; do not mistreat me, Elicia. You need not be so full of yourself now that Sempronio is here, or put on airs, for he would rather have me as a counselor than you as a friend, even though you love him so much. Go to the room where I keep the ointments and, in the black cat's skin where I had you put the wolf's eyes, you will find it. And take down the goat's blood and a few of the hairs you cut from its beard.

. . . .

ELICIA. Here, Mother; here they are. And Sempronio and I are going up.

CELESTINA (*alone*). I conjure you, gloomy Pluto, lord of the depths of hell; emperor of the court of the damned; sovereign captain of condemned angels; lord of the sulfurous fires that erupt from boiling Etna; director and overseer of torments and tormentor of sinful spirits; ruler of the three Furies, Tisiphone, Megaera, and Alecto; regulator of all blackness in the regions of the Styx and Dite, with all their lakes and tenebrous, infernal shadows and abysses; governor of flying harpies, and all the company of fearsome and terrifying hydras. I, Celestina, am the best known of those who summon you, I conjure you through the virtue and force of these crimson letters, through the blood of that nocturnal winged creature with which they are written, through the gravity of the incantations and magical signs this paper contains, through the powerful serpents' venom from which this oil was compounded, and with which I anoint this thread. Come in all haste to obey my will, wrap yourself within its loops and do not let go until Melibea, at the suitable opportunity, buys it. And stay entangled in it, so that the more she looks upon it, the more her heart will soften and accede to my petition; may her heart open and be struck with uncontrollable love for Calisto, so much that setting aside all modesty she will bare herself to me and will reward my actions and message. Once this is done, ask and demand my obedience. If you do not act swiftly you will find in me a mortal enemy; I will flood your sad, dark dungeons with light, I will attack your constant lies, I will denounce your horrible name with cruel curses. And I will conjure you again and again. And thus, trusting in my great power, I am setting off for that place with my thread, in which I believe I have you carefully entwined.

ACT FOUR

(Celestina, Lucrecia, Alisa, Melibea)

PLOT

Celestina walks down the road, talking to herself, until she reaches the door of Pleberius, where she finds Lucrecia, Pleberius's servant. She starts a conversation with her. They are overheard by Alisa, mother of Melibea, and when she learns it is Celestina, she bids her come in. A messenger arrives to summon Alisa. She leaves. Celestina is left in the house with Melibea, and she reveals the reason for her visit.

SCENE 1

CELESTINA (*alone*). Now that I am alone, I want to think very carefully about why Sempronio feared my coming here, because those things that are not carefully thought out, though they may sometimes work out well, ordinarily produce illogical results. Time spent on speculation never fails to produce good fruit. For although I have dissembled with Sempronio, it could well be that if my purpose in these plans for Melibea were found out I could pay with nothing less than my life, or be left with nothing, or should they choose not to kill me be tossed in a blanket or cruelly lashed. And then these hundred coins would be bitterly won. Ay, so many cares. What a bind I have got myself into! To show myself to be diligent and strong, I am playing my life on the boards. What shall I do, harassed and needy that I am, when withdrawing is without profit and persevering is fraught with danger? Shall I go forward or shall I turn back? What doubt-ridden and cruel bewilderment! I do not know which is the wiser course. Danger awaits in daring, and in cowardice, defeat and disgrace. Where does the ox go that is no longer able to plow? Every road has its dangerous and deep ravines. If I am caught in the act, I will never escape but either suffer death or be placed in the stocks with the procuress's hood on my head. If I do not go, what will Sempronio say? That *these* were my powers, my knowledge and strength, my artifice and offers to help, my astuteness and concern? And his master, Calisto, what will he say, what will he do, what will he think but that there is new deceit in my actions and that I have revealed our scheme to have greater profit from the other side, as a two-faced cheat and liar. Or, if such odious thoughts do not occur to him, he will nonetheless rant like a madman. He will throw angry insults in my face; he will recite a thousand disadvantages that my hasty decisions have caused him, saying "You old whore, why did you inflame my passions with your promises? Deceitful old convent-trotter, you have busy feet for everyone else, for me, only your busy tongue; for others, works, for me, words; for others, remedies, for me, pain; for others, endeavor, for me, naught; for others, light, for me, darkness! Well then, you perfidious old slattern, whence your offer to help me? Your words gave me hope; hope held off my death, gave me life, made me a happy man. But as there is no result, you will not lack for pain, nor I for misery and despair." Ay, what tears! No good here, no good there; trouble on both sides! When there is no middle between extremes, it is wise to choose the safer course. I would rather offend

Pleberius than anger Calisto. So I will go there; the shame of staying like a coward is greater than the punishment of daring to do what I promised, for Fortune always favors the attempt. I see her door now. I have found myself in worse situations. Courage, Celestina, courage! Do not lose heart! There are always many who will plead my case for a lesser punishment. All the omens are lined up to be favorable, or else I know nothing of this art; of the four men I met on the way here, three are named Juan—there's a good sign—and two are cuckolds. The first word I heard when I came out was related to love. And I have not stumbled once, as I usually do. The stones seemed to move aside and make room for me to pass, and my skirts were no impediment nor am I weary from walking. Everyone bade me a Good Day. Not one dog barked at me nor did I sight a raven or crow or any other black as night bird. And best of all is that I see Lucrecia at Melibea's door. She is Elicia's cousin. She will not give me trouble.

SCENE 2

LUCRECIA (*alone*). Who is that old woman hurrying this way and tripping over her skirts?

CELESTINA. Peace be on this house!

LUCRECIA. Mother Celestina, you are welcome. What God brought you to these unaccustomed parts?

CELESTINA. Love, Daughter, and wanting to see you. I bring Elicia's greetings to all of you, and would like to see your mistress and her daughter, the old and the young. For I have not visited you since I moved to a different part of the city.

LUCRECIA. And did you come only for that? I am surprised, for that is not your custom, nor do you usually move a step unless profit is assured.

CELESTINA. But, silly girl, what greater profit than doing what you like? And also, since there is always something we old women need, and that is especially true of me because I must tend to the daughters of others, I go about selling a little thread.

LUCRECIA. That is just what I mean! I still have my wits. I know that you never put in a needle without pulling out an iron post. But my old mistress has been weaving a cloth; she has need of thread and here you are selling it. Come in and wait here and things will go well.

SCENE 3

ALISA. Who are you talking with, Lucrecia?

LUCRECIA. Señora, with that old woman with the knife scar across her face, the one who used to live near the tanneries down by the river.

ALISA. I do not know her as well as I did. If you want me to recognize someone by telling me what is least known about her, that is like catching water in a basket.

LUCRECIA. Jesú, Señora. This old woman is better known than goat's rue. I do not know how you can have forgotten that she was pilloried for witchcraft, that she sold girls to priests, and defiled a thousand marriages.

ALISA. What is her trade? Maybe I will recognize her by that.

LUCRECIA. Mistress, she perfumes linen caps, makes face powders, and has at least thirty other trades. She knows a lot about herbs, she physics babies, and some even call her Old Lapidary for what she knows about stones.

ALISA. None of this you say tells me who she is. Tell me her name, if you know it.

LUCRECIA. If I know it, Señora? There is no child or elder in the whole city who does not know it. Why would I not know it?

ALISA. Then why do you not say it?

LUCRECIA. I am embarrassed.

ALISA. Silly girl. Go on, say it. Do not vex me by being so slow.

LUCRECIA. Celestina, speaking with respect, is her name.

ALISA (*she laughs*). You should be struck with a goiter for making me laugh so hard; you must feel strongly about that old hag if it embarrasses you to speak her name. I'm beginning to remember who she is. She is a fine one all right! Say no more. She has come to ask me for something. Tell her to come up.

LUCRECIA. Come up, Auntie.

SCENE 4

CELESTINA. My dear señora, may the grace of God be with you and with your noble daughter. My suffering and illness have kept me from visiting your house as was called for. But God knows my honest nature, my true affection; distance between dwellings does not take the love from our hearts. And so it is that what I have long wished to do, necessity has made me do. Along with other adversities, I have suffered a lack of funds. I knew no better remedy than to sell a little of the thread I had put aside for some lace-trimmed caps I was commissioned to do. I learned from your servant that you had need of some thread. Although I am poor, and not in God's mercy, what I have is for you, if you wish to make use of it, and of me.

ALISA. Good neighbor, your explanation and your offer move me to compassion; so much that I would prefer to increase your funds rather than decrease your supplies. I thank you for what you have said. If the thread is good, you will be well paid.

CELESTINA. Good, Señora? As good as my life and my old age and that of anyone who would share my oath. Fine as the hair of your head, consistent, straight as a vihuela string, white as a snowflake, all spun by these very fingers, reeled and wound. See these little skeins. I was paid three coins yesterday for an ounce, a joy to this sinful soul.

ALISA. Daughter Melibea, keep this honorable woman with you, for it is already late for me to visit my sister, the wife of Cremes, whom I have not seen since yesterday; she has sent her page to fetch me for she has taken a turn for the worse.

CELESTINA (*apart*). Ah, the Devil is hereabouts, providing an opportunity for me by making the sister's illness worse. Ho, good friend. Be steadfast! This is the time, now or never. Stay with her; you, the one I am addressing, take her away from here.

ALISA. What are you saying, good friend?

CELESTINA. Señora, I merely curse the Devil and my sin, for as your sister is worsening, we will have no opportunity to do our business. And what is her ailment?

ALISA. A pain in her side, so bad that from what the page says I am afraid I may not find her alive. For my sake, neighbor, in your devotions pray God for her health.

CELESTINA. I promise, Señora, that when I leave here I will go by those monasteries where I have friars who are devoted to me, and I will pass to them the charge you gave me. And further, before I have breakfast, I will say my rosary four times.

ALISA. Well, Melibea, make our neighbor happy by giving her whatever is reasonable for the thread. And you, Mother, forgive me; on another day we will have more time together.

CELESTINA. Señora, where there is no fault, to forgive would be excessive. God has forgiven you, for you leave me with good company. God is allowing your daughter to enjoy her noble youth and flowering maidenhood, and this is the time for her to experience greater pleasures and delights. By my faith, old age is the inn of illness, the hostelry of recollection, a friend to quarrels, a never-ending misery, an incurable sore, an herb from the past, pain of the present, sad worry of the future, a neighbor of death, a roofless hut that lets in rain everywhere, and a wicker staff that bends beneath the slightest weight.

SCENE 5

MELIBEA. Why, Mother, do you speak such ill of something everyone wants to live to enjoy?

CELESTINA. They who do are wishing hard work and misfortune for themselves. They want to get there because by doing so they are still alive, and living is sweet, but living they grow old. So the boy wishes to be a lad, and the lad old, and the old man still older, even with aches and pains. It is all about living, for as it is said, even with pip the hen lives on. Ay, but what I could tell you, Señora, of life's afflictions, its disadvantages, its fatigues, its cares, its illnesses, its cold, its heat, its discontent, its conflicts, its grief, the wrinkled face, the hair losing its original, youthful color, the difficulty hearing, the sight fading as the eyes sink in their sockets, the lips thinning, the teeth falling out, the strength flagging, the gait stumbling, the cautious eating. And, ay, Señora, if what I have recounted is accompanied by poverty and there is a deep longing for food and the cupboard is bare, all else will be as nothing. I have never known a worse ache than hunger.

MELIBEA. I do know that everyone speaks of the fair according to what they get from it; so the rich sing a different tune.

CELESTINA. My dear daughter, every road has its three leagues of rocks and gullies. The rich man loses his good fortune, glory, and repose down conduits that do not seem to be sewers as they are of brick covered over with flatteries. He who is at peace with God is rich. It is safer to be scorned than feared. The poor man sleeps better, for he does not have to guard what he won with hard work and would grieve to lose. My friend has no pretenses but the rich man does. I am loved for myself, the rich man for his possessions. He never hears the truth; everyone says things that are sweet to his palate, and everyone envies him. You seldom find a rich man who does not confess that it would be preferable to live in a middling estate or in honest poverty. Riches do not make one rich, but busy; they do not create a master, but a steward. Rather than possess riches, men are possessed by them. Wealth has brought death to many and stolen pleasure from all, and nothing is more inimical to good practices. Have you not heard it said that "Men with riches dreamed their dream and waked to find nothing in their hands?" Every rich man has a dozen children and grandchildren who have but one prayer, one plea to direct to God: that he be taken from them. They long for the hour when they will have him in the earth, and everything his in their hands, the moment they have laid him in his eternal home—at the least possible expense.

MELIBEA. Mother, that being the case, you must suffer greatly for the years you have lost. Would you like to go back to the beginning?

CELESTINA. No, Daughter; demented is the traveler who annoyed by the day's fatigues wants to go back to the beginning of the journey and travel again to the same place; for all those unpleasant things in life are far better possessed than anticipated, because the farther one is from the beginning the nearer one is to the end. There is nothing sweeter or more welcome to the weary traveler than an inn. So it is that, although youth is a happy time, the wisely old man does not desire it, because he who lacks reason and good sense loves almost nothing but what he has lost.

MELIBEA. If only to live longer, it is good to want what I want.

CELESTINA. The butcher, Daughter, is gone as quickly as the lamb. No one is so old that he cannot live another year, or so young he cannot die. So in this matter you have little advantage.

MELIBEA. You frighten me with what you have said. Your arguments make me think that I have seen you before. Tell me, Mother, are you that Celestina who used to live near the tanneries down by the river?

CELESTINA. As long, Daughter, as God wills it.

MELIBEA. You have grown old. They speak wisely who say that the days mark their passing. In truth, I would not have recognized you were it not for that scar on your face. I fancy you were beautiful, but you look like a different person. You are very changed.

LUCRECIA (*apart; she laughs*). Yes, the old devil has changed! Beautiful indeed with the knife slash across half her face!

MELIBEA. What are you saying, stupid girl? What is it you are saying? What are you laughing at?

LUCRECIA. That after such a short time you did not recognize Mother by her face.

MELIBEA. Two years is not such a short time, and besides, she is all wrinkles now.

CELESTINA. Daughter. When you stop time from moving forward I will not have changed. Have you not read, "The day will come when you do not know yourself in the glass?" But my hair turned gray early and I look twice my age. But 'pon my sinful soul and your lovely body, of the four girls my mother bore, I was the youngest. So you see, I am not as old as I am judged to be.

MELIBEA. Friend Celestina, I have enjoyed seeing you and getting to know you. It has also been pleasant to talk with you. Here is your money, now go with God, for it seems you must not have eaten.

CELESTINA. O my angelic girl! O precious pearl, how sweetly you speak! My pleasure has been hearing you speak. And surely you know the words that issued from the divine mouth itself—against the wicked tempter—man does not live by bread alone? So it is that eating alone does not sustain us; especially me, for I often fast for one or two days as I go about my missions for others. And why do you believe there is virtue in this world if it is not to work on behalf of others, or die for them? This has always been my byword, to work serving others rather than be idle indulging myself. So, with your permission, I will tell you the true cause for my visit, for it is different from what you have heard till now, and we would both regret it if I left without your learning it.

MELIBEA. Tell me, Mother, all your needs; for if I am able to remedy them, I will gladly do so because of our past acquaintance, and because of being neighbors, which places an obligation on all good people.

CELESTINA. My needs, Daughter? I put those of others first, as I have said; for mine never step outside my door, their feet never touch the ground. I eat when I can, drink when I have it. Even though I am poor and widowed, I never, praise God, am short a copper for bread and a few maravedís for wine; once I had no cares— there was always an extra wineskin in my house, and one full and another empty. I never went to bed without first enjoying a crust soaked in wine, and—to tone the womb—a dozen or two draughts to follow. Now that I have to look out for myself, they bring my wine in a cracked jug that does not hold two measures. Six times a day, for my sin, I have to go, gray hair streaming down my back, to fill it at the tavern. But may I not die my death until there is a skin or a good-sized jug sitting inside my door. For on my faith, there is no other provision so good, and, as it is said, "Go down the road with bread and wine, and for anything more you will never pine." So it is that where there is no man, nothing goes well: "The bobbin's not wound when there's no man around." We came to this subject,

Daughter, because of what you were saying about the needs of others, not mine.

MELIBEA. Ask what you would wish, whoever it is for.

CELESTINA. Gracious maiden, of such fine breeding! Your soft way of speaking and happy face, added to the generosity you show to this poor old woman, allow me to dare tell you. I have come from a man sick to death, who believes that with only one word from your noble lips, which I will carry to him buried deep in my bosom, he will be healed, owing to the deep devotion he feels for your kindness.

MELIBEA. Honorable old woman, I cannot understand if you do not tell me what your request is. On the one hand, you vex me and stir my anger; on the other, you move me to compassion. I would not know how to give a proper answer based on the little I have heard you say, but I feel blessed that my word is needed for a Christian's health, because to do a kindness is to liken ourselves to God, and the one who gives it also receives it when it is addressed to a deserving person. And beyond that, it is said that he who is able to heal someone who suffers, and fails to do it, is responsible for his death. So please do not let reticence or fear keep you from stating your request.

CELESTINA. I lost all fear, Daughter, seeing your beauty. For I cannot believe that without reason God made some females with more perfect faces than others, more endowed with graces and beautiful features, if not to make them the storehouse of virtue, of mercy, of compassion, the minister of graces and gifts, as He did you. And since as we are all human, born to die, it is true that he who was born only for himself cannot say "born," for that would mean he was like the animals, among which there are even some few that are merciful, as is said of the unicorn, which kneels before a maiden, or the dog, which with all its vigor and ferocity when it springs to bite will not harm you if you throw yourself to the ground; this an act of mercy. And birds? The rooster eats nothing it does not share, calling the hens to eat of its grain. The pelican opens its chest to feed its chicks from its very innards. Storks keep their old parents in the nest for the same amount of time they fed them as chicks. Since nature endowed animals and birds with this knowledge, why should we humans be more cruel? Why do we not give part of our favors and our persons to our neighbors, especially when they are laid low by a secret malady, the kind that can be healed only by the thing that causes it?

MELIBEA. God help us, do not delay longer but tell me who this ailing person is who suffers such a bewildering indisposition that his suffering and its remedy are found in the same source!

CELESTINA. You must be aware, Daughter, that in this city there is a young caballero, a nobleman of pure blood, Calisto by name.

MELIBEA. Enough, enough! Good woman, say no more; go no further. This then is the sufferer for whom you have presented such a preamble in your plea, for whom you have come to seek death for yourself, for whom you have taken such perilous steps, you shameless, bearded old crone? What can that wretch feel that you come with such passion? His illness must be madness! What do you think? If you had found me free of suspicions concerning that madman, what words would you have used to ensnare me? It is not for nothing said that the most dangerous part of the wicked man or woman is the tongue. May you burn at the stake, you deceitful procuress, you vile convent-trotter, you witch, you enemy of decency, you cause of secret sins! Jesú, Jesú! Lucrecia! Take her from my sight. I am through; she has left no drop of blood in my body! The person who gives ear to such women deserves this and more. Were it not that it would reflect upon my purity, and spread the word of the audacity of this brash man, I would, you wicked drab, have seen that your words and your life were quickly ended.

CELESTINA (*apart*). If my spell fails, I will have come at an accursed hour! Ho, hear me; I know whom I am speaking to! Come, Brother, or all will be lost!

MELIBEA. You are still mumbling in my presence, is it to increase my anger and double your punishment? Do you want to ruin my reputation in order to save a madman? Leave me sad for making him happy and you carry off the reward in exchange for my perdition, the reward for my sin? Ruin and destroy my father's house and honor to gain those things for an accursed bawd like you? You think I have not heard where your footsteps are going and understood your corrupt message? Well I can swear to you that the only reward you could take from here would be to prevent you from further offending God by putting an end to your days. Answer me, traitor, how did you dare do this?

CELESTINA. Fear of you, Daughter, has impeded my apology. My innocence makes me bold but your wrath perturbs me. And what I most regret is unjustly to be the object of your anger. Please God, Daughter, let me finish what I have to say, and neither will he be guilty or I condemned; you will see that it is more a service to God than a dishonest proposal, more to give health to a sick man than to harm the physician's reputation. Had I thought, Daughter, that you would so quickly succumb to noxious suspicion, your permission would not have been enough, and I would never have dared speak to you concerning Calisto, or any other man.

MELIBEA. Jesú! I do not want to hear another word about this crazed wall jumper, this night specter, this leggy stork, this badly woven figure in a tapestry, lest I drop dead on the spot! This then is the man who saw me the other day and began to rant and rave and act the gallant. Tell him, my good woman, that if he thought everything already won and the field his, I listened because I thought it better to listen than to publicize his flaws; I wanted more to treat him as a madman than to spread word of his outrageous boldness. So advise him to leave aside this proposition and all will be well; if not, it could be that all his lifetime he has never paid so dearly for someone to speak on his behalf. For he knows a person is not vanquished until she believes she is, and that I was left untouched and he strutting; madmen tend to believe that all others are of their ilk. Carry his message right back to him. You will have no other answer from me, and do not expect one, and furthermore, it would be to plead to one who can have no mercy. And give thanks to God that you leave this fair a free woman. I have been told who you are, and warned of your qualities, although today I did not recognize you.

CELESTINA (*apart*). Stronger was Troy, but I have tamed even wilder maidens. No storm lasts forever.

MELIBEA. What are you saying, enemy? Speak so I can hear you. Do you have any excuse that will satisfy my anger and justify your error and audacity?

CELESTINA. As long as your ire endures, my explanation will add harm. That you are severe does not surprise me; it takes very little heat to make young blood boil.

MELIBEA. Little heat? You may call it little since you are left alive, and I querulous at your daring. What word could you want from me for that man that would work to my well-being? Answer me, for you say you have not finished; perhaps it will expunge what has happened here.

CELESTINA. He requests a prayer, Daughter, one he was told you know. One prayed by Saint Apollonia for toothache. And also the girdle you wear clasped around your waist, for it is widely known that it has touched all the relics in Rome and Jerusalem. The caballero I told you of is suffering, longing for that blessing. This is why I came, but since in my telling I incurred your wrathful response, he must suffer the pain as payment for sending such an unfortunate messenger; for as I found no mercy among your many virtues, I would similarly expect that were I sent to the sea I would find no water. But you know now that the pleasure of vengeance lasts but a moment and that of mercy for eternity.

MELIBEA. If it is the girdle you wanted, why did you not tell me that? Why did you not say that in a few words?

CELESTINA. Daughter, because the purity of my intent made me believe that even though I spoke briefly I gave no cause to suspect evil, and if my proposal lacked a proper preamble it was because truth does not demand colorful words. Compassion for his suffering and confidence in your munificence choked out expression of the cause. And as you know, Daughter, pain is distracting, and that distraction frees and agitates the tongue (which always is linked to the brain). God's mercy, do not blame me! And if error has been done, it does not lead to harm for me for I have no guilt other than being messenger for the guilty one. Do not snap the rope at the thinnest strand; do not be like the spider web, which demonstrates its strength only against the weakest creatures. Do not have the just pay for the sinners. Follow the way of divine justice, which says, "The one that sins, let that soul perish," and also the human, which never condemns the father for the sin of the son, nor the son for that of the father. Nor is it right, Daughter, that Calisto's audacity should bring about my perdition, for because of his privilege it would not take much to make me the one condemned. I have no office but to serve my fellow beings. From this I live and clothe myself. It has never been my wish to anger some to please others, though in my absence you may have been told something different. In the end, Daughter, the wind of common gossip cannot sway the truth. I am alone in my honest undertaking, and in all this city I know few who are dissatisfied. I work with everyone and go where I am sent, as if I had twenty feet and as many hands.

MELIBEA. That does not surprise me, for it is said that a single master of vice is enough to corrupt a great city. It is true that I have heard so many tales about your cunning ways that I am not sure I believe it was a prayer you were asking for.

CELESTINA. May I never pray again, and if I do may it not be heard, if anything different could be wrung from me though I suffer a thousand torments.

MELIBEA. I am too recently irate to laugh at your apology, for I know that neither oath nor torture could make you speak the truth, as that is not within your code of conduct.

CELESTINA. You are my mistress. I must calm your words, I must serve you, you must command me. Your harsh words are the harbinger of a new skirt for me.

MELIBEA. You have earned it!

CELESTINA. If I have not won it with my tongue, I have not lost it with my intention.

MELIBEA. You so strongly assert your ignorance that you make me believe it may be true. In that case, on the strength of your questionable apology I will delay issuing your sentence and not rule on your request without further deliberation. You should not be surprised at my recent outburst because of two things you said, either of which was enough to drive me out of my mind: you told me the name of this caballero of yours, and you asked for a word from me without telling me why. That could only make me suspect some harm to my honor. But since it comes without ill intent, there can be forgiveness for what has happened; to some degree my heart is eased, knowing it is pious and saintly work to heal those suffering from heart and ill health.

CELESTINA. And so ill, Daughter! God's bones! If you knew him well you would not judge him by what you have said and shown with your ire. By my faith and my soul, there is no drop of bile in him. Gifts and favors, two thousand; in generosity an Alexander; in strength, a Hector; in bearing, a king; entertaining, cheerful. Melancholy will never reign in him. Of noble blood, as you know. A great jouster; seeing him armed, you would say a Saint George. Strength and spirit Hercules could not equal. His mien, his features, demeanor, eloquence, it would take yet another tongue to tell. All together, he is like an angel from heaven. By my faith, that handsome Narcissus who fell in love with his own reflection when he saw it in the waters of the fountain was not as august. But now, Daughter, he finds himself felled by a single tooth that never stops paining him.

MELIBEA. And how long has it been . . . ?

CELESTINA. About twenty-three years, Daughter; for this Celestina standing here saw him born and welcomed him into the world.

MELIBEA. That is not what I am asking, I have no need to know his age; I wanted to know how long he has had the toothache.

CELESTINA. A week, Daughter: it seems a year by how thin he is. And the best remedy he has is to take up his vihuela and strum so many and such mournful songs that I do not think them different from those the emperor-musician Hadrian composed about the departing soul in order to confront imminent death without swooning. I know very little about music, but to me it seems he makes that vihuela talk. And if he happens to sing, more birds flutter down to listen than did to that Amphion who was said to move trees and stones with his singing. And once he was born, Orpheus was no longer praised. Ask yourself, Daughter, whether a poor old woman like me would not rejoice to give life to someone with so many graces. No woman sees him who does not praise God for creating him as he is. If he happens to talk with her, she is no longer mistress of herself but does what he bids. And since I have such good reason,

Daughter, judge my proposal to be good, my actions as wholesome and empty of suspicion.

MELIBEA. O how my lack of patience weighs on me. Though he is unaware and you innocent, you have nevertheless suffered the alarms of my wrathful tongue. But that I had reason relieves me of the guilt raised by your suspicious words. In payment for your ordeal, I want to fulfill your request and give you my girdle. And because there will be no time to write the prayer before my mother returns, if that is not enough, come secretly for it tomorrow.

LUCRECIA (*apart*). Ay, ay, my mistress is lost! She wants Celestina to come secretly? There is a trick in this! She must have more in mind than what she has said!

MELIBEA. What did you say, Lucrecia?

LUCRECIA. Mistress, what has been said is enough; it is late.

MELIBEA. Well, Mother, do not report to that caballero what has happened, so he will not consider me cruel or rash or dishonest.

LUCRECIA (*apart*). I do not lie when I say this is going badly.

CELESTINA. I am amazed, Daughter Melibea, that you have any doubt about the secret. Have no worry, I know how to suffer and conceal anything. I see very well that your strong suspicion misinterpreted my intent, as suspicion often does. I am going now, very happy to leave with your girdle, and I believe his heart is thankful for the mercy you have done us, and that I will find him much relieved.

MELIBEA. I will do more, if need be, to compensate for what you have suffered.

CELESTINA (*apart*). More will be needed, and you will do more, although you may not be thanked!

MELIBEA. What do you say, Mother, in the way of thanks?

CELESTINA. I say, Daughter, that we are all grateful to you and we will serve you and all be in your debt. The surest payment is when there is most to be fulfilled.

LUCRECIA (*apart*). Turn those words around!

CELESTINA (*apart*). Daughter Lucrecia! Shh! Come to my house and I will give you a bleach that will make your hair shine brighter than gold. Do not tell your mistress. And I will even give you powders that will rid you of that unpleasant breath, it smells less than sweet; in all the kingdom no one but I knows how to make it, and a woman can suffer nothing worse.

LUCRECIA (*apart*). May God grant you a good old age, for I had greater need of all this than for food!

CELESTINA (*apart*). Then why are you muttering against me, crazy girl. Say no more; you may well need me in a matter of greater importance. Do not provoke your mistress, make her angrier than she has been. Let me go quietly.

MELIBEA. Mother, you were saying?

CELESTINA. We were agreeing about something, Daughter.

MELIBEA. Tell me, for it irritates me when things are said in which I have no part.

CELESTINA. Daughter, I was telling her to remind you of the prayer so you can have it written, and to learn from me to have patience when you are angry, following, as I did, the counsel that said to leave the angry one for a short period and the enemy a long one. You were angry, Daughter, about what you suspected in my words, but you were not my enemy. But even were it what you believed, those words were not bad in themselves; every day men suffer over women and women over men, and this is effected by nature, and nature is commanded by God, and God does no evil. And so my request remained, as I wished it, praiseworthy in itself, branching as it does from such a strong tree, and I innocent of blame. I would give you more reasons than these, except that loquaciousness is irritating to the one who listens and harmful to the one who speaks.

MELIBEA. You have had a good touch in all this, as much in speaking little during my anger as in tolerating a great deal.

CELESTINA. Daughter, I bore it with fear, because you had good reason for anger. And when power is added to anger, it can produce a thunderbolt. For this reason I let your severe words pass me by until the store was emptied.

MELIBEA. This caballero is in your debt.

CELESTINA. Daughter, he deserves more. And if I have achieved something for him with my prayer, I have harmed him with the delay. I will leave now to go to him, with your permission.

MELIBEA. Had you asked for it earlier, I would gladly have given it to you. Go with God, for neither you nor your message has benefited me, nor can your leaving do me harm.

ACT FIVE

(Celestina, Sempronio, Pármeno, Calisto)

PLOT

After taking leave of Melibea, Celestina makes her way through the streets, talking to herself. Once home, she speaks with Sempronio, who is waiting for her. They continue on together, talking, until they reach Calisto's house and are seen by Pármeno, who notifies his master, Calisto, that they are arriving, and he orders Pármeno to open the door.

SCENE 1

CELESTINA (*alone*). O such danger! O cunning daring mine! O great suffering! I was very near death had my cleverness not known to trim the sails of my petition. O threats from that fiery maiden! O wrathful maiden! And you, Devil, you I conjured, how faithfully you kept your word in everything I asked of you! I am in your debt! You tamed that cruel female with your power, and with her mother's absence provided the opportune opening for my words, as I wished. O Celestina, old girl! Are you happy? You know that with a good beginning half is done. O my snake oil! O my white thread! How well you worked in my favor! If not, I would have broken all my bonds, now, past, and future, and never again had faith in herbs or stones, or words. So be cheerful, old woman; you will take in more from this transaction than from fifteen patched maidenheads. Curse these long skirts, you keep getting in the way of my reaching the place where my new ones are to be found. Good fortune, how you aid the daring and belay the timid! Never by fleeing has a coward fled death. How many would have failed in what I have achieved! And what would many of these new mistresses of my trade have done in such narrow straits but say something to Melibea that would have lost what I, with clever silence, have gained? That is why it is said: "Let him play who knows the tune," and, "Better the physician with experience than one who learned from books," and also, "Experience and hard knocks make a man skillful," as it has me, an old woman who knows to lift her skirts when she wades across a stream. Ah, girdle, girdle I hold in my hand! If I live I will make you drag her to me by force, this pretty one who did not want to speak to me with courtesy!

SCENE 2

SEMPRONIO. Either I do not see well or that is Celestina. She is coming at a devilish trot, skirts boiling. And talking to herself.

CELESTINA. Why are you crossing yourself, Sempronio? I think because you saw me.

SEMPRONIO. I will tell you. Rarity is the mother of wonder; wonder conceived in the eyes travels through them to the mind; the mind is forced to communicate that by way of external signs. Who ever saw you in the street, head lowered, eyes to the ground, not looking at anything, as now? Who ever saw you muttering along the way, spurred on like someone racing to claim a benefit. This new behavior is enough to make someone who knows you marvel. But with that aside, tell me, God willing, what news? Tell me if it is good or bad, for I have been waiting for you here since it struck one, and have no sign but how long you have taken.

CELESTINA. Son, that ridiculous belief is not always reliable, my slow return may not have signaled good news; I could have taken an hour longer and left my nose behind, or two, and left nose and tongue; the longer, the dearer the cost.

SEMPRONIO. For all that is love, Mother, do not go without telling me what happened.

CELESTINA. Friend Sempronio, I cannot stop now, nor is this the proper place. Come with me. Once we are with Calisto you will hear wondrous things; the bloom will be taken from my message if I tell it too many times. I want you to learn from my own lips what has been done, for though you are to have some little share of the reward, I want all the thanks for the work.

SEMPRONIO. A little share, Celestina? I do not like the sound of that.

CELESTINA. Hush, foolish boy; share or little share, whatever you want I will give you. Everything mine is yours. We will enjoy, we will profit, we will never quarrel over the dividing. And also, you know how much more we old folks need than boys do, especially you who go to a table already set.

SEMPRONIO. I need things beside food.

CELESTINA. What, Son? A dozen laces and a band for your cap, and a bow to take from house to house shooting your arrows at little birds, ogling them at their windows. At girls, I say, foolish lad, who as yet do not know how to fly, if you understand my meaning. There is no better go-between than a bow, since your arrow may enter uninvited, like someone seeking wool. But O, Sempronio, pity the one who must maintain her honor while growing old, as I am!

SEMPRONIO (*apart*). Fawning old crone! Ancient bawd, seeped in evil! Greedy and avaricious gullet! She wants to deceive me as well as my master and make herself rich. Well, may she make little progress! I do not plan to share it with her! Who in some clumsy fashion climbs, sooner falls than higher ascends. What a terrible thing to know man! It is rightly said that no object, no animal, is so difficult. What a deceitful old woman! The Devil led me to her! Better to have fled this viper than to have picked her up. The fault was mine, but I gained, because for good or ill she will keep her promise.

CELESTINA. What are you saying, Sempronio? Who are you talking with? Are you nibbling at my skirt tails? Why do you not come ahead?

SEMPRONIO. What I am saying, dear mother, is that I do not marvel that you are changeable, most women are. You told me that this would take a while, but now you are rushing off, without a thought, to tell Calisto everything. Do you not know that the thing held dear is the one long desired, and that every day my master suffers will double our reward?

CELESTINA. The wise man changes his course, the fool perseveres. New enterprise, new counsel is required. I did not think, young Sempronio, that I would have such good fortune. A prudent messenger does what the occasion demands. The quality of what is done cannot cover time not wisely spent. And in addition, I know that your master, according to what I have sensed of him, is generous if somewhat capricious. He will give more on a day of good news than on a hundred in which he wanders in pain and I trot back and forth. Delayed, then sudden, pleasure creates confusion, and great confusion hinders deliberation. So to what can good come if not to good, and good tidings but to long-lasting reward. Hush, fool, let this old woman do her work.

SEMPRONIO. But tell me what happened with that gentle maiden. Give me some word from her lips. God's fury! I suffer to know as much as my master does.

CELESTINA. Quiet, dolt! Your attitude has changed. I see in you that now you would rather have the taste than the smell of this business. Let us go quickly, for your master will be maddened by how long I have been gone.

SEMPRONIO. Even without that he already is.

SCENE 3

PÁRMENO. Señor, Señor!

CALISTO. What do you want, fool?

PÁRMENO. I see Sempronio and Celestina hurrying toward the house, making little stops from time to time, and when they do they are drawing lines on the ground with the sword. I do not know what it can be.

CALISTO. O raving, negligent fool! You see them coming, can you not tell me as you run to open the door? O God on high! O sovereign Deity! What can they be bringing? What news do they have? They have taken so long that I was more concerned about their returning than I was about the matter of my remedy. O my poor ears! Prepare yourself for what is coming, for on Celestina's lips, this moment, lies the relief or pain of my heart. If only these few minutes would pass in a dream until I know the first and last of her words! Now I know as truth that it is more agonizing for the criminal to await the merciless sentence of death than it is the execution itself. Ho, Pármeno! Apathetic wretch, hands of a dead man! Draw that exasperating bolt and let the honorable mistress, on whose tongue my life lies, come in.

CELESTINA (*apart*; *outside*). You hear, Sempronio? Our master is in a different mood. His words are very different from what we heard from him and Pármeno on our first visit. We appear to be moving from bad to good. There is no word he says that does not mean a skirt or two for old Celestina.

SEMPRONIO (*apart*; *outside*). Well, as you go in pretend you do not see Calisto, and say something good.

CELESTINA (*apart*; *outside*). Shhh, Sempronio; for although I have risked my life, Calisto and his plea, and yours, deserve more, and I expect even greater favors from him.

ACT SIX

(Calisto, Celestina, Pármeno, Sempronio)

PLOT

Celestina goes inside Calisto's house. With great apprecia-
tion and eagerness, Calisto asks her what happened at Melibea's.
While they are talking, Pármeno, listening to Celestina, puts in
an objection to every statement. Sempronio reprimands him. Finally Celestina tells Calisto of the negotiation and of Melibea's
girdle. Taking leave of him, she goes to her home, and Pármeno
goes with her.

SCENE 1

CALISTO. What were you saying, dear señora and mother?

CELESTINA. O Señor Calisto! You here? My new lover of
the beauteous Melibea, and with great reason! And how will you
repay the old woman who today has put her life on the line for
you? What woman has ever seen herself in such perilous straits as I,
who remembering it shrinks and feels all the blood in her veins
drying up? I offered my life for less than I would give for this frayed
old cloak.

PÁRMENO (*apart*). You will look out for yourself, you will find lettuces between the cabbages. You have climbed up one rung, and from now on it will all be skirts. All of it for you and not one thing you can share. The old crone wants to feather her nest. You will prove me right and my master crazed. Listen to every word, Sempronio, and you will see that she does not want to ask for money because money can be divided.

SEMPRONIO (*apart*). Hush, do not be foolhardy. Calisto will kill you if he hears you.

CALISTO. Mother, dear Mother, be briefer with your story or take this sword and kill me!

PÁRMENO (*apart*). The poor devil is quivering like quicksilver; he can barely stand. He would like to lend her his tongue so she would speak faster. His life does not mean much to him, we will be wearing mourning if this affair advances.

CELESTINA. Sword, Señor, or what? May a sword kill your enemies and he who wishes you evil. I want to give you life with the hope I bring from the one you most love.

CALISTO. Hope, Señora?

CELESTINA. It can well be called hope, for the door is open to my return, and she would rather receive me in this ragged skirt than another in silk and brocade.

PÁRMENO (*apart*). Sempronio, stitch these lips together, I cannot bear it. There is the accursed skirt again.

SEMPRONIO (*apart*). God's bones, will you keep quiet or shall I throw you to the Devil? If she keeps going on about the skirt, she does it with good reason: she needs one. Where the abbot chants, there he is clothed.

PÁRMENO (*apart*). And she dresses like she chants. This old whore would like in one day, at one swoop, to shed the rags she has not been able to better in fifty years.

SEMPRONIO (*apart*). And she taught you this, everything you know? This is how she brought you up?

PÁRMENO (*apart*). I will put up with her begging and stealing, but not her taking everything for herself.

SEMPRONIO (*apart*). She knows no way but to be greedy. Let her get her house in order and later we will secure ours, or she will regret the day she met us.

CALISTO. With God's pity, Señora, tell me what you did. How did you get in? What was she wearing? What part of the house was she in? What face did she show you at the beginning?

CELESTINA. The face, Señor, that brave bulls in the ring show to those who place the banderillas, the face boars turn to harassing hounds.

CALISTO. And you call those signs of well-being? Then what ones would be fatal? Not, of course, death itself; that would be a relief to this torment of mine, for it is greater and pains me more.

SEMPRONIO (*apart*). Is this my master's former fire? What has happened? Can this man not stand hearing what he has so long wanted?

PÁRMENO (*apart*). And you want *me* to hush, Sempronio: For if our master hears you, he will punish you as soundly as he does me.

SEMPRONIO (*apart*). O may you burn in Hell. You say harmful things of everyone, and I offend no one. O may you be devoured by an unbearable, deadly pestilence, you belligerent, envious, accursed man! *This* is the friendship you have worked out with Celestina and me? Go away, and may it be straight to bad fortune.

CALISTO. If, my señora and queen, if you do not wish my spirit to despair and my soul to depart, condemned to perpetual pain from hearing these things, tell me briefly whether your glorious petition came to a good end, and also of the cruel and unforgiving expression of that angelic and lethal face, for all that is more a sign of loathing than of love.

CELESTINA. The greatest glory of the secret office of the bee, and one the prudent should imitate, is that all things touched by her are converted into something better than they are. This is how I have treated Melibea's headstrong and disdainful words. I have turned all her rigor into honey, her anger into meekness, her haste into calm. For why else do you think old Celestina, whom you magnificently reward beyond her worth, went there if not to soften her anger, endure her passion, be shield to your absence, catch in my cloak the blows, the indifference, the scorn and disdain that girls display when they make their first forays into love, so that later their gift be held in higher esteem? For they speak most harshly of the one they most love. And if that were not so, if they all said "yes" when they saw themselves loved, there would be no difference between the love of public whores and that of sheltered maidens. And although burning and afire with love, modesty demands that they show a cold exterior, a calm face, a pleasant disdain, an unwavering spirit, and a chaste resolve, along with bitter words that make their tongues marvel at their suffering and force them to express the opposite of what they feel. So in order for you to rest and find your repose while I will tell you in full detail the progress of our talk and how I found my way into the house, know that by the end her argument and words were very favorable.

CALISTO. First, Señora, now that you have given me strength to endure the rigors of her response, tell me everything you demand and wish, and I will give you my full attention. My heart is already calm, my thought already at rest, my lost blood already flowing through my veins, already I have lost my fear, already I am happy. Let us go up; yes, you lead, upstairs. In my chamber you will tell me in great detail what I have here heard in summary.

PÁRMENO (*apart*). Blessed Virgin! What roundabout way is this madman seeking to escape from us so he may weep his pleasure with Celestina and reveal to her a thousand secrets of his delirious, lascivious appetites, to ask and answer every curiosity six times without the presence of anyone to tell him how long-winded he is. But let me tell you, my crazed master: we come right behind you!

CALISTO. Look how Pármeno is talking, Señora; he comes as if crossing himself because of what you accomplished with such diligence. By my faith, he is astonished, Señora Celestina. And he is crossing himself again. Here, Señora, come sit here, for I want to kneel before you and hear your gentle answers. And now tell me, what was your ruse to get inside?

CELESTINA. Selling a little thread, a stratagem by which, with God's help, I have snared more than thirty of her sort, and some even higher.

CALISTO. That would be in stature, Mother, but not gentility, not estate, not grace and discretion, not lineage, not deserved presumption, not virtue, not speaking.

PÁRMENO (*apart*). His clock's chain has slipped some links and is striking out of order. It never strikes fewer than twelve; it is always midday! Count, count, Sempronio; your jaw is dropping as you listen to his mad ravings and her lies.

SEMPRONIO (*apart*). Poisonous vilifier! Why do you close your ears to what makes everyone else prick up theirs? Are you a snake that flees the voice of the charmer? As this talk is all about love, even though lies, you should enjoy listening.

CELESTINA. Now, Señor Calisto, listen and you will see what your good fortune and my solicitude accomplished. When I was just beginning my sale and putting a price on my thread, Melibea's mother was called to go visit an ill sister of hers. And as it was necessary for her to leave, she left Melibea in her place to . . .

CALISTO. O unequaled joy! O singular opportunity! O opportune time! O how I wish I could have been there beneath your cloak, listening to the words of one in whom God gathered such extreme charms!

CELESTINA. Under my cloak, you say? Ay, poor thing I am. You would have been seen through thirty holes, unless God mended it!

PÁRMENO (*apart*). Take me out of here, Sempronio. I have no more to say. You listen to everything yourself. If this lost soul, my master, were not measuring in his head how many steps there are from here to Melibea's house, picturing her expression, and contemplating her as she would have bargained for the thread, his thoughts entirely occupied with her, he would see that my counsel favored his well-being more than Celestina's deceptions.

CALISTO. Here, lads, what is this? I am trying to listen to something that will determine my life. Are you two as usual whispering to make me angry and bring ill fortune my way? For my sake, be still! You will die of pleasure to hear of this señora's industry. Tell me, Señora, what did you do when you found yourself alone with her?

CELESTINA. I received such a charge of pleasure that anyone who saw me would know it from my face.

CALISTO. I am feeling it now; and how much more the person contemplating the image right before her. Were you struck dumb by that unexpected opportunity?

CELESTINA. Rather, seeing myself alone with her gave me more daring to say what I wanted. I bared my heart. I told her of my mission, how you longed for a favorable word from her lips that would heal your immeasurable pain. And she stood looking at me, astonished by this new message, straining to hear who it might be who was in pain because he had such need of a word from her, who it was her tongue might heal, and when I named your name she cut short my words and clapped a hand to her forehead, like someone who had heard something very frightening, saying I should speak no more and should leave her presence if I did not want her servants to be executioners and end my days. All of which merely aggravated my daring; she called me witch, procuress, deceiver, bearded old evildoer, and many other offensive names you use to frighten children in their cradles. And after that, a thousand faints and swoons, a thousand miracles and frights, her senses disturbed; she was wildly flinging her arms and legs this way and that, wounded by the golden arrow that pierced her at the sound of your name, writhing, clasping her hands like someone in despair, then pulling at them as if she would tear them apart, eyes rolling in every direction, feet tapping on the hard floor. And I, during all this, cornered, shrinking, silenced, was entirely delighted with her ferocity. The more deeply she was upset, the happier I became, because that much closer was her surrender and her fall. But all that time her wrath was frothing out, I did not let my thoughts be vague or idle but used it to reorient my plan.

CALISTO. Tell me, Mother; I have been going over it in my mind while I listen to you and have not found an answer that was good or suitable to cover or color what you said without leaving a terrible suspicion in regard to your request. Let your wisdom, in which you seem to be more than a woman, be known, for as you had foreseen her response, you had time to form your reply. What more did that Tuscan Adeleta do, whose fame, had you been alive, would have been overshadowed? Three days before he died, she prophesied the death of her aged husband and of his two sons. I believe what is said, that the weaker female is more adept in instantaneously conceived schemes than are males.

CELESTINA. Scheme, Señor? I told her that your pain was a toothache and that the words you wanted from her were those of a devout prayer she knew to cure that ill.

CALISTO. O what brilliance! O what a unique woman in your trade! O cautious female! O quickly found remedy! O discreet messenger! What human mind could think of such a refined elixir? I truly believe that if that Aeneas and Dido had lived in our age, Venus would not have worked so hard to bring Dido's love to her son, making Cupid take on the form of Ascanius to deceive her, but would have hastened things by using you as intermediary. Now I would consider my death well lived placed in such hands, and I will believe that even if my desire does not have the effect I wish, that nothing permitted by natural order could have worked better for my well-being. How does it seem to you, lads? What else can one think? Has such a woman ever been known in the world?

CELESTINA. Señor, do not interrupt my story. Let me speak, for night is coming. You know that he who works evil abhors the light, and that I might have a bad encounter on the way to my house.

CALISTO. What? What? O, yes. I have torches and pages to accompany you.

PÁRMENO (apart). Ah, yes indeed. So no one will rape the little girl. You go with her, Sempronio; she is afraid of the crickets that sing in the dark.

CALISTO. Were you saying something, son Pármeno?

PÁRMENO. Señor, it will be good if Sempronio and I go with her, for it is getting very dark.

CALISTO. Well said; it soon will be so. Continue your story and tell me what else happened. How did she respond to the request for the prayer?

CELESTINA. That she would give it with pleasure.

CALISTO. With pleasure? O God, what a magnificent gift!

CELESTINA. But I asked for more.

CALISTO. What, my honorable old friend?

CELESTINA. A girdle she wears cinched around her waist, saying that it would be beneficial to your malady because it had touched many relics.

CALISTO. And what did she say?

CELESTINA. A plum! Give me a plum and I will tell you.

CALISTO. By God's grace. Take this house and all there is in it and tell me, or ask what you will!

CELESTINA. In exchange for the cloak you give to this old woman, she will put into your hands something Melibea wears on her body.

CALISTO. You say cloak? And a skirt! And everything I have!

CELESTINA. I need a cloak, that will be enough. Go no further, and have no suspicion regarding my request. It is said that to offer much to one who asks little is a kind of refusal.

CALISTO. Run, Pármeno, summon my tailor and then have him cut a cloak and a skirt of that Flanders cloth we sent to have the nap raised.

PÁRMENO (apart). You see, you see! Everything for the old woman; she comes loaded with lies like a bee, and as for me, they leave me to live like a pauper. This is what she has been working around to all day.

CALISTO. What does it take to make the Devil go? There is no man as badly treated as I, maintaining grumbling, soothsaying young servants, enemies of my well-being. Where are you going, you envious villain, praying like that? What are you saying that I cannot understand? Go quickly to do what I order and do not anger me, for my pain has been enough to finish me off; there will be a coat for you in that piece as well.

PÁRMENO. All I am saying, Señor, is that it is very late to get the tailor.

CALISTO. Have I not said you are a diviner? Well, wait till tomorrow, and you, Señora, for my sake, have patience; what is postponed is not lost. And make me display the blessed girdle that was worthy to embrace such a form. My eyes, with all my other senses, will feast on it, for they have all been inflamed. My badly wounded heart will rejoice, for it has not had a moment of pleasure since I set eyes on that beautiful maiden. All my senses went to my heart, raced to it with their work panniers. Each caused it the most pain it was able: the eyes, seeing her, the ears, hearing her, the hands, touching her.

CELESTINA. You are saying you have *touched* her? That frightens me.

CALISTO. I mean in dreams.

CELESTINA. Dreams?

CALISTO. I see her in dreams so many nights that I fear what happened to Alcibiades or Socrates will be visited upon me. The former dreamed he found himself wrapped in his mistress's mantle, and the next day he was killed and there was no one to lift him up from the street or cover him except her, with her cloak. The latter heard himself called by name, and he died three days later. But in life or in death, I would be ecstatic to wear her garment.

CELESTINA. You suffer deeply, for when others are resting in their beds, you are preparing suffering for the morrow. Have courage, Señor; for God made no man to abandon him. Give room to your desire. Take this girdle; and if I do not die I will deliver its mistress to you.

CALISTO. O my new companion! O fortunate girdle; you had the power and merit to encircle the body I am not worthy to serve! O prayer knots of the Passion, you enfolded my desires! Tell me, my knots, were you present when the one you serve and I adore, the one for whom I labor day and night with no benefit or gain, uttered her joyless reply?

CELESTINA. The old saying is: "He who strives least, gains most." But I will see that you, by striving, attain what you would never gain with negligence. Be consoled, Señor, for Zamora was not won in a day; do not for that lose faith in the combatants.

CALISTO. Ah, what misery! Cities are enclosed by stone, and stone conquers stone. But this my mistress has a heart of steel. There is no metal that can penetrate it, no shot that will pierce it. Put ladders to her wall, her eyes can shoot arrows, her tongue will be filled with reproaches and indifference; the stronghold is such that no one can put up a wall within half a league.

CELESTINA. Hush, Señor; for the daring of a single man won Troy. Do not lose faith, for one woman can conquer another. You have had few dealings with me; you do not know what I can do.

CALISTO. All you tell me, Señora, I want to believe; you brought me this jewel. O my glory, embracer of that angelic waist! I look upon you and cannot believe it. O girdle, girdle! Were you enemy? Tell me true. If you were, I forgive you, for it is just that the good forgive guilt. I do not believe you were an enemy, for if you were against me you would not have fallen into my power so quickly, unless you come to apologize. I conjure you to answer, by virtue of the great power my mistress Melibea holds over me!

CELESTINA. Enough of this nonsense, Señor. I am weary of listening to you, and your hands are destroying the girdle.

CALISTO. O misery! How I wish that heaven had ordained that you be made and woven from my arms and not of silk as you are, for each day they would delight in surrounding and clasping with due reverence that dear being that you, dear girdle, without sensing or taking pleasure of such glory, continually embrace. O what secrets you have seen of that excellent image!

CELESTINA. You will see more, and with more sensation, if you do not lose it by all your talking.

CALISTO. Hush, Señora, this girdle and I understand each other. O my eyes, remember that you were cause and door through which my heart was wounded, and the thing that is the cause is seen to do the harm. Remember that you are also responsible for my ill health, and look again, see the remedy has come to this house.

SEMPRONIO. Señor, does fondling the girdle replace taking pleasure of Melibea?

CALISTO. What! Madman, raving fool, killjoy! What are you saying?

SEMPRONIO. That all this talking kills you and those who hear you, and by going in that direction you will lose either your life or your reason; the absence of either is enough to leave you in the dark. Abbreviate your arguments; let Celestina give you hers.

CALISTO. Are you annoyed, Mother, by my long exhortations, or is this servant of mine drunk?

CELESTINA. Although he is not, Señor, you must cut short your argument, put aside your long lamentations, treat the girdle as a girdle so you will know to speak differently when you see Melibea; do not let your tongue make the person and the garment equivalent.

CALISTO. O Señora, Mother, consoler! Let me have my pleasure with this herald of glory! O tongue! Why are you diverted to other subjects and ceasing to adore the excellence of one you may never see in your power? O hands! With what boldness, with what little reverence, you hold the remedy for my wound! Now the poison on the sharp tip of that arrow can no longer harm me. I am safe, because the one who inflicted the wound will cure it. O Señora, joy of elder women, delight of young girls, repose for the exhausted like me! Do not let my fear of you cause more pain than that caused by my shame. Loose the rein on my contemplation; let me go out into the streets with this jewel, so that they who see me will know that there is no man as fortunate as I.

SEMPRONIO. Do not inflame your wound by burdening it with more desire. It is not, Señor, this girdle alone your remedy depends on.

CALISTO. I am well aware of that, but I do not have the will to keep from adoring such a precious symbol.

CELESTINA. Symbol? That symbol is gladly given; but know that she gave it in God's love to cure your tooth, and not to close your wounds. If I live, she will turn the page.

CALISTO. And the prayer?

CELESTINA. She did not give it to me just now.

CALISTO. And why was that?

CELESTINA. Time was short. But it was left that if your pain did not lessen I would return for it tomorrow.

CALISTO. Lessen? My pain will lessen when her cruelty lessens.

CELESTINA. Enough, Señor. Enough said, enough done. She feels compelled, from everything she showed, to do anything for this illness I want to ask, if she is able. Look, that is enough for a first visit. I am going now. And you, Señor, if you go out tomorrow, you must wear a cloth around your jaw, so if you are seen by her my petition will not be judged false.

CALISTO. I will wear four, whatever you wish. But tell me, please God, did anything else happen? I am dying to hear words from those sweet lips. How were you so bold that without knowing her you acted like a friend, just going in and making a plea?

CELESTINA. Without knowing her? They were my neighbors for four years. I saw them and spoke and laughed with them day and night. Her mother knows me better than she knows her own hands, though Melibea has grown to be a discreet and genteel young woman.

PÁRMENO (*apart*). Ha! Sempronio, I want you to hear what I whisper to you.

SEMPRONIO (*apart*). Tell me, what is it?

PÁRMENO (*apart*). As Celestina is listening so attentively, it gives our master a reason to go on and on. Go to her; nudge her foot. Let us signal her not to wait any longer but go; no madman born speaks long when left alone.

CALISTO. You call Melibea genteel, Señora? It seems you say it in jest. Has her equal ever been born in the world? Did God create a sweeter form? Can such features, a model of beauty, be painted? If Helen were alive today, the one for whom so many Greeks and Trojans died, or the beautiful Polyxena, they would obey this comely mistress for whom I pine. Had she been present in that contest among the three goddesses for the golden apple, they would never have given it the name discord because, without dissent, they would have conceded and agreed that it be given to Melibea, and thus it would have been called the apple of concord. For women who know of her curse themselves, and wail to God because he did not remember them when he made this my sweet mistress. They use up their lives, envy gnaws their flesh, they inflict brutal martyrdom upon themselves, thinking that with artifice they will equal the perfection nature effortlessly bestowed on her. They thin their eyebrows with eyebrow pluckers and plasters and fine cords; they look for golden herbs, roots, branches, and flowers to make bleaches so their hair will be like hers; and they maul their faces, covering them in various hues of unguents and ointments, acid lotions, white and red paints, and powders that for the sake of brevity I will not detail. Now the one for whom all this was done, does she deserve to be served by a wretch like me?

CELESTINA (*apart*). I understand you, Sempronio. Leave him; he is going to fall off the ass he is riding, and it will be the end.

CALISTO. She, whom nature conspired to make perfect; the one who when the graces were distributed among women were brought together in her. In her was made a display of the most beauty could achieve, so that all who saw her would know the greatness of her Painter. Only a bit of clear water and an ivory comb are needed to surpass all those born with charm and elegance. These are her weapons; with them she kills and conquers, with them she captured me, with them she keeps me bound to her with a strong chain.

CELESTINA. Quiet now, do not exhaust yourself, for the file I have is stronger than the chain that torments you. I will cut it, so that you are left free. Therefore, allow me to leave, for it is very late. And let me take the girdle, because I have need of it.

CALISTO. O wretch that I am! Adverse Fortune continues to follow me. I would like to be accompanied this long, dark night, by you or the girdle or both. But as there is nothing perfect in this life of pain, let my solitude be complete. Pármeno! Sempronio!

PÁRMENO. Señor?

CALISTO. Accompany the señora Celestina to her house, and may as much pleasure and joy go with her as sadness and loneliness stay with me.

CELESTINA. God be with you, Señor. Tomorrow I will be back, where my cloak and her answer will meet, for there was not enough time today. Accept your suffering, Señor. Think of other things.

CALISTO. That I cannot do, for it is heresy to forget the one who gives me pleasure in life.

ACT SEVEN

(Celestina, Pármeno, Areúsa, Elicia)

PLOT

Celestina speaks with Pármeno, urging him to peace and friendship with Sempronio. Pármeno recalls to her the promise she made to give him Areúsa, whom he loves very much. They go to Areúsa's house. Pármeno stays the night. Celestina goes to her house; she knocks at the door; Elicia comes to open, berating her for her late arrival.

SCENE 1

CELESTINA. Pármeno, my son, given all that has happened, I have not had an opportune moment to tell you and show you the great affection I have for you, and in that same vein, how everyone has heard from my lips the good things I have said about you in your absence. It is not necessary to repeat the reason, for I had you as a son, at least an adopted son, and you behaved like a natural son, but this is how you repay my presence, taking everything I say amiss, whispering and muttering against me in front of Calisto. I

97

had thought that after you submitted to my good counsel that you would not turn and reject it. It seems to me that you carry pointless complaints from the past, and are speaking off the top of your head rather than using reason. You are sacrificing benefit to content your tongue. Hear me, if you have not till now, and see that I am an old woman, and that good counsel resides in the elderly, and that what is characteristic of youth is their own pleasure. I truly believe that your error is based on age alone. I pray God that you will behave with more kindness toward me in the future, and that you will change your wicked notions, or, as it is said, change your habits as your hair changes color. I mean, son, growing old, and seeing new things each day. Because youth focuses only on the present, it impedes and occupies you, but maturity does not omit the present or the past or the future. If, Pármeno my son, you had remembered the love I had for you, the first place you would have lodged when newly come to this city would have been with me. But youth cares little for those of us who are old; you want things to your own taste; you never think that you have, or have to have, need of the old; you never think of their illnesses; you never think that you may lose the flower of youth. But, my friend, for matters as essential as these, a knowledgeable old woman is good help, a friend, mother, and more than mother: a good inn where you can safely rest, a good hospital for curing ills, a good purse in need, a good coffer for storing money in prosperity, a good winter fire spiked with spits, a good summer shade, a good tavern for eating and drinking. What, my foolish lad, have you to say to all this? I can tell by what you have said that you are befuddled. But I want nothing more from you; God asks nothing of the sinner but that he repent and change his ways. Look at Sempronio; I made him a man—apart from God's work. I would like you two to be like brothers, because if things are good with him, so they will be with your master, and with everyone. You see that he is well regarded, diligent, courtly, a good servant, amusing. He wants your friendship; your good fortune will increase if each of you offers his hand to the other, and your master will have no favorites but the two of you. He knows you must love if you want to be loved, for you do not catch trout unless you are willing to get into the water. Nor does Sempronio owe you anything. It is very stupid not to want to love but to hope to *be* loved, and madness to repay friendship with hatred.

PÁRMENO. Mother, I confess to you that I erred a second time, and with your forgiveness for what has passed, I want you to direct what is to come. But with Sempronio, it seems impossible to maintain a friendship. He is chaotic, disorderly, and I am impatient; how do you make those two friends?

CELESTINA. But once you were not that way.

PÁRMENO. By my faith, the older I grew the more I forgot my earlier patience. I am not the one I was, and Sempronio himself has nothing to benefit me.

CELESTINA. You know a certain friend in an uncertain moment, and he is proved in times of adversity; then he comes with good intention to visit the house that prosperity has abandoned. What shall I tell you, my son, of the virtues of a true friend? There is nothing more loved or more rare. He will refuse you nothing. You and Sempronio are equals: having similar habits and hearts is what most sustains friendship. Remember, son, that you have something that is being kept for you, though you will earn more than the fortune you learned of. Your father, who amassed it, did well. It cannot be given to you until you are living more quietly and reach a certain age.

PÁRMENO. What do you call "quietly," Aunt?

CELESTINA. Son, to live for yourself, and not in the houses of others, which is what you will do as long as you do not learn to profit from serving. I was so sad to see you in worn clothing that today, as you saw, I asked Calisto for a cloak. Not for me but because with the tailor in the house and you before him without a jacket one would be given you. So it was not for my benefit, as I thought I heard you say, but for yours; for if you wait for the customary reward from these fine gentlemen, what you receive in ten years can be tied up in a pouch. Enjoy your youth, a good day, a good night, good food and drink. When you have them, do not let them go, whatever the cost. Do not weep over the fortune your master inherited, thinking you can take it with you from this world, for we hold fortunes only in our lifetimes. O my dear son Pármeno—as I looked after you for so long I can easily call you son—take my advice, for it comes from an honest desire to see you achieve honor. O how happy I would be if you and Sempronio could come to an agreement, be good friends, brothers in all things, or if I could see you come to my poor house to be merry, to see me, and even to take your pleasure with a girl for each of you!

PÁRMENO. Girls, Mother?

CELESTINA. Ah yes, girls; with myself around I have been enough with old women! Sempronio has a girl, and he does not have as good a reason or the affection I have for you. What I tell you comes straight from my heart.

PÁRMENO. Mother, do not be deceived.

CELESTINA. And though I were, it would not pain me greatly, for I also do this for God's love, and because I see you in a land not your own, and even more to honor the bones of the one who entrusted you to me. For you will become a man and you will have a good and true knowledge of things, and you will say, "Old Celestina gave me good counsel."

PÁRMENO. Though I am still a boy, I know it even now. And although today you saw what I was saying, it was not because I objected to what you were doing, but because I had given good counsel to my master and he scarcely gave me thanks. From now on we will follow closely behind him. Do what you will and I will say nothing. I already stumbled by not believing you regarding this business with him.

CELESTINA. You will stumble and you will fall over this and other matters as long as you do not take my counsel, which are those of a true friend.

PÁRMENO. Now I consider the time well spent I served you as a boy, for it bears abundant fruit for the future. And I will pray to God for my father's soul, for leaving me such a tutor, and my mother's, who delivered me to such a good woman.

CELESTINA. Do not speak her name, son, please God, or my eyes will fill with tears. Did I ever have such a friend in this world, such a companion, such a solace for my labors and fatigue? Who supplied my needs, who knew my secrets, to whom did I bare my heart, who was all my well-being and rest but your mother, who was more than my sister and fellow godmother? O how gracious she was. How assured, how sincere, and brave as a man. Without pain or fear she would walk from cemetery to cemetery at midnight, looking for the paraphernalia of our office, as if it were day. There were no Christians or Moors or Jews whose burials she did not visit; in the daytime she looked them over, by night she dug them up. She was as happy with the dark of night as you with a bright day; she called night the cape of sinners. For did she not have skill, along with other graces? One thing I will tell you, so you can see what a mother you lost, even if it is better kept to yourself . . . but I can tell you anything: she used her eyebrow pluckers to pull seven teeth from a hanged man while I took his shoes. She entered a magic circle better than I, and with stronger effect, even though I was much better known than I am now; and for my sins everything was forgotten with her death. What more can I tell you than devils themselves were afraid of her. She terrorized and frightened them with the raw power of her voice. So she was as well known by them as you in your house. They would come tumbling over each other at her call. They did not dare tell her a lie because of how she dominated them. After I lost her, I never again heard the truth from them.

PÁRMENO (*apart*). How could God favor this old trull more than she favors me with these praises of my mother's words!

CELESTINA. What are you saying, my most upright Pármeno, my son, my more than son?

PÁRMENO. I am asking how my mother had that advantage, since the conjuring words that you and she used were the same.

CELESTINA. How? You marvel at that? Do you not know the saying "Great the distance between Pedro and Pedro"? Your mother's ways did not spread to all of us. Have you seen that some are good at their trade and others better? That is how your mother was, may God be with her, the foremost of our trade, and for that known and loved by everyone from caballeros to clerics to married men, old men, lads, boys. And young girls and damsels as well? They prayed to God for her life as they did for their own parents. She had dealings with them all, she spoke with them all. When we went down the street, everyone we met were her godchildren; her principal occupation for sixteen years was being a midwife. So although you did not know her secrets because of your tender years, now it is right for you to know, for she is dead and you are a man.

PÁRMENO. Tell me, Mother, when the tribunal ordered your arrest, and I was in your house, did you two know each other well?

CELESTINA. Did we? You are asking as a jest? We did it together; together they heard us, together they arrested and charged us, together they sentenced us, which that time was, I believe, the first. But you were very young; I am amazed that you remember, for it is the most forgotten event in this city. Things that happen in the world. Every day you will see who sins and pays for it, if you visit that market.

PÁRMENO. That is true; but the worst of sin is continuing to do it; for as man does not control his first movements so it is with the first error, about which is said, "Who errs and corrects his ways . . ."

CELESTINA (*apart*). You lash out at me, stupid boy? Are we looking for truths? Well wait, for I will jab you where it hurts.

PÁRMENO. What are you saying, Mother?

CELESTINA. Son, I am saying that, not counting that time, your mother was arrested four times, just her, may God be with her. And even the time they took her for being a witch because they found her at night taking dirt from a crossroad by candlelight, and kept her half a day on a scaffold in the plaza wearing a painted prisoner's miter on her head. But these are things that happen; men have to suffer in this sad world in order to earn the right to live. And with her good sense she took it as a minor thing, and none of it kept her from practicing her trade even better than before. We are talking about this because of what you said about continuing what once was an error. She had skill in everything; as God is my witness, even on that scaffold, to judge from her bearing, she had no concern for anyone below. So it is that those who are somebody, as she was, and know that and have worth, are the ones who err most quickly. Think of Virgil, and how much he knew, but you have already heard how he was suspended in a basket hung from a tower, with all Rome looking on. But he did not for that cease to be honest and upright, nor was the name Virgil lost or forgotten.

PÁRMENO. What you say is true; but that was not the work of the tribunal.

CELESTINA. Hush, stupid. You know very little about attacks by the church, or how much better punishment is at the hand of the law than from a different source. The priest knew that better who, coming to console her, may she be with God, said that the Holy Scripture teaches, "Blessed are they who are persecuted for righteousness' sake; for theirs is the kingdom of heaven." Consider whether it is too much to suffer in this world in order to know glory in the next. And worse, according to what was said, unjustly, and with no reason, and with false witnesses and harsh torture, they made her confess to what she was not. But with her good effort, and as a heart accustomed to suffering makes things lighter than they are, she held it as nothing. A thousand times I heard her say, "If I do not walk as well, it was worth it, for now I am better known than I was before." All this happened to your good mother here, so we must believe that God will reward her there if what our priest told us is true, and that consoles me. But like her, you must be a true friend to me and work to be good, for you have a model to follow. And what your father left is in safe hands.

PÁRMENO. I believe that, Mother, but I would like to know how much it is.

CELESTINA. Not now. The time will come, as I told you, for you to know and hear.

PÁRMENO. Well, let us leave the dead and inheritances; for if he left me little I will find little. Instead let us speak of matters at hand, for that will do more than recalling the past. You will surely remember that not long ago, in my house, I told you I was dying for Areúsa's love, and you promised you would see that I have it.

CELESTINA. Yes, I promised you that. I have not forgotten, and do not think I am so old I have lost my memory, for three times in your absence I have spoken with her. I believe by now she will be about ripe for you. If we make our way to her house she will not be able to escape. This is the least I am going to do for you.

PÁRMENO. I had no confidence that I would ever have her because I have been unable to make her stay long enough to say a word, and as it is said that "A bad sign of love is to turn your face and flee," I was left without confidence.

CELESTINA. I do not worry greatly about that, as you did not realize or know, as you do now, that you have on your side the supreme mistress of such labors. But now you will see how much you profit because of me, how much I can do with girls like her, how much I know about love. Slow down. Here is her door. We will go in quietly; the neighbors will not hear us. You stay and wait here beneath this staircase. I will go up to see what I can do regarding the matter we have discussed, and with good fortune we may do better than either you or I may have thought.

SCENE 2

AREÚSA. Who is there? Who is it coming up to my chamber at such an hour?

CELESTINA. Someone who wishes you no ill of course. Who never takes a step without thinking of your gain. Who remembers more about you than about herself: someone who, though an old woman, loves you?

AREÚSA (*apart*). Devil take that old bawd! Who is she bringing like a hobgoblin at this hour? (*Aloud*) Dear aunt, what is this nice, very late, visit? I had already undressed to go to bed.

CELESTINA. With the chickens, Daughter? That is no way to make your fortune. Come now. Get up! Others may weep their needs, but not you. The one who feasts is the one who pays! Anyone would love such a life!

AREÚSA. Jesú! I have to dress again, I am cold.

CELESTINA. No, do not do that, 'pon my life; just get into bed and talk to me from there.

AREÚSA. Happy to, for I need it badly; I have been feeling ill all day. So need, more than laziness, bid me to take the sheets for petticoats.

CELESTINA. Well, you do not have to sit up; lie down and get under the covers, you look like a siren.

AREÚSA. A nice thing to say, dear aunt.

CELESTINA. Ay. What a nice smell when you move. Everything is just right! I have always appreciated you, your cleanliness and finery. How fresh you are. May God smile upon you! What sheets, what a cover pane, what pillows, how white everything is! So my old age should be, the way all this looks to me. Little pearl of gold, you will see how much someone who visits you at such an hour loves you. Let me look you over at length, it gives me such pleasure.

AREÚSA. Stop there, Mother! Do not come over here; you tickle me and make me laugh, and laughing makes me hurt more.

CELESTINA. What hurts you, my love? 'Pon my life, are you gulling me?

AREÚSA. Misery strike me if I am jesting! For four hours I have been dying of this woman pain, and now it has risen to my breasts, and it wants to take me from the world. I am not as well off as you think.

CELESTINA. Well, make room for me. I will feel you all over, for I still know something of this ailment, for my sins; each of us has or has had her turn of it, along with the anguish that comes with it.

AREÚSA. But where I feel it is higher, over my stomach.

CELESTINA. May God and Saint Michael Archangel bless you! How plump and fresh you are! What breasts and all so lovely! Up till now I have always thought you beautiful, seeing what everyone could see, but now I tell you that, as far as I know, in all this city you will not find three bodies like yours. You do not look fifteen. O, I would be a man and win the chance to be allowed such a sight! God's bones! You do commit a sin by not giving part of these charms to all those who love you so much. God did not give them to you for you to waste the freshness of your youth beneath six folds of woolen and linen. Do not be miserly with what has cost you so little. Do not hoard your loveliness, for it is by its nature as good an exchange as money. Do not be the dog in the manger that not only does not eat but lets no one else eat either, and since you cannot enjoy your own beauty let he who can do so. Do not believe that you were created for no reason; when a she is born a he is born, and when a he, a she. Nothing is superfluous in the world, nor anything that nature does not provide for. What a sin it is to weary and torment men when they can be helped.

AREÚSA. You praise me now, Mother, but no one loves me! Give me a remedy for my ailment, and do not be making fun of me.

CELESTINA. We are all, for our sins, experts in this too common pain! What I have seen many do, and something I often resorted to, I will tell you because as the qualities of people differ so too do medicines work different effects. Any strong odor is good, like pennyroyal, rue, wormwood, smoke from partridge feathers, rosemary, musk, or incense; used with great diligence, they lessen pain and gradually return your womb to its place. But there is something I always found better that all those, but because you have been acting so saintly I do not want to tell you that one.

AREÚSA. What, Mother? I beg you. You see me in pain and yet you conceal what would give me relief.

CELESTINA. You understand me very well. Do not pretend to be dumb!

AREÚSA. Enough! May I be struck if I understand you! What do you want me to do? You know that my friend left yesterday for the war, alongside his captain. Do you want me to betray him?

CELESTINA (*apart*). You will see. (*Aloud*) And what harm and what betrayal?

A R E Ú S A . But it would be. He gives me everything I need. He honors me, he favors me, and he treats me as if I were his señora.

C E L E S T I N A . But though all of that may be true, as long as you do not have a child you will always have the ailment and pain you have now, of which he must be the cause. And if you do not believe pain will tell you, believe that your color will, and you will see what comes of being alone.

A R E Ú S A . It is nothing but my bad luck, a curse my parents cast on me; but this is not the time to go into that. Let us leave that, for it is late. Tell me the reason for your good visit.

C E L E S T I N A . You already know what I have told you about Pármeno. He complains that you still do not want to see him. I do not know why that is, unless because you know I love him and consider him a son. Well, of course, I look at your situation another way, for even your neighbor women seem nice to me, and my heart is happy every time I see them, because I know they talk with you.

A R E Ú S A . You may be mistaken, dear aunt.

C E L E S T I N A . I know that I believe in actions, for empty words are sold anywhere. But love is always repaid with pure love, and good actions with good actions. You already have the bond between you and Elicia, whom Sempronio visits in my house. Pármeno and he are companions; they serve this señor you know, someone from whom you too might receive favor. Do not deny what little effort it would cost you. You and Elicia, cousins, they, companions; how could we want a better pairing? He is here with me. Would you like for him to come up?

A R E Ú S A . This is so distressing! What if he has heard us?

C E L E S T I N A . He hasn't, he is downstairs. I would like to ask him up. Grant him the grace of seeing that you recognize him, and talk to him and put on a good face. And if it seems a good idea, let him take pleasure with you and you with him. For although he gains a lot, you lose nothing.

A R E Ú S A . I do know, Mother, that all your arguments, these and those past, are directed to my benefit. But how do you want me to do this thing? I have someone I must explain things to, as I have told you, and if he gets a sniff of this he will kill me. I have envious neighbors; they will tell it. So if nothing worse happened than my losing him, it would be more than I gain in pleasing the one you send me to.

C E L E S T I N A . You fear that, but I took care of it; we entered very quietly.

A R E Ú S A . I am not talking about just tonight, but about many others.

C E L E S T I N A . How? Are you one of those? Is that how you behave? You will never have a house with an upper floor. You are afraid of the one who isn't here? What would you do if he were in the city? As it happens, I never cease to give counsel to fools, and there still are some who err. But I do not marvel at that, for the world is wide and those who are experienced few. Ay, ay, Daughter! If you could see how wise your cousin is, and how she has profited from my training and counsel, and how well versed she is! She does not even take my chastisement badly, for she can always boast of one in her bed, and another at the door, and another sighing for her in his house. And she satisfies them all and shows them all a good face, and they all believe they are much loved, and each of them thinks there is no other and that he is her only one, and that only he gives her what she has need of. And you believe that if you have two, the slats of your bed would reveal that? Can your needs be fed from a single dribble? There will not be much food on your table. I would not want to live on your crumbs! One man never satisfied me, and I never focused all my affection on one. Two can do more, and even more four, and they give more and have more and offer more to choose from. There is nothing as lost, Daughter, as the mouse that has only one hole; if that one is closed off the mouse will have nowhere to hide from the cat. And he who has but one eye, think of what danger he walks in. A poor soul alone neither sings nor weeps; a single action does not make a habit; a friar is seldom seen alone in the street; it is a wonder to see a single partridge take wing in summer; a single dish, eaten continuously, quickly loses savor; one swallow does not a summer make; one witness does not generate confidence; she who has but one garment soon wears it out. What is it you want, Daughter, from this number *one*? I will tell you more drawbacks concerning it than the years I have on my back. Have at least two, for two is laudable company. The way you have two ears, two feet and two hands, two sheets on your bed, two shifts to change into. And if you want more, the better it will be; for the more Moors, the more plunder. Honor without benefit is nothing but a ring on your finger. And since both will not fit well in the same sack, seize the profit. Son Pármeno, come up!

AREÚSA. No, do not come! Strike me dead! I will die of embarrassment. I do not really know him. I have always been shy around him.

CELESTINA. I am the person who will take that shyness from you, cloak those feelings, and talk for you both; he is as shy as you.

SCENE 3

PÁRMENO. Mistress Areúsa, God bless your gracious presence.

AREÚSA. Good señor. You are welcome here.

CELESTINA. Come over here, you ass! Why are you going to sit over there in the corner? Do not be embarrassed, please remember that the Devil took the shy man to the palace for his undoing. I want

both of you to hear what I say. You already know, my friend Pármeno, what I promised, and you, my daughter, what I have asked of
you. With the difficulty of your private capitulation left behind, few
arguments are necessary, for time will not allow. Pármeno's love for
you has brought him suffering, so, seeing his pain, I know you will
not want to be the cause of his death, and I even recognize that he
attracts you enough that you will not object to his staying the night.

AREÚSA. 'Pon my life, Mother, that cannot be! Jesú, do not ask
that!

PÁRMENO (*apart*). Mother, for the love of God, I cannot leave
here without a favorable agreement; seeing her, my love has mor-
tally wounded me. Offer her whatever my father left me. Tell her
that I will give her everything I have. Come, tell her that! For it
seems to me she does not want to look at me.

AREÚSA. What did he whisper in your ear? Does he think I have
to do anything you ask?

CELESTINA. He said nothing, Daughter, other than he takes
great pleasure in your friendship, because you are so worthy, so well
fit for benefit. And he adds that since all this is being done through
my intercession, he promises that from this day on he will be a good
friend to Sempronio, and join in everything he might wish against
his master in a negotiation we have under way. Is that true, Pármeno? Do you promise to do as I have I put it?

PÁRMENO. Do not doubt it, I promise.

CELESTINA (*apart*). Ha, my ruinous lad! I have your word!
And none too soon. (*Aloud*) Come here, you neglectful, bashful
boy. Before I leave I want to see whether you have what it takes.
Have some sport with her here on the bed!

AREÚSA. He would not be so discourteous as to come where it is
forbidden without permission.

CELESTINA. Are you bound up in courtesies and permissions? I will not stay longer. I truly believe that you will wake without dolor and he without color. But as he is a fuzzy-cheeked little cock-a-doodle-doo, it is my opinion that the cock will be doodling for three full nights before it ceases to crow. The doctors of my land used to send me young men like this to gobble up alive, when I had my teeth.

AREÚSA. O Señor, do not treat me like this! Be civil, for the sake of courtesy. Respect the gray hairs of that honorable old woman, for gray they are! Leave, for I am not one of those you think I am! I am not one who sells her body publicly. This you do to please me? I will leave this house if you touch a thread of my clothing before my aunt, Celestina, has left.

CELESTINA. What is all this, Areúsa? What this strange behavior, this coyness, this new reserve? You would think, Daughter, that I do not know anything about this, that I never saw a man and a woman together, and that I never did it myself, or took pleasure from what there was to take pleasure of, and that I do not know what happens, or what is said and done! So sad to hear the likes of that! So be advised of one thing; I was like you, I had men. But I never drove an old man or old woman from my side, or ignored their counsel in public or in my secret thoughts. For the death I owe God I would greatly prefer a slap across the face. You would think I had been born yesterday, to judge by your reticence. To make yourself appear honest, you make me appear stupid and shameful, with no experience or ability to keep secrets, and you diminish me in my trade in order to lift you up in yours. For between porter and porter there is little difference but the heft of the keg. But I praise you more behind your back than you praise yourself.

AREÚSA. Mother, if I was mistaken, forgive me. And come closer, and he can do what he wants. I would rather have you content than myself; I would rather poke out my eye than offend you.

CELESTINA. I am not offended, we will talk later. Be with God. I am leaving; all your kissing and frolicking makes me envious; the taste of it was left on my gums, that was not lost with my teeth.

AREÚSA. Go with God.

PÁRMENO. Mother, do you ask me to go with you?

CELESTINA. That would be to take from one saint to give to another. God be with you; I am an old woman and I do not fear being raped in the street.

SCENE 4

ELICIA. The dog is barking. Yes. That devil of an old trollop is coming.

CELESTINA. (*She knocks loudly.*)

ELICIA. Who is it? Who is knocking?

CELESTINA. Come down, Daughter, and open the door.

ELICIA. This is when you get home? Wandering at night is what gives you pleasure! Why do you do it? What took you so long this time? You go out but never come back home. This is a habit you have: tending to one you leave a hundred unhappy. Today you were sought by the father of the betrothed girl you took to the clergyman last holy day; he wants to see her married three days hence and you must patch her up as you promised so her husband will not detect she is not a virgin.

CELESTINA. I do not remember, Daughter, which one you mean.

ELICIA. How can you not remember? You forget a lot. O how memory deteriorates. But you yourself told me, when you took her, that you had renewed her seven times.

CELESTINA. Do not be surprised I forgot, Daughter. She who spills her memory in many places will not find it in any. But tell me, will he be back?

ELICIA. Be back! He gave you a gold bracelet as payment for your labor. And you think he will not be back?

CELESTINA. O, the gold bracelet girl? Now I know the one you mean. Why did you not get the instruments and do something for her? When a girl needs that you should, after all the times you have watched me, try it yourself. If you do not, you will spend your lifetime as a poor creature with no trade and no income. And when you are my age, you will weep over the soft life you lived, for idleness in youth leads to a repentant and hard-working old age. I did much better when your grandmother, may she be with God, taught me this trade; by the end of a year I knew more than she did.

ELICIA. I do not wonder; for often, as is said, the good disciple surpasses the maestro. But that happens only when one is eager to learn. No learning is well employed by one who has no liking for it. I loathe this trade; you thrive on it.

CELESTINA. You have your say. You must want to be old and poor. Do you think you will always be at my side?

ELICIA. God a'mercy, let us put aside our irritations and, for a time, counsel. Let us be happy. If we have enough to eat today, we will not think of tomorrow. The one who has everything dies as quickly as the one who is poor, the doctor like the pastor, the pope like the sacristan, the master like the servant, he of fine breeding like the lowborn, you with your trade like me with none. We do not live forever. We take our pleasure and take our ease; few see old age, and of those who do, none died of hunger. I want nothing in this world but my daytime, my daily bread, and a corner in Paradise. Although the rich are better provided to attain glory than he who has little, none is content, and no one says, "I have more than enough." There is none who would not have my pleasure in exchange for his money. Let us put our cares behind us and go to bed, it is late. A good night's sleep with no fear will make me richer than all the treasure in Venice.

ACT EIGHT

(Pármeno, Areúsa, Sempronio, Calisto)

PLOT

Morning comes. Pármeno awakes. Taking his leave of Areúsa he goes to the house of Calisto, his master. He finds Sempronio at the door. They agree to be friends. Together they go to Calisto's bedchamber. They find him talking to himself. Once up, he goes to the church.

SCENE 1

PÁRMENO. Is day breaking, or what is so light in this chamber?

AREÚSA. Day breaking? Sleep, Señor, we have no more than gone to bed. I have scarcely closed my eyes, is it already day? Please God, open that window there above the headboard and you will see.

PÁRMENO. I am clearheaded, sweet mistress. It is broad day, you can see light streaming in beneath the doors. O what a traitor I am! What a plight I have fallen into with my master! I deserve no little punishment. How late it is!

AREÚSA. Late?

PÁRMENO. Very late.

AREÚSA. Then you pleasured my soul, for the pain in my womb has not eased. I do not know how that can be.

PÁRMENO. Well, what do you want, my life?

AREÚSA. For us to talk about my ailment.

PÁRMENO. Mistress of my life, if what we have discussed is not enough you must forgive me what more is needed because it is already late in the day. I will be back tomorrow, and all the times later that you command. That is why God made one day to follow another, because what does not get done in one will be accomplished in the next. And so we may see each other even more, accept this gift: come at midday to eat with us in the house of Celestina.

AREÚSA. That would please me, greatly. Go with God. And pull the door to behind you.

PÁRMENO. God be with you.

SCENE 2

PÁRMENO (*alone*). What singular pleasure! What singular joy! What man has ever been more fortunate than I? What one more joyful, more blessed to be given such an excellent gift, and being so quickly requested so quickly given? Of course, if in my heart I could suffer the deceits of this old crone, I would crawl on my knees to please her. How can I repay her for this? O God on high! Whom can I tell of this pleasure, to whom shall I reveal such a monumental secret, with whom do I share my glory? The old crone rightly told me that no prosperity is good without company. Pleasure not communicated is not pleasure. Who could feel my happiness as strongly as I? I see Sempronio at the door to the house. He has risen very early. I have work with my master if he has sallied out, but he will not have, for that is not his custom. However, as he is not in his right mind, I would not be surprised to find his habits have changed.

SCENE 3

S E M P R O N I O . Brother Pármeno, if I knew that place where a wage is earned while sleeping, I would make a great effort to go there. There no advantage is given to anyone; I would earn as much as the next. And what were you doing that you were too lazy or too thoughtless to return? I know not what to think of your late arrival unless you stayed to warm the old woman's cockles or rub her feet, as you did when you were a boy.

P Á R M E N O . O Sempronio, friend and more than brother! Do not, I pray God, corrupt my pleasure; do not let your ire intrude upon my repose, nor muddy with such turbid waters the clear stream of my thought; do not sully my pleasure with your envious chastisement and odious reprimands! Welcome me with happiness, and let me tell you the marvels of my night's good fortune.

S E M P R O N I O . Tell it, tell it! Is it about Melibea? Have you seen her?

P Á R M E N O . What do you mean, Melibea! It is another I love, and one who, if I am not deceived, can rival her in grace and beauty. Yes, the world and all its charms are not rolled up in Melibea.

S E M P R O N I O . What raving is this, fool? I would like to laugh, but I cannot. Are all of us now in love? It will be the end of the world! Calisto loves Melibea, I love Elicia, and as you are envious you have looked for someone over whom you can lose what few brains you have.

P Á R M E N O . Then is it madness to love, and I am crazed and have no sense? For if madness truly equaled pain, wailing would never wane.

SEMPRONIO. By your standards you are mad. I have heard you offer useless counsel to Calisto and contradict Celestina when she speaks. And, to impede any benefit we both might win, you appear content not to do your part. Well, you have fallen into my hands, where I can do you harm, and I will.

PÁRMENO. It is not, Sempronio, true strength or power to harm and belittle but instead to profit and protect; even greater is to want to do it. I have always thought of you as a brother. May it not be, pray God, what is often said, that a small incident may part friends of like mind. You treat me very badly. I do not know the source of this rancor. Do not antagonize me, Sempronio, with such piteous arguments. Very rare is patience that is not brought down when battered by pointed affronts.

SEMPRONIO. I do not deny that, but throw another sardine in the pot for the stableboy, now that you have a fine lady friend.

PÁRMENO. You are angry. I will suffer you, even if you treat me worse, for it is said that no human passion is perpetual or lasting.

SEMPRONIO. You treat Calisto badly, counseling him to do what you flee from doing, saying that he should stop loving Melibea, that he become like an inn sign that offers comfort to others but none to himself. O Pármeno, now you see how easy it is to criticize someone else's life and how difficult to manage one's own! I will say no more, for you are evidence of it. And from here on we will see how you do, for already your soup bowl needs filling, like everyone else's. Had you been my friend, you would have helped me when I had need of you, and aided Celestina in my benefit instead of driving a nail of malice into each word. You know that when nothing is left of the wine but dregs it drives drinkers from the tavern; so, too, adversity or necessity the false friend when base metal is discovered beneath the gilt.

PÁRMENO. I have heard that said, and experience tells me it is so: in this sad life pleasure does not come without its opposite, anguish. We see joyous, serene, bright sunshine replaced by dark clouds and rain; comfort and pleasure by sorrow and death; laughter and delight by weeping and mortal passion; and finally, tranquility and repose by grief and sadness. Who could arrive as happy as I am now, and who could suffer such a dismal welcome? Who could see himself, as I do, elevated to such glory as I with my beloved Areúsa? And who could fall so precipitously, being as badly treated as I by you? For you have not given me opportunity to say how strongly I am with you, how I will support you in all your plans, how much I regret the past, how much counsel and scolding I have received from Celestina to your favor and benefit, to all in fact. This game between our master and Melibea is in our hands, and we must profit from it now, or never.

S E M P R O N I O . I am well pleased to hear what you say, and hope that your actions, which I will wait to see to believe you, are as good. But, God help us; tell me, what is this you say about Areúsa? It seems you know the Areúsa who is cousin to Elicia.

P Á R M E N O . Yes, and if we had not been so close, why am I so happy?

S E M P R O N I O . What is this idiot saying! I cannot speak for laughing! What do you mean, "so close"? Was she at the window, or what?

P Á R M E N O . Close enough to raise the question of whether I left her pregnant.

S E M P R O N I O . You frighten me. A steady effort will have effect; a dripping spout wears a hole in stone.

P Á R M E N O . You will see that I thought about it so steadily yesterday that now she is mine.

S E M P R O N I O . The old bawd is in this somewhere.

P Á R M E N O . In what do you see her?

S E M P R O N I O . In her telling me that she loved you a lot and that she would get you the girl. How fortune favored you. All you did was go there and make a request. That is why it is said that, "More fortu-

nate is he whom God assists than he who rises in morning mists."
But you had the godfather for it.

PÁRMENO. Say godmother, for that is closer to it. As they say, he
who shelters beneath a good tree . . . I was late at it, but early rewarded. O my brother, what I could tell you of that woman's graces,
of her way of speaking, and the beauty of her body! But we will leave
that for a better time.

SEMPRONIO. Who could she be but Elicia's cousin? You cannot tell me anything that is not better in Elicia. I believe everything
you say. But what did it cost you? Did you pay her anything?

PÁRMENO. Of course not. But even if I had, it would have been
well spent; there is nothing she cannot do. When such women are
had they are bought dear. They cost what they are worth. And what
is worth a lot never costs little, except my mistress Areúsa. I invited
her to the midday meal at the house of Celestina, and if you like, we
will all go there together.

SEMPRONIO. All, Brother?

PÁRMENO. You and she, and the old woman and Elicia will
already be there. We will make merry.

SEMPRONIO. God's mercy, how you have cheered me! You are
generous. I will never fail you. I see you are a man, and I strongly believe God will do well by you! All my anger for the things you have
said in the past you have turned to love. Now I do not doubt your co-
operation with us to be as it should. I want to embrace you; may we be
like brothers and may the Devil be banished to hell! Let the past be
like the fable of Saint John; following that model we will have peace
for the whole year, for friends' anger inevitably leads to the restitution
of love. Let us eat and be merry, and let our master fast for us all.

PÁRMENO. And what is he doing, this disconsolate man?

SEMPRONIO. He is lying on the platform of his bed, where
I left him last night, neither asleep nor awake. If I go in there, I

hear him snoring; if I leave, he sings or raves. I have not gone near enough to see whether he is suffering or resting.

PÁRMENO. What are you saying? He has never called me or remembered me?

SEMPRONIO. He does not remember himself, why would he remember you?

PÁRMENO. Even in this, things are going well. As this is his state, while he is waking I want to send food ahead to be prepared.

SEMPRONIO. What are you planning to send to ensure that two silly girls will see you as a man without fault, well brought up and generous?

PÁRMENO. In a house well provided the meal will be prided. What there is here in the larder will be a-plenty: bread, Monviedro wine, a side of bacon, and more, six pairs of chickens the master's tenants brought in the other day. If he should ask for them, I will make him believe that he has eaten them. And the doves he asked to be kept for today I will say were getting high. You will be my witness. We can see that he is not sickened by eating them, and our table will be as it should. While there we will speak in detail of his affliction, and of how we and the old bawd may profit from that love sickness.

SEMPRONIO. Better to say from his pain and grief! For 'pon my faith, I feel that this time he will either die or go mad. But since that is how it is, hurry; let us go up to see what he is doing.

SCENE 4

CALISTO (*singing*). My death will not be long to come
I walk with peril at my side,
for my desire demands of me
what hope has yet denied.

PÁRMENO (*apart, outside*). Listen, Sempronio, listen. Our master is making a song.

SEMPRONIO (*apart, outside*). O whoreson troubadour! The great Antipater of Sidon, the great poet Ovid, they whose arguments came in meter to their lips. Yes, yes, he is one of those. That devil troubadour will sing again. He is raving in his dreams.

CALISTO (*singing*). My heart, it is well deserved
that you suffer and pain endure
for being so quickly overcome
by your beloved's sweet allure.

PÁRMENO (*apart, outside*). Did I not say he was singing?

CALISTO. Who is that talking in the great hall? Sempronio! Pármeno!

PÁRMENO. Señor?

CALISTO. It is night? Is it time to sleep?

PÁRMENO. Even later, Señor, past time to rise.

CALISTO. What are you saying, fool? The whole night has passed?

PÁRMENO. And even a good part of the day.

CALISTO. Tell me, Sempronio, is this madman lying, making me believe it is day?

SEMPRONIO. Señor, forget Melibea for a bit and you will see the light. You have gazed upon her so long that you are dazzled, like a partridge by a hunter's lantern.

CALISTO. Now I believe you, I hear the bell tolling for mass. Hand me my clothing; I will go to the church of the Magdalene. I will pray to God to direct Celestina and put my remedy in Melibea's heart or put a quick end to my dismal days.

SEMPRONIO. Do not exhaust yourself so, do not want everything in one hour; it is not the way of the prudent to wish great efficacy in what may end sadly. If you ask something to be done in one day that would ordinarily fill a year, your life will go very quickly.

CALISTO. By that do you mean that I am as impatient as the servant of the Galician squire who went barefoot all one year and then wanted to kill the cobbler for not making him shoes in one day?

SEMPRONIO. God forbid I say such a thing, for you are my señor. And in addition, I know that just as you praise my good counsel, you would punish me for something badly stated. It is true that praise of good service or good words is never equal to reprimands and punishment for something badly done or spoken.

CALISTO. I do not know who taught you so much philosophy, Sempronio.

SEMPRONIO. Señor, colors not identical to black are not completely white, nor is all that glisters gold. Your so quickly aroused desires, not weighed with reason, make my counsel seem clear. Yesterday, did you not want Melibea to be brought immediately, tied and bound in her girdle, as if you had sent for any old piece of merchandize in the plaza for which it cost no greater effort than to go there and pay? Give, Señor, a little rest to your heart, for in such a short space of time there is no room for great adventure. An oak is not felled with a single blow. Suffer and make preparations, for prudence is praiseworthy and expectation a fine weapon in fierce combat.

CALISTO. You speak wisely, if you accept the nature of my ailment.

SEMPRONIO. What, Señor, are brains for if desire prevails over reason?

CALISTO. Madman. Madman! The healthy man says to one ill, "May God grant you good health!" I want no counsel, nor expect more arguments from you; they merely feed and fan the flames that are consuming me. I shall go alone to mass and not return until you summon me, seeking the reward that comes from my pleasure at Celestina's good visit. Nor shall I dine until then, though Apollo's horses be grazing in the emerald-hued meadows, as they are wont to do when their day's journey has come to an end.

SEMPRONIO. Cease, Señor, these circumlocutions, cease this poesy, for a reference that is not shared by all, one in which all do not participate, one which few understand, is not worthwhile. Say "even though the sun has set," and all will know what you say. And as you will have no meal, take with you some conserve.

CALISTO. Sempronio, my faithful servant, my good counselor, my loyal servitor, may it be as it appears to you; because I am sure, given your unblemished service, that you value my life as much as yours.

SEMPRONIO (*apart*). Do you believe that, Pármeno? I know you would not swear to it. Remember, if you go to get the conserve, slip away with a pot to take to the fair beauties that mean much more to us. And to a good listener . . . You can tuck it into your codpiece.

CALISTO. What are you saying, Sempronio?

SEMPRONIO. I was, Señor, telling Pármeno to get some citron conserve.

PÁRMENO. I have it with me.

CALISTO. I'll take it!

SEMPRONIO (*apart*). Watch how the devil gobbles it. He would like to swallow it whole to hurry things along.

CALISTO. My soul is calm again. Be with God, my sons. Wait for the old woman and come for a reward.

PÁRMENO. Go with the Devil, toward calamitous years! And when you eat the citron, may it have the effect of the poison that turned Apuleis into an ass.

ACT NINE

(Sempronio, Pármeno, Celestina, Elicia, Areúsa, Lucrecia)

PLOT

Sempronio and Pármeno talk as they make their way to Celestina's house. Once there, they find Elicia and Areúsa. They all sit down to eat. During the meal Elicia argues with Sempronio. She gets up from the table. They calm her. As they talk among themselves, Lucrecia, Melibea's servant, arrives to tell Celestina that Melibea wants to see her.

SCENE 1

SEMPRONIO. Pármeno, take down our cloaks and swords, if you please; it is the hour for us to go to dinner.

PÁRMENO. Let us go quickly. I believe they will be complaining that we are late. Not down that street but this other, so we can go into the church and see if Celestina has finished with her devotions. We must take her with us.

SEMPRONIO. A fine hour she chose to be praying!

PÁRMENO. What can be done at any time cannot be said to have a wrong time.

SEMPRONIO. That is true, but you do not know Celestina. If she has things to be done, she does not remember God, or the holiest of priests. When she has something to gnaw on in her house, the saints are safe, but when she goes to the church with her beads in hand, she has found the cupboard bare. Although she brought you up, I know her better than you do. When she is telling her beads she is counting the number of maidenheads she is scheduled to repair, and how many enamored men there are in the city, and how many girls she has entrusted to her, and which stewards give her a good portion and which are best, and what their names are so when she meets them she will not speak like a stranger, and which canon is the youngest and most generous. When she moves her lips it is to fabricate lies, to plot the deceptions that will produce a wherewithal: this is how I will open, he will say this, I will reply that. That is how the old trollop we so revere makes a living.

PÁRMENO. I know more than that, but because you were angry the other day when I told Calisto about her, I will say no more.

SEMPRONIO. Though what we learn we may use to our benefit, we need not publish it to our harm. I know that if our master learned it, he would toss her out for who she is, and not go to her for healing. Then after he rid himself of her, he would necessarily turn to another, of whose work we can expect no part, as we do from this one, who either willingly or forced will share with us part of what she is given.

PÁRMENO. You have spoken well. But hush now, for the door is open. She is at home. Knock before you go in, for if by chance they are in dressing gowns they will not want to be seen that way.

SEMPRONIO. Go in; do not worry, we are all part of the household. They are setting the table.

CELESTINA. O my beloveds, my pearls of gold! Would that the year bring what your coming brings to me!

PÁRMENO (*apart*). What a welcome from our noble señora! Now, Brother, you see some of her trumpery at work.

SEMPRONIO (*apart*). O, let it go, that is how she makes her way in the world, but I do not know from what devils she learned all her wiles.

PÁRMENO (*apart*). Need and poverty, hunger; there are no better teachers in the world, no better energizers and enliveners of wit. But who taught the magpies and parrots to imitate our voices, our way of speaking, with their musical tongues?

CELESTINA. Girls, girls! O you silly girls! Come down here right now, for there are two men here who want to ravish me!

ELICIA. But we waited and they did not come! And they were invited well ahead of time! My cousin has been here for three hours. That lazy Sempronio must have been the cause of such tardiness; his eyes do not want to see me now.

SEMPRONIO. Hush, mistress mine, my life, my love; he who serves another is not free, so my subjection relieves me of guilt. Let us not be angry but sit down to eat.

ELICIA. Just like that! Yes, at sitting down to eat he is very diligent! He sits down, his hands are clean, and no contrition to be seen!

SEMPRONIO. Let us quarrel later, and eat now. Sit down, Mother Celestina, you first.

CELESTINA. You sit, my sons, there is room a-plenty for all of us, thanks be to God; may we have it as well in Paradise when we go there! Sit in order, each with his beauty. As for me, being alone, next to me will be this jug and cup, for my life is no more than conversation over a cup. Now that I am old, I know no better office at table than to pour the wine, because if you handle honey, some is bound to stick to you. On winter nights there is no better bed warmer, and if I drink two of these jugs when I go to bed, I feel no cold throughout the night. During the Christmas holy days, I line my garments with it, it warms the blood, it keeps me who I am, it makes me happy as I go about, and keeps me fresh; when I know there is a generous supply in the house, I have no fear of a lean year, and a crust of mouse-nibbled bread will keep me three days. Wine banishes the heart's sadness better than gold or coral; it puts vigor in a young man and in an old man strength; it gives color to what has faded, courage to the coward, diligence to the indolent, comfort to the brain; it warms stomach chills, sweetens a sour breath, makes the impotent virile, helps reapers bear their hard labors, helps one through bad times, and cures colds and toothaches; it keeps on sea voyages without going bad, something water cannot do. I could tell you of more virtues than you have hairs on your heads. I know no one who does not enjoy speaking of it. It has but one flaw, and that is that good wine is dear and the bad does harm. What keeps the liver healthy sickens the purse. But still, with all my difficulties, I look for the best in the little I drink. Only a dozen or so quaffs each meal. I never exceed that number unless I am an invited guest, as I am now.

PÁRMENO. Mother, all those who write on the subject say that three is good and modest.

CELESTINA. Son, the text must be mistaken: they have written three for thirteen.

SEMPRONIO. Mother Celestina, it is good eating and talking together, but later there will not be time to learn the state of matters between our wretched master and that gracious and charming Melibea.

ELICIA. Get out of here, you vexatious oaf! May what you have eaten not sit well, for what a meal you have given me! 'Pon my soul, I would like to throw up everything I have inside me, I am so nauseated from hearing you call that woman "charming"! *Charming*, you say? Jesú! Jesú! And how sick and angry I am to see how little shame you have. *Who* is charming? May God sicken me if you mean Melibea, she has not a whit of charm, but there is always someone who is grateful merely if his eyes come unstuck in the morning! I want to cross myself at your stupidity and ignorance. Who would want to argue her beauty and *charm* with you! Charming? *Melibea* is charming? When she is, these ten fingers of mine will march two by two. Her beauty is the kind you can buy in a shop. Actually, on the street where she lives, I personally know four damsels on whom God bestowed more grace than He did on Melibea; if she has a hint of beauty it comes from the fine clothing she wears. Put them on a pole, and *it* will be charming. I do not say this to praise myself, but I believe that I am as beautiful as your fine Melibea!

AREÚSA. O but you have not seen her as I have, Sister. God demands I tell you that if you run into her before breakfast, you would be so nauseated you would not eat all that day. All the year she shuts herself in to apply a thousand filthy unguents to her face. And when she has to go out where she can be seen, she coats her face with gall and honey and other things that out of respect for the table I will leave unsaid. It is riches that make these girls beautiful and praised, not the graces of their bodies. Let me say that though she is a virgin, she has breasts that look as if she has borne three babies; they look like two prodigious gourds. Her belly I have not seen, but judging from the rest, I believe that hers must be as flabby as that of an old woman of fifty. I do not know what Calisto has seen in her to make him leave behind others he could have had more easily and with whom he would have had more pleasure, but a corrupted taste often judges bitter to be sweet.

SEMPRONIO. Sister, it seems to me here that each of you peddlers is praising her own needles; for what you say is the opposite of what is heard about the city.

AREÚSA. Nothing is further from the truth than popular opinion. You will never live a happy life if you are ruled by the will of many. Because these are true conclusions: anything the crude and unrefined think is vanity; what they speak is false, what they censure is good, and what they approve is bad. And since this is their most predictable custom, do not for that judge the goodness and beauty of Melibea to be what you report.

SEMPRONIO. Mistress Areúsa, those who have common speech do not pardon the faults of their betters, and thus I believe that if Melibea had a flaw, it would have been discovered by those who are more often with her than with us. And even conceding what you say, Calisto is a caballero, Melibea a woman of breeding, and those born of noble ancestry seek out one another. It should not therefore be any surprise that he loves her more than another.

AREÚSA. Base is he who behaves basely. Actions determine nobility; we are all, after all, children of Adam and Eve. On our own each of us should try to be good and not look for virtue in the nobility of ancestors.

CELESTINA. Children, 'pon my life, let us put an end to such annoying discussion. And you, Elicia, go back to the table and cool your anger.

ELICIA. And what if it does not sit well, and what if I swell up and burst from eating it? Must I eat with that jackanapes who has insisted to my face that his rag of a Melibea is more charming than I am?

SEMPRONIO. Hush, my life, it was you who made that comparison. All comparisons are odious; that is your doing, not mine.

A R E Ú S A . Come eat, sister. Do not give satisfaction to those stubborn idiots; if you do not, I too will have to get up from the table.

E L I C I A . To accommodate your humor, I will satisfy my enemy and be pleasant to everyone.

S E M P R O N I O . (*Laughs.*)

E L I C I A . And why are you laughing? I hope a tumor will eat away that disagreeable mouth of yours.

C E L E S T I N A . Do not answer her, Son; if you do we will never be finished. Let us come to an agreement concerning what to do next. Tell me, how was Calisto? How did you two leave him? How were you able to slip away?

P Á R M E N O . He went off shooting sparks of hellfire, desperate, lost, half crazed, to the mass at the Magdalene, to pray God to grant you grace to chew the bones of these young cockerels, and declaring that he would not return to his house until he hears that you have come with Melibea up your sleeve. Your gown and cloak, and even my jacket, are as good as in our hands. I am not sure about the rest. And when we will have payment in coin I do not know.

C E L E S T I N A . Whenever it be. A benefit that comes late is still a benefit. Everything earned with minimal labor is happily received; most of all, that coming from where it makes so little difference, from a man who has so much to spare that with no more than what is unneeded in his house I could emerge from beggary. What they spend does not hurt people like him when they know the reason they are giving it. When they are bedazzled by love they do not feel anything; they see nothing, they hear nothing. I reach this judgment on the basis of others I have known who were even less impassioned and enveloped in the fire of love than what I see in Calisto. They do not eat or drink, laugh or weep, sleep or stay awake, talk or keep silent, suffer or find repose; they are not content or plaintive, according to the confusion caused by the sweet and fiery wound in their hearts. And if a need of nature obliges them to perform a task, it is so immediately forgotten that if eating, the hand forgets to lift the victuals to their lips. If you speak to them, they are unable to give a suitable reply. Their bodies are there, their hearts and feelings with their beloveds. Love has great power: it can travel across not just the earth but even seas. It holds dominion over all manner of men. It shatters all obstacles. It is anxious, fearful, and restless; it studies everything around it. So if you have been lovers, you will judge that I speak the truth.

SEMPRONIO. Mother Celestina, I agree entirely with your reasoning, for here is someone who for some time has made me into a second Calisto, my emotions lost, my body weary, my head empty, my days sleeping badly, my nights all wakeful, my morning greetings predawn, making faces, leaping walls, putting my life on the line every day, challenging bulls, racing horses, tossing rings, throwing the javelin, tiring friends, breaking swords, climbing ladders, wearing armor, writing couplets, painting emblems, trying new things, the thousand acts of a man mad with love. But I consider it all worthwhile, for I won a true jewel.

ELICIA. You think then you have won me! Well let me tell you straight out that you no more than turn your head and there will be another in this house I love more, someone more amusing than you, one who does not go about looking for ways to make me angry. You take a year to come see me and then you are late and bring your malevolence with you!

CELESTINA. Son, let her speak, for she is raving. The more you hear, the more she is confirming her love. This is all because you praised Melibea. The only way she knows to make you pay is to say these things, and it is my belief that she cannot wait to see the meal over to . . . well I know what. As for her cousin, I know her. Enjoy the freshness of youth, for he who has time but waits for still better will some day regret he did, as I do now for those hours I lost when I was a girl, when I was valued, when I was loved. For now, by the rood! I am aged, and no one loves me. God knows how much I want it. Put your arms around each other and kiss, for I have nothing left but to enjoy watching. As long as you are at table, everything from the waist up is allowed. When you move away from it, I will set no limits because the King sets none. What I know from my girls is that they never have to beg you. And toothless old Celestina will gum the crumbs from the table. May God bless you; how good to see you laugh and be gay, my moonstruck young whoresons, my prankish rogues. Will this clear away the storm clouds of your little squabbles? Watch there, do not overturn the table!

SCENE 3

ELICIA. Mother, someone is knocking at the door; that will be the end of our fun.

CELESTINA. Go look, Daughter. See who it is. With luck it will be someone who will join in and add to the revelry.

ELICIA. Either the voice deceives me or it is my cousin Lucrecia.

CELESTINA. Open the door and have her come in, and a warm greeting to her. For even she can understand some of these things we are talking about, though being kept in so much has prevented her from enjoying her youth.

AREÚSA. Take my word that is true; for the girls who serve señoras know neither pleasure nor the sweet rewards of love. They never have contact with relatives or with equals they can talk with girl to girl, not with anyone who says things like, "What did you have for dinner?" "Are you pregnant?" "How many hens do you have?" "Take me to your house for a bite!" "Point out your lover to me!" "How long since he has come to see you?" "How are you doing with him?" "Who are your neighbors?" and things on a similar level. Ah,

Aunt, how hard and serious and arrogant the word *señora* is continually in your mouth. That is why I have lived on my own ever since I have known who I am. I never prized being called by any name but my own, especially those that señoras use now. Spend the best of your time with them and they pay you for ten years' service with a frayed, cast-off skirt. Insulted, badly treated, continually subjected, the girls dare not speak up. And when a girl has served her prescribed time and the señora is obligated to give her a dowry and find her a husband, they set a trap for her and throw her together with a servant or with the son of the house, or bring the husband into it and pretend to be jealous, or introduce men into the house, or claim the girl stole a cup or lost a ring. Then they beat her and throw her out the door with her skirts over her head, saying, "There you go, you thief, you whore; you will no longer despoil my house and my honor!" So, expecting a benefit, she gets only the fit; expecting to be married, she is harried; and expecting a wedding jewel or dress, she comes out naked and oppressed. These are their rewards, their benefits and pay. Obliged to find the girl a husband, the señora strips her of her clothes. The finest privilege she has is to go from street to street, from señora to señora, carrying messages. She never hears her own name from her mistress's mouth, only "Over here, whore!" "Over yonder, whore!" "Where are you going, pimple-face?" "What did you say, trouble-maker?" "Why did you eat that, you little glutton?" "Why did you not scrub the fry pan, pig?" "Why did you not clean my cloak, filthy creature?" "Why did you say that, stupid?" "Who lost the plate, slattern?" "You clever thief, where did the hand towel go? You must have given it to that ruffian of yours!" "Come here, strumpet. The speckled hen is nowhere in sight; look for her, hurry. If you do not, you will notice it in your wages!" And after that, beaten a thousand times with a clog, and suffering whippings and strappings. No girl knows how to please them, no one can endure them. Their pleasure is to yell, their glory to quarrel. The more the girl does, the less happy the señora. That is why, Mother, I have preferred to live in my little house, free and my own mistress, and not in their rich palaces, submissive and enslaved.

CELESTINA. You have good sense. You know what you are doing. As wise men say, "A crumb of bread eaten in peace is worth more than a well-stocked larder with quarrels." But let us leave off this discussion and let Lucrecia in.

SCENE 4

LUCRECIA. Good appetite to you, Mother, and to your company. God bless so many honest people.

CELESTINA. So many, Daughter? You think this is *many?* It seems you did not know me in my prosperous times twenty years ago. Ay, who saw me then and who sees me now! I do not know why your heart is not breaking with sorrow. I saw, my love, at this table where your cousins are sitting now, nine girls of about your age; the eldest was not more than eighteen and none was younger than fourteen. The world, like the waterwheel, turns with some of its buckets filled and others empty. It is the law of fate that nothing remains the same for very long, its order is change. I cannot without weeping tell how I was respected then, although, for my sins and bad fortune, that has gradually tapered off. As my days declined, so did my livelihood diminish. It is an ancient proverb that everything in the world waxes and wanes. Everything has limits, everything has degrees. My honor reached its zenith in relation to who I was; necessarily, it too had to deteriorate and sink low. I am approaching the end. In this I see that I have little life left. But I know that I climbed in order to descend, I flourished in order to dry up, I had pleasure in order to grow sad, I was born in order to live, I lived in order to grow, I grew in order to become old, I became old in order to die. And as this has been verified, I will suffer my misfortune with less pain, although it is not possible to say goodbye to emotion completely, as it is formed of sensitive flesh.

LUCRECIA. Mother, you have had difficult times working with so many girls; they make up a difficult herd to drive.

CELESTINA. Work, my love? No, I would say rest and relaxation. All of them have honored me, I was respected by all of them; none strayed from my circle of affection. What I said was the right thing. I gave each of them her part. They chose no one beyond those I sent them; lame, one-eye, one-arm, they considered sound the one who paid me most. Mine was the profit, theirs the hard work. As for servants, because of the girls did I not have them? Caballeros, old and young men, religious men of all ranks, from bishop to sacristan. As I walked into the church, an assortment of headgear came off in my honor, as if I were a duchess. He who had little negotiating to do with me considered himself worst off. They would see me from half a league away, and would leave their devotions; one by one and two by two they came to see if I had something to tell them about their young mistresses. One might be saying mass and on seeing me be so flustered that he could not say or do anything correctly. Some addressed me as "Señora," others as "Aunt," others said "my love," and still others, "honorable old woman." There in the church they arranged their comings to my house, there the goings to theirs; there they offered me monies, there promises, there other gifts, kissing the hem of my cloak, and some even my face, to keep me more content. Now fate has brought me to such a state that you say to me: "Good appetite! Meaning may that old piece of leather provide you good appetite!"

SEMPRONIO. You frighten us with such tales, telling us about these religious men and blessed tonsures. May it not be true of all of them!

CELESTINA. No, Son, nor does God command that I raise such a suggestion. For there were devout old men with whom I had very few profitable dealings, and even those who would not allow their eyes to rest upon me. But I believe that was from envy of the others who did speak to me. As the clergy is numerous, there were all kinds, some very chaste, others who believed their charge was to maintain one of my girls. I think even now there are many of those. They would send their squires and young servants to see me home, and I would scarcely arrive at my house before through my door came chickens and hens, geese, ducklings, suckling pigs, doves, sides of bacon, and wheat cakes. As each of these men received tithes for the Church, they came to me to list them in my records so that I and their devoted young mistresses could dine. And wine? Did I not have more than enough? The best that was drunk in the city, come from many places. From Monviedro, from Luque, from Toro, from Madrigal, from Sant Martin and many other places, and so much that although I retain the differences in tastes and bouquets in my mouth, I do not hold their many lands in my memory. It is too much to think that an old woman, by just sniffing a wine, could say where it is from. There were other priests with no income, who the minute they were offered the votive bread and kissed the gold fringe on their stole, ran to my house. As thick as a rain of stones on a target, youths laden with provisions poured through my door. I do not know how I am able to live after falling from such a privileged state.

AREÚSA. God preserve us, we have come to enjoy ourselves; do not weep, Mother, do not fret, for God will remedy everything.

CELESTINA. I have so much, Daughter, to weep about, remembering such happy times and the life I had and how I was served by everyone. There was never a new fruit that I was not first to enjoy before others even knew they had ripened. It was in my house that fruit was to be found should it be sought for some pregnant girl.

SEMPRONIO. Mother, there is no benefit in remembering those good days; they cannot be brought back but bring only sadness, as is happening now. You have drained pleasure from our hands. Clear the table. We are off to celebrate and you to give an answer to this young damsel who has come here.

SCENE 5

CELESTINA. Daughter Lucrecia, having abandoned these arguments, I would like for you to tell me what brought us your good visit.

LUCRECIA. Truth is, I have already forgotten my principal demand and message, hearing the memory of that very happy time as you have told it. I could pass a year without eating, listening to you and thinking about the good life those girls must have enjoyed, which seems to me to be that I am now living. My visit, Mother, is what you will know: to ask you for the girdle. And in addition, my señora begs to be visited by you, and very soon, because she is exhausted from swoons and heartaches.

CELESTINA. Daughter, such little pains are more show than substance. I am amazed to hear that such a young woman is suffering a heart problem.

LUCRECIA (*apart*). May you be dragged to the scaffold, traitor! You do not know what it is! The old bawd casts her spell and leaves; then she pretends to be surprised.

CELESTINA. What are you saying, Daughter?

LUCRECIA. That we must go quickly, Mother, and that you will give me the girdle.

CELESTINA. We will go, and I will bring it.

ACT TEN

(Melibea, Lucrecia, Celestina, Alisa)

PLOT

As Celestina and Lucrecia are walking to the house of Melibea, Melibea is alone, talking to herself. They reach the door. Lucrecia goes in first. She motions Celestina in. Melibea, after a long conversation, confesses to Celestina that she is burning with love for Calisto. They see Alisa, Melibea's mother, coming. They quickly say goodbye. Alisa asks Melibea about her dealings with Celestina, and then discourages further conversation with her.

SCENE 1

MELIBEA (*alone*). O how wretched I am. What poor judgment! Would it not have been better for me to yield to Celestina's entreaty yesterday, when she asked on behalf of that caballero who captivated me at first sight; he would have been happy and my health would have been restored and I not forced to reveal my wound when he was not grateful; now, when not confident of a good answer from me, he may have set his eyes upon loving another? How much greater gain a requested promise than an offering under pressure! O my faithful servant Lucrecia! What will you say of me, will you think I have any good sense left when you see me tell the world what I never wanted to reveal to you? Will you be frightened by the crumbling of the honor and self-respect I always knew as a sheltered damsel? I do not know whether you will have perceived the source of my pain. O if only you were bringing with you the woman who intercedes for my well-being! O sovereign God above! It is You to whom all with tribulations call, You whom the suffering seek for remedy, the wounded for medicines; it is You whom skies, sea, and earth, the very depths of hell, obey; it is You, the one who made all things submissive to man, I humbly ask to bestow upon my wounded heart the patience to conceal my terrible passion! Do not strip away the fig leaf I have placed before my amorous desire, pretending my pain to be other and not what is tormenting me. But how shall I be able, when I am so cruelly aggrieved by the poison dealt me at the sight of that caballero. O shy and timid womankind! Why are women not given the power to reveal their anguishing and ardent love, as men are? O that Calisto should not live with a complaint, nor I with pain.

SCENE 2

LUCRECIA (*apart, outside*). Aunt, wait here at the door for a moment. I will go in to see who my mistress is talking with. (*Inside*) Come in, come in, it is with herself.

MELIBEA. Lucrecia, pull across that portière. You are welcome, wise, honorable woman. How does it seem to you that my happiness and good fortune turned so abruptly that I should have need of your wisdom, and that so soon you would have to pay in the same coin for the favor you asked of me for that caballero you cured by virtue of my girdle?

CELESTINA. What, Daughter, is this illness that reveals signs of your torment in the heightened colors of your face?

MELIBEA. O Mother mine, inside my body, serpents are eating this heart of mine.

CELESTINA (*apart*). Aha, that is good; that is what I wanted! You will pay, foolish girl, for your excessive wrath.

MELIBEA. What are you saying? Seeing me, have you sensed the seat of my malady?

CELESTINA. You have yet, Daughter, to describe the nature of your illness. Do you want me to divine the cause? What I can tell you is that it pains me greatly to see such sorrow on your lovely countenance.

MELIBEA. Then make me happy, for you are esteemed, and I have heard great accounts of your wisdom.

CELESTINA. Daughter, God alone knows everything, but as in our search for good health and healing many were granted skills to prepare medicines, some from experience, some by art, some by natural instinct, some little part fell to this poor old woman by whom, at this moment, you can be served.

MELIBEA. O how pleasant and agreeable to listen to you! How healing to someone ill the happy face of her visitor. It seems to me that I see in your hands the broken pieces of my heart, knowing that if you so wished, you could with very little effort join them together simply by virtue of your tongue, in the same way that after seeing in dreams the healthful root in a dragon's mouth the great Alexander, king of Macedonia, cured his servant Ptolemy of a serpent's venom. Well then, for the love of God, set aside all else and set about more diligently to study my illness, and offer the remedy.

CELESTINA. A large part of well-being is the desiring of it, and for that reason I believe your pain to be less dangerous. But for me, through God, to be able to offer a suitable and healthful remedy I must first know three things from you. The first: in what part of your body is the sensation most painful? Second, whether it is newly felt, because tender infirmities are sooner healed in their early stages than when they have made a habit of survival. Beasts of burden are better broken at an early age rather than when their hide has toughened if they are to go tamely to the yoke; plants grow better when transplanted tender and new rather than moved when already bearing fruit; much more easily does one rid oneself of a new sin than one that by long custom we commit every day. The third question: whether the malady originates from some cruel thought that settled in the place where you have pain. When I know these things, you will see my healing do its work. Therefore, you must tell your physician, as you tell your confessor, the whole truth and hold nothing back.

MELIBEA. Dear Celestina, my wise friend and esteemed teacher, you have opened wide the path along which my illness can be specified. And you ask as a woman expert in healing such illnesses. My malady lies in the heart. The left breast is its lodging place, and its rays extend through all my body. Second, the illness is newly born in my body, and I never thought that pain could deprive me of good judgment as this is doing; it contorts my face, ruins my appetite, prevents me from sleeping, and veils all reason for laughter. The cause or thought, which is the last thing you asked about my malady, I do not know how to tell you. Because neither the death of kin nor loss of riches, neither impairment of vision nor delirious dream, not anything can I feel that it was other than the upset you caused me with the request I suspected came from that caballero Calisto, when you asked me for a prayer.

CELESTINA. What, Daughter? Is he an evil man? Does he have such a bad reputation that merely the sound of his name brings poison with it? Do not believe that this is the cause of your feeling; I suspect a different source. And since that is so, if you give me permission, Señora, I will tell you what it is.

MELIBEA. How is that, Celestina? What is this new arrangement you ask? Do you need permission to restore my health? What physician ever asked a warrant to treat a patient? Tell me, for you always have it from me, as long as you do not demean my honor with your words.

CELESTINA. I see, Daughter, that on one hand you groan about pain, and on the other fear the remedy. Your fear makes me afraid, the fear brings silence; the silence intervenes between your wound and my medicine, and that will be why neither will your pain cease nor my visit be of help.

MELIBEA. The longer you delay my healing the more the pain and torment grow and multiply. Either your medicines are powders of infamy and liquors of corruption, compounded with another, crueler sorrow than the one felt by the patient, or you have no knowledge at all. And if one or the other were not an obstacle, you would give me a different remedy without fear, for I am asking you to do that, as long as my honor is left untouched.

CELESTINA. Daughter, you need not again be strong enough to endure the burning turpentine and sharp needles that inflict pain and double the torment, not that first stitch on healthy flesh. If you would be healed and have me show you the tip of my subtle needle without fear, make a ligature of calm for your hands and feet, a blindfold of mercy for your eyes, a curb of silence for your tongue, and fill your ears with a cotton of suffering and patience if you would see an old mistress of such wounds at work.

MELIBEA. O I am dying with your delay! Say, for God's sake, what you want; do what you know to do, for your remedy cannot be so harsh that it can equal my pain and torment. Taint my honor, damage my reputation, punish my body! Although it be to rip my flesh and tear out my painful heart, I give you my word that you will be safe and, if I feel relief, well rewarded.

LUCRECIA (*apart*). My señora has lost her wits. This is a terrible illness. She is bewitched by this old spellbinder.

CELESTINA (*apart*). I am never without some devil. God freed me from Pármeno but set Lucrecia in my path.

MELIBEA. What did you say, my valued adviser? What was the girl saying to you?

CELESTINA. I heard nothing from her. But whatever she may have said, she knows that spirited surgeons encounter no greater impediment to bold healing than weak-hearted souls who with their loud lament, their sorrowful speech, their pitiful pacing, strike fear in the patient, make him lose confidence in the possibility of good health, who anger and disturb the physician and that disturbance affects the hand and shakes the needle. What one may know clearly is that for your health it is obligatory for there to be no other person present; you must, therefore, order them to leave. And to you, Daughter Lucrecia, my apologies.

MELIBEA. Leave us immediately!

LUCRECIA (*apart*). I am, I am! All is lost. (*Aloud*) I am leaving now, Señora.

SCENE 3

CELESTINA. Your great pain gives me daring, as does the fact that even with your suspicions you have already swallowed some part of my cure: it is still necessary, however, to bring brighter medicine and more salutary relief from the house of that caballero Calisto.

MELIBEA. Hush, Mother, please God. Do not bring anything from his house for my benefit, nor utter his name here.

CELESTINA. Suffer, Daughter, with patience, for this is the first, the principal, stitch. Do not break the thread, lest all our work will be lost. Your wound is deep; it will take a harsh cure, and what is hard is softened more efficiently by another hardness. The wise say that the physician's healing leaves a large mark behind, and that danger is never vanquished without danger. Be patient, for what is unpleasant is seldom healed without unpleasantness; a nail is driven out with another, and one pain with another. You must not hate or detest, nor allow your tongue to speak ill of, a person as virtuous as Calisto, for if you knew him . . .

MELIBEA. O dear God above! You are killing me! Have I not said not to praise that man, or name him, whether for good or bad?

CELESTINA. Daughter, this is a different, a second, stitch, which if you with your grave suffering do not allow, my coming will have achieved very little; but if, as you promised, you do allow it, you will be left in good health and without debt, and Calisto without a complaint, and paid. Early on I advised you of my cure and of this invisible needle that, though not touching you, you will feel when it is but mentioned on my lips.

MELIBEA. You refer so many times to this caballero of yours that neither my promise nor having given you my word is enough to make me listen to what you say. For what will he be paid? What do I owe him? How am I in his debt? What has he done for me? What has he to do with the condition of my malady? I would rather you tear my flesh and take out my heart than to say those words here.

CELESTINA. Without ripping your clothing, love dove into your bosom; I will not slash your flesh to heal it.

MELIBEA. How do you call this pain that has taken command of the best of my body?

CELESTINA. Sweet love!

MELIBEA. Tell me what that is, for only hearing it I am happy.

CELESTINA. Love is a hidden fire, a pleasant wound, a delicious poison, a sweet bitterness, a delectable hurting, a happy torment, a sweet, fierce wound, a gentle death.

MELIBEA. Ay, wretch that I am! For if it is as you tell it, my health will be doubtful. For given the opposition I hear between those words, what to one is beneficial will add to the other's torment.

CELESTINA. Do not, Daughter, lose faith in the noble health of youth; for when God on high sends the wound, he follows with the remedy. Even better, I know a flower blooming in splendor that will free you from all this.

MELIBEA. How is it called?

CELESTINA. I dare not say it.

MELIBEA. Say it, do not be afraid.

CELESTINA. Calisto! . . . O God's bones, Daughter Melibea! What weakness is this? What this swooning? O such misery! Look up! O luckless old woman! Is this how my plan is to end? If she dies, they will kill me; even if she lives I will be caught out, for she cannot help but spread word of her malady and my cure. My dear daughter, dear angel, what have you felt? What has happened to your eloquent tongue? Where is your joyful color? Open your bright eyes! Lucrecia! Lucrecia! Come here. Quick! You will find your mistress in a faint in my hands. Run quickly for a jug of water!

MELIBEA. Slowly, slowly, I am trying. Do not raise a furor in the house.

CELESTINA. O what distress! Do not faint again! Señora, talk to me. I want to hear you speak.

MELIBEA. I will, and much better! Hush, do not exhaust me.

CELESTINA. But what do you command me to do, beautiful pearl? Where was your pain? I believe my stitches are pulling apart, the thread breaking.

MELIBEA. My honor is breaking, my modesty too, my shyness is fading, and, as is natural, as they are so used to being with me, they could not take flight from my face without taking with them, for a while, my color, my strength, my tongue, and a large portion of my senses. And now, my new teacher, my faithful confidante, all that you so clearly know now, I tried in vain to conceal. Many, many days have gone by since that noble caballero spoke to me of love. At the time I was as angered at his vexing words as later, when you spoke his name, I was happy. Your stitches have closed my wound. I am come to do your will. You took him the deed to my freedom wrapped in my girdle. His toothache was my greatest torment, his pain my agony. I praise your forbearance, your sane daring, your generous labors, your solicitous and loyal acts, your pleasant conversation, your vast knowledge, your deep solicitude, your beneficial persistence. That señor owes you a lot, and I more, for all my reproaches were not enough to lessen your effort and perseverance. I put my trust in your astuteness; when most affronted, you were more diligent, when least favored, you made more effort, when answered most coolly, you were most cheerful, and when I was most wrathful, you were most humble. With my fear deferred, you have slipped from my breast what I never thought to disclose to you or any other.

CELESTINA. Dear daughter and young mistress, do not marvel, because these aims, when effected, provide me the audacity to suffer the harsh and dread rebukes of sheltered damsels like you. Truth is that before I determined to act, both on the way to and in your house, I had strong doubts whether to present my petition to you. Given your father's great power, I was afraid; knowing the gentility of Calisto, I dared; in view of your discretion, I doubted; seeing your virtue and humanity, I strove to continue. On the one hand, I found fear, and on the other, confidence. And since now, young señora, you have chosen to disclose the great mercy you have shown us, speak your will, fling your secrets into my lap, leave to me an agreement to this disagreement. I will tell you how your and Calisto's desires will soon be fulfilled.

MELIBEA. O my Calisto, my señor, my sweet and gentle joy! If your heart feels as mine does now, I marvel that my absence allows you to live. O Mother, Señora Celestina, if you want to save my life, find the way for me to see him soon.

CELESTINA. See *and* speak.

MELIBEA. Speak? That is impossible.

CELESTINA. Nothing men want badly is impossible.

MELIBEA. Tell me how.

CELESTINA. I have thought on it. I will tell you: through cracks between the doors of your house.

MELIBEA. When?

CELESTINA. Tonight.

MELIBEA. You will have my praise if you arrange it. Tell me, what hour?

CELESTINA. At twelve.

MELIBEA. Then go, my señora, my loyal friend, and speak with the caballero. And have him come very quietly. There, at the hour you have chosen and, if he is willing, we will reach an accord.

CELESTINA. I am gone, your mother is coming this way.

SCENE 4

MELIBEA. Friend Lucrecia, my loyal servant and faithful confidante, you have seen that things are no longer in my hands. I am captive to the love of that caballero. Pray to our Lord God to conceal all this with a secret seal that I may pleasure in such a gentle love. I will place you high in my esteem, as your faithful service deserves.

LUCRECIA. Señora, long before now I have felt your wound and gauged your desire. Your passion has brought me great sorrow. The more you have wanted me to cover over the flame that was burning you, the more your flames were visible in the color of your face, in the agitation of your heart, in the trembling of your limbs, in your apathy at table, in your loss of sleep. You left constant signs of pain, as if they were dropping from your hands. But as in times when a strong wish or excessive appetite arises in their masters, it falls to servants to obey with physical diligence and not with insincere verbal advice. I suffered with pain, kept silence with fear, I loyally aided you to conceal, and though I suffered I believed that hard counsel was better that soft flattery. But as now you have no choice but to die or to love, it makes good sense to choose as better what in fact *is*.

SCENE 5

ALISA. What are you doing here every day, neighbor?

CELESTINA. Señora, yesterday I was a little short in a weight of thread and because I gave my word, I came to deliver it. And having done, I am going. Be with God.

ALISA. And He with you. Daughter Melibea, what did that old bawd want?

MELIBEA. She wanted to sell me face powders.

ALISA. I believe that more than what the old drab said. She thought I would be annoyed by her visit and she lied to me. Be on your guard against her, Daughter, for she is very treacherous: the cunning thief is always found around the houses of the rich. With her treachery and her fraudulent merchandise she knows how to alter intentions. She damages reputations; she enters a house three times and suspicion is rife.

LUCRECIA (*apart*). Our mistress awakes a little too late!

ALISA. Because I love you, Daughter, if she comes back without my seeing her, do not consider her coming a good thing and do not welcome her. Let her find honor in your answer and she will never return; true virtue is more to be feared than the sword.

MELIBEA. She is one of those? Never again! I am happy, Mother, to be warned, and to know whom I must guard against.

ACT ELEVEN

(Celestina, Sempronio, Calisto, Pármeno, Elicia)

PLOT

Celestina, after leaving Melibea, makes her way down the street alone, talking to herself. She sees Sempronio and Pármeno, who are going to the church of the Magdalene to find their señor. Sempronio talks with Calisto. Celestina follows them. They all go to Calisto's house. Celestina gives him her message and tells him of the arrangements she has made for him with Melibea. As they are engaged in this conversation, Pármeno and Sempronio are talking between themselves. Celestina says goodbye to Calisto, goes to her house, knocks at the door. Elicia comes to let her in. They have their supper and turn in for the night.

SCENE 1

CELESTINA (*apart*). God help me! How I long to be in my house with all this happiness I am carrying! I see Pármeno and Sempronio on their way to the Magdalene. I will go after them, and if Calisto is not there, we will go to his house to claim my reward for the pleasure he will know.

SEMPRONIO. Señor, you have stayed long enough to give everyone something to talk about. God's truth, you have tried to avoid being the subject of talk, but the extremely devout are deemed hypocrites. What will they say but that you have been seen kissing the feet of all the saints? If you are tormented, suffer it in your house, not where the very earth can hear you. Do not disclose your pain to strangers, for now it is in the hands of the tambourine mistress, who knows the tune very well.

CALISTO. Whose hands do you mean?

SEMPRONIO. Celestina's.

CELESTINA. Who is it I hear speaking Celestina's name? What are you saying about this slave of Señor Calisto? I followed you down Arcidiano Street, trying to catch up with you, but these blessed long skirts kept me from it.

CALISTO. O jewel of the world, succor of my torment, mirror that reflects truth to my eyes! My heart is made happy by your honorable presence, your noble years. Tell me, what do you come with? What news do you bring? I see you happy but I do not know on what my life depends.

CELESTINA. On my tongue.

CALISTO. What are you saying, my repose and my glory? Tell me more.

CELESTINA. Let us go outside the church, Señor, and from there to the house, where I will tell you something that will make you truly happy.

PÁRMENO (apart). The old bawd is in good humor, Brother, she must have succeeded.

SEMPRONIO (apart). Listen to her.

CELESTINA. All this day, Señor, I have been working on your enterprise, though it meant neglecting others from which I expect good payment. I left many people complaining in order to keep you content. I have lost more than you think. But everything in good hour, for I bring a happy message. I bring you many good words from Melibea and leave her at your service.

CALISTO. What is this I am hearing?

CELESTINA. That she belongs to you more than to herself; she is more at your command and wishes than she is at her father Pleberio's.

CALISTO. But speak to the conventions of courtly love, Mother. Say no such thing, lest these youths will say you are mad. Melibea is my beloved, Melibea is my goddess, Melibea is my life. I am *her* captive, I *her* servant.

SEMPRONIO. With such lack of confidence, Señor, such a low value of self, with your thinking so little of yourself, you are saying things to interrupt Celestina's words. You are upsetting us with your ravings. Why are you crossing yourself? Give her something to compensate her labors; that will do well, for those words say she expects a reward.

CALISTO. You speak wisely. My dear mother, I know for certain that my trivial reward will never equal your labor. Instead of a cloak and skirt, and to prevent some share from going to the tailor, take this little chain. Put it around your neck and proceed with your account and my joy.

PÁRMENO (*apart*). A *little* chain, he calls it! Do you hear, Sempronio? He has no idea of its value. Well, I tell you that I would not accept four ounces of gold for my share, however the old trull divides it.

SEMPRONIO (*apart*). Our master will hear you. We have things in him to soothe and in you to heal, the way he is angered by your muttering. In the name of love, Brother, just listen and say nothing; that is why God gave you two ears and one tongue.

PÁRMENO (*apart*). Let the Devil hear! Our master is hanging from the old bawd's lips, deaf, mute, and blind, become a person with no sound, and even if we gave him our most vulgar fingers and thumb, he would say that we were lifting our hands to God, praying for a good end to his pursuit of love.

SEMPRONIO (*apart*). Hush, listen closely to Celestina. In my heart she deserves it all, and any more she is given. She has a lot to say.

CELESTINA. Señor Calisto, you have been very generous to a feeble old woman like me. But as every gift or favor is judged large or small depending on the one who gives it, I do not want to bring into consideration my inconsequential merit before someone who exceeds me in quality and quantity, for measured against your munificence, it is nothing. In payment I restore your health, which was lost, your heart, which was missing, your good sense, which was wavering. Melibea pines for you more than you for her. Melibea loves you and longs to see you. Melibea spends more hours thinking of you than she does of herself. Melibea calls herself yours, and to her that is *freedom*, and with it she quenches the flames that are burning her more than you.

CALISTO. Lads, am I standing here? Lads, am I hearing this? Lads, look and see if I am awake. Is it day or night? O God in Heaven, Celestial Father, I pray that this not be a dream! But I am awake! If you are mocking me, Señora, to pay me with words, do not fear. Speak the truth; you deserve more than you have received from me.

CELESTINA. Never does the heart wounded with desire take good news as real, nor bad as doubtful. But whether or not I mock, you will see her this night, according to the agreement I made with her, at her house when the clock strikes twelve, and speak with her through the doors. From her lips you will know more fully my solicitude and her desire, and the love she has for you, and who has brought it about.

CALISTO. Yes, yes! Can I expect that? Is it possible for such a thing to happen to me? Surely I will die between now and then. I cannot endure such glory, being undeserving of such great favor, being unworthy to speak with such a dear woman, and with her wish and will.

CELESTINA. I have always heard that it is more difficult to suffer good fortune than it is adversity, for the one offers no repose and the other no consolation. How, Señor Calisto, would you not look at who you are? How would you not look at the time you have spent in her power? And how not look at whom you chose as intermediary? Until now you have always doubted you could approach her, and have suffered, but now that I affirm the end to that pain you want to put an end to your life? Look, just look. Celestina is here at your side, and even if you lacked everything required to be a lover, Melibea would see you as the most accomplished gallant in the world. She would level craggy peaks before your feet, and calm raging waters that you might cross without getting wet. You have no idea whom you are giving your money to.

CALISTO. Here, Señora, what are you telling me! That she comes willingly?

CELESTINA. On her knees.

SEMPRONIO. I hope this is not a sorcerer's trick to take us all. Look, Mother, that is how they wrap poison paste in bread, so you do not notice the taste.

PÁRMENO. That is the best thing I ever heard you say. The hasty surrender of Mistress Melibea makes me very suspicious, her concession to all Celestina's wishes, deceiving our will with her ready, dulcet words, only to steal away to a different place as those gypsies from Egypt do when they read destiny on our palms. So many injuries are avenged, Mother, with sweet words. The man disguised as a bullock and wearing soft bells drives partridges into the net, the song of the siren ensnares the naïve sailor with its sweetness. And so with her meekness and ready concession, she may want to take a number of us without danger to herself; she will use Calisto's honor and our deaths to affirm her innocence. Like the little lamb that suckles its mother and any other that will have it, she will from her safe haven wreak vengeance on Calisto through all of us, and with the many people she has she can capture master and servants in one nest, and you will be scratching yourself by the fire, saying, "The man who rings the alert is safe in the tower."

CALISTO. Quiet you idiotic, suspicious blackguards. You seem to suggest that angels know how to work evil. Yes, Melibea is a cloaked angel living among us.

SEMPRONIO (*apart*). Still you persist in your heresy. Listen to him, Pármeno, but do not worry, for if there is double-dealing he will pay for it; our feet will fly.

CELESTINA. Señor, you are in the right, and you two are laden with vain suspicions. I have done everything that was mine to do. I leave you a happy man. God liberate and mend you. I leave content. If you should need me for this or any other service, I will be happy to answer your call.

PÁRMENO. (*Apart; he laughs.*)

SEMPRONIO (*apart*). What, for God's sake, are you laughing about, Pármeno?

PÁRMENO (*apart*). About the old slattern's haste to leave. She cannot wait to get the chain out of the house. She cannot believe she has it in her power, or that it has in fact been given her. She considers herself as little worthy of such a gift as Calisto believes he deserves Melibea.

SEMPRONIO (*apart*). What do you want a whorish old go-between who knows and understands things we do not talk about, and who is known to restore seven maidenheads for a few coins, to do but, after finding herself laden with gold, be eager to get to a safe place with her chain, fearing that, after she has done what was her part to do, it will be taken from her? Well, watch out for the Devil, old crone, or when it comes time to divide we will have your soul.

CALISTO. God be with you, Mother. I want to sleep and rest a while to make up for these last nights, and to prepare for the one to come.

SCENE 4

CELESTINA. (*She knocks.*)

ELICIA. Who is that knocking?

CELESTINA. Open, Daughter Elicia.

ELICIA. Why are you coming so late? You should not do that, you are an old woman. You will trip, and where you fall you will die.

CELESTINA. I have no fear of that, for by day I find the way to where I am going that night. I never climb up on the high footpath but walk in the middle of the street. Because as is said, "The one who walks along the wall will not go far before a fall," and also, "He who is most sane always walks the level lane." I would rather muddy my shoes than bloody my headdress and the paving stones. But that is not what is bothering you here.

ELICIA. What is there to bother me?

CELESTINA. That the company I left you with went away, and you were left alone.

ELICIA. Four hours have gone by since then, you think I am remembering that?

CELESTINA. The sooner they left you, the more, with good reason, you felt it. But let us set aside their going and my late arrival. Let us think of eating and sleeping.

ACT TWELVE

(Calisto, Sempronio, Pármeno, Lucrecia, Pleberio, Celestina, Alisa, Elicia)

As midnight approaches, Calisto, Sempronio, and Pármeno, well armed, leave for Melibea's house. Lucrecia and Melibea are near the door, waiting for Calisto. Calisto arrives. Lucrecia speaks first. She calls Melibea. Lucrecia goes away. Melibea and Calisto talk through the crack between the doors. Pármeno and Sempronio converse at a distance. They hear people in the street. They get ready to flee. Calisto bids Melibea farewell after they agree upon a meeting the next night. Pleberio, at the sound of the noise in the street, wakes. He calls to his wife, Alisa. They ask Melibea whose footsteps they heard in her chamber. Melibea answers her father, Pleberio, pretending she was thirsty. Calisto and servants start for his house, talking along the way. Calisto lies down to sleep. Pármeno and Sempronio go to Celestina's house. They demand their part of the payment. Celestina dissembles. They quarrel. Pármeno and Sempronio lay hands on Celestina: they kill her. Elicia screams. The authorities arrive and arrest them.

CALISTO. Lads! What hour is striking?

SEMPRONIO. Ten.

CALISTO. O how the forgetfulness of servants perturbs me. My resolve and caution this night, and your carelessness and forgetting, would make a rather long account. How stupid, Sempronio, knowing how much its being ten or eleven means to me, that you said the first thing that came to mind. Never such distress! Imagine if by chance I had dozed, and had accepted Sempronio's answer to make ten of eleven, and so eleven of twelve. Melibea would have come to the door, I would not have been there, she would have gone back to her chamber, and there would have been no end to my malady or fulfillment of my desire. It is not for nothing it is said that it is easy to ignore another's malady.

SEMPRONIO. To me, Señor, it seems as much error, knowing, to ask, as not knowing to answer. (*Apart*) My master wants to quarrel and does not know how.

PÁRMENO. It would be better, Señor, if you spent the remaining hour in preparing weapons rather than looking for a quarrel. Being well prepared, Señor, is half the battle.

CALISTO (*apart*). This fool has wise things to say. Anger in such a time is not good. I do not want to think about what might come but, rather, about what did, not about the harm that might have resulted from his negligence but the benefit that will come from my vigilance. I must set aside my anger, which either will leave me or compose me. So, Pármeno, take down my armor, and you two arm yourselves and thus will go protected. As is said, "Planning 'fore done, battle half-won."

PÁRMENO. Here you have them, Señor.

CALISTO. Help me put them on. Sempronio, you go look to see if anyone is in the street.

SEMPRONIO. Señor, there is no one to be seen, and even if there were, the darkness would prevent our being seen or recognized.

SCENE 2

CALISTO. Well, let us go down this street; even though it is not the shortest way we will be better concealed. It is striking twelve o'clock; we are in good hour.

PÁRMENO. We are very near.

CALISTO. And we arrive in good time. Stop, Pármeno; you go look between the doors to see if my sweet mistress has come.

PÁRMENO. Me, Señor? It is not God's command that I botch something that was not my doing. At this first meeting, Señor, it would be better if *you* were there, because seeing me she might be upset that what she wanted to keep hidden, what she does with such fear, is known by many. She might even think you are tricking her.

CALISTO. O, how well you have spoken! Your subtle advice has given me life, for it is no more needed for me to be carried home dead than for her to be turned back by my lack of foresight. I will go there; you two stay here.

SCENE 3

PÁRMENO. What do you think, Sempronio, of our idiot master's idea to use me as shield in the first dangerous encounter? How do I know who is behind those closed doors? How do I know whether there is any trickery? How do I know whether Melibea is in this way planning to pay our master for his boldness? And even more, we are not absolutely certain the old crone is telling the truth. So, Pármeno, had you not known to speak, they would have your soul without your knowing who did it. Do not fawn over your master as he would like and you will never weep over the troubles of others. Do not, in what involves you, take Celestina's counsel and find yourself in the dark. Give your advice and loyal warning and they will give you a thrashing. If you change who you are, you will sleep well. I want to celebrate that I was born today, for I escaped a great danger.

SEMPRONIO. Quiet, Pármeno. Do not be jumping about so. Do not make such a happy celebration. You give every reason to be heard.

PÁRMENO. Hush, Brother. Why would I be happy? I made Calisto believe that I was not going because he should be the one, and it was for *my* safety! Who has known better than I to secure the advantage? From here on, if you are alert, you will see me do many things, though not everyone will notice, neither Calisto nor so many involved in this affair of his. Because I am sure that for Calisto this maiden is bait on the hook, meat set out for the vultures, and those who come will pay dearly for their share.

SEMPRONIO. Those suspicions will do you no harm, even if they turn out to be true. Just be alert, and at the first voice you hear, we will make smoke.

PÁRMENO. You and I think alike, we are of one mind. I am wearing the breeches and leggings you told me of, so I will be fleetest of all. I am pleased, Brother, that you have advised me of something I would have been ashamed to do. For if our master is heard, he will not, I fear, escape the hands of Pleberio's people and be able later to demand to know how we did it and to accuse us of running away.

SEMPRONIO. O friend Pármeno! How happy and profitable is agreement between companions! If Celestina were not good for anything more, it is enough that we have come together through her doing.

PÁRMENO. No one can deny what shows itself to all. It is clear that as we each were ashamed to be accused of cowardice, we would have awaited death here with our master, deserving it no more than he.

SEMPRONIO. Melibea must have come to the door. Listen, they are talking quietly.

PÁRMENO. I fear that it is not Melibea but someone imitating her voice!

SEMPRONIO. God save us from traitors; I hope they have not claimed the street we would use to flee. I am not afraid of anything else.

SCENE 4

CALISTO (*apart*). This noise is more than that made by one person. I must speak, whoever it may be. Psst, my señora Melibea.

LUCRECIA (*apart, inside*). That is Calisto's voice. I will go closer. Who is speaking? Who is outside?

CALISTO. The one who comes to follow your command.

LUCRECIA (*apart, inside*). Why do you not go, Señora? Go without fear, it is the caballero.

MELIBEA (*apart, inside*). Quiet, silly girl. Look carefully. Is it he?

LUCRECIA (*apart, inside*). Go, Señora. It is he. I know his voice.

CALISTO. I am certain I am being tricked. It was not Melibea who spoke to me. I hear noise. I am lost. Well, alive or dead, I am not leaving.

MELIBEA (*apart, inside*). Go, Lucrecia, go take a rest. (*Aloud*) Psst, Señor! What is your name? Who commanded you to come here?

CALISTO. The one who deserves to command the entire world, the one whom I do not have the dignity to serve. Do not, Your Grace, fear to reveal your refinement to this captive. The sweet sound of your voice, which has never left my ears, affirms you to be my mistress Melibea. And I am your servant Calisto.

MELIBEA (*inside*). The brazen boldness of your messages has forced me to this conversation with you, Señor Calisto. For having recently had from me a reply to your argument, I do not know what more you think to draw from your love for me than what I then showed you. Divert your mad, vain thoughts that my honor and my person may be safe from inevitable suspicion. It is for this that I have come here, to reach agreement regarding your farewell and my repose. You do not want to put my reputation on a scale tilted by slandering tongues.

CALISTO. To a heart strongly prepared against adversities, nothing can come that will breach the strength of its wall. But this sad person—who came unarmed and without foreseeing deceits and traps to penetrate the gates of your security, no matter what he met— has reason to be tormented, finding destroyed all the storerooms in which sweet news was lodged. O ill-fated Calisto! O how you have been mocked by your servants. O deceitful Celestina! Let me die, and do not come again to revive my hope and fan the flames that already afflict me. Why did you bring me a false message from my mistress Melibea? Why have you with your tongue given me cause for despair? Why did you tell me to come here, to be shown disfavor, interdiction, doubt, hatred, from the very lips of the one who holds the keys to my damnation or my glory? O enemy! Did you not tell me that this my mistress looked upon me with favor? Did you not tell me that it was her wish for this her captive to come to this place, not to be banished again from her presence but to lift the banishment placed by an earlier command? In whom may I place my trust? Where is truth? Who is free of deceit? What place is free from falsehood? Who is the visible enemy? Who the true friend? Where is treachery not practiced? Who dared give me such cruel hope of passion?

MELIBEA (*inside*). Leave off, my señor, your legitimate complaints, for neither is my heart large enough to suffer them nor my eyes able to conceal my feelings. You weep with sadness, judging me cruel; I weep with pleasure, seeing you so faithful. O my dear señor, my life! How happy I would be if only I could see your face as well as hear your voice! But as nothing more can be done at the present, accept what I say now as signature and seal of the words I sent you written on the tongue of that solicitous messenger. All that she told you, I confirm; I hold it all to be good. Dry your eyes, Señor, command me at your will.

CALISTO. O my sweet mistress, my hope of glory, rest and relief of my suffering, joy of my heart! What tongue will be enough to give you thanks to equal the great, the incomparable favor that at this point of such anguish you offer, in wishing that such a weak and unworthy man may draw pleasure from your most gentle love? Of which, though infinitely desiring, I have always judged myself unworthy, seeing your magnificence, considering your high estate, admiring your perfection, contemplating your gentility, observing my little worth and your supreme merit, your superb graces, your praised and manifest virtues. Then, O God on high! how shall I be ungrateful to You, who so miraculously have worked to my benefit Your singular marvels? O how many the days before this moment had this thought come to my heart, but, being impossible, was driven from my memory, until just now the radiance of your bright face has brought light to my eyes, inflamed my heart, awakened my tongue, increased my worth, reduced my cowardice, banished my timidity, doubled my strength, freed my feet and hands from numbness, and, finally, endowed me with such daring that with its great power it has brought me to this sublime state in which I now find myself, hearing your soft voice and words, which, had I not known it before, and not recognized your sweet scent, I could not have believed was free of deception. But as I am certain of the purity of your blood and your actions, I must look to see if it is I, Calisto, to whom such blessing is being granted.

MELIBEA (*inside*). Señor Calisto, your great merit, your boundless graces, your high birth have, after I had a complete account of you, been cause for my being unable to tear you from my heart. And although I have struggled for many days to hide it, I have since that woman brought your sweet name to my mind been unable to keep secret my desire. I have come to this place and time, where I beg to hear your orders, and ask that you direct my person as you wish. I curse these doors that prevent our pleasure, their strong locks and my weakness, else you would have no cause for complaint, nor I for discontent.

CALISTO. Tell me, dear mistress Melibea, how you can allow a piece of wood to impede our pleasure? I never thought that anything but your wish would stand in our way. Accursed, frustrating doors! I pray God that the fire that is devouring me may envelop you, for only the third part would immediately consume you. O God's mercy, my sweet Melibea, allow me to call my servants to burst them open.

PÁRMENO (*apart*). You hear, Sempronio? You hear? He wants to come find us to do something that will make this a memorably bad year. I like nothing about this visit. I believe this devotion was begun in a malevolent hour. I will not wait here any longer.

SEMPRONIO (*apart*). Hush, hush. Listen. She will not allow us to come in.

MELIBEA. Do you, my love, want to ruin me and destroy my reputation? Rein in your wishes. Hope is certain, the time brief until all will be as you order. You feel your pain and I that of both of us; you, only your sadness, but I yours *and* mine. Be content to come tomorrow at this hour to my garden wall. For if you burst open these cruel doors now, even if we are not heard, with the dawn, in my father's house, there would be terrible suspicion I had erred. And you well know that the greater the error, that much more badly treated the one who errs; soon it would be published around the city.

SEMPRONIO (*apart*). It is a bad hour that we came here this night. And the dawn will find us here, going by the time our master is taking. Even with the best luck, lingering as we have we will be heard in Pleberio's house, or his neighbors'.

PÁRMENO (*apart*). I have pleaded with you for two hours to leave; something will happen, I know.

CALISTO. O my sweet mistress and all my being! Why do you call error what has been given me by God's own saints? I was praying today before the altar of the Magdalene when that solicitous woman brought to me your joyous message.

SCENE 5

PÁRMENO. Stop your raving, Calisto, stop! I have faith, Brother, that this is not Christian. What the treacherous old troll has wrought with her pestiferous witchcraft *she* says was effected by the saints. And with this confidence, he wants to burst open the doors. He will not have struck the first blow before he will be heard, and captured by the servants of Melibea's father, who are sleeping nearby.

SEMPRONIO. Do not be afraid, Pármeno, we are far enough away. At the first sound we will profit from a speedy withdrawal. Let him do it, for if he does wrong, he will pay.

PÁRMENO. You speak well. I am with you. So it will be. We will flee from death, for we are still young. Not wanting to die or to kill is not cowardice but normal and proper conduct. Pleberio's men are crazed; they do not value eating and sleeping as much as fighting and creating an uproar. A greater madness would be to stay and skirmish with an enemy that does not love victory and triumph as much as continual war and battle. O how pleased you would be, Brother, if you could see me. Half-turned, to be on guard, legs spread apart, left foot forward, poised to flee, the tails of my doublet tucked into my belt, shield under my arm, so it will not get in my way. God's bones, I am so afraid that I believe I could run like a buck.

SEMPRONIO. I am even more ready, for I have belted on my shield and sword so they will not fall as I run, and my helmet is in the hood of my cape.

PÁRMENO. And the stones you were carrying in it?

SEMPRONIO. I turned them out to lighten my load. It would have been too much to carry the breastplates you found were hampering you. A good thing I refused to bring them, they would have held us back if we had to run. Listen, listen! You hear, Pármeno? They are headed for trouble. We are dead! Hurry, run! Head for Celestina's house, we do not want to be cut off from our house.

PÁRMENO. Hurry, hurry! You are too slow! O, I am a gone sinner if they catch up with us. Leave your shield, everything.

SEMPRONIO. What if they have already killed our master?

PÁRMENO. I do not know. No talking. Run. And keep quiet, for he is my least concern.

SEMPRONIO. Psst, psst, Pármeno! Turn back, quiet, turn back. That is just the night watch going down that other street.

PÁRMENO. Look carefully. Do not trust your eyes, for often they want to see one thing for another. There is not a drop of blood in my veins. I have already tasted death; it seemed to me that they were raining blows on my shoulders. I do not remember ever being so frightened, or seeing myself in such a pickle, though I was for many years in other houses, and in places where I labored hard. I served the priests of Guadalupe for nine years, where I and others were a thousand times punched and pummeled in a fray, but never have I been so afraid of dying as tonight.

SEMPRONIO. And I? Did I not serve the priest at San Miguel, and the innkeeper on the plaza, as well as the gardener Mollé-jar? And I also had my quarrels with those who threw stones at the birds that settled in one of his large poplars, because they damaged the produce. But may God protect you from being seen with armor; that is truly to be feared. Not for nothing it is said, "Weighed with spear, weighed with fear." Go back, go back, it is definitely the night watch.

SCENE 6

MELIBEA (*inside*). Señor Calisto, what is that I hear in the street? It sounds like the voices of people fleeing. Look out for yourself, you are in danger.

CALISTO. O sweet mistress, do not fear, I come in safety. It must be my people you hear. They are fierce men who will disarm any who go by; that is someone is running from them.

MELIBEA (*inside*). And do you have many with you?

CALISTO. No, only two. But even if six were against them, it would not be too difficult for my two to take their weapons and send them on their way, in accord with their spirit. They are well chosen, Señora, I do not travel by the light of straw torches. If it were not for your honor, they would make kindling of these doors, and if we were heard they would rescue us from your father's men.

MELIBEA (*inside*). O please God, do not do that! But I am greatly relieved that you are accompanied by such loyal men. The bread eaten by brave servitors is well employed. Since nature chose to grant them such favor, Señor, may you treat them well, and reward them so that they keep your secret. And when you reprimand their boldness and daring, along with punishment slip in some favor, so that their brave spirit not be diminished at the time it is called for.

PÁRMENO. Psst, psst! Señor! Come quickly. You must leave. A large group of men is approaching with torches, and you will be seen and recognized; there is no place to hide.

CALISTO. O misery! I am obliged, mistress mine, to leave your company! Of course fear of death is inappreciable compared to your honor. But as it is so, may the angels be with you. I will return, as you command me, to the garden.

MELIBEA (*inside*). So be it, and may God go with you.

SCENE 7

PLEBERIO. Señora, wife, are you sleeping?

ALISA. No, Señor.

PLEBERIO. Do you hear noise in your daughter's chamber?

ALISA. Yes, I hear it. Melibea! Melibea!

PLEBERIO. She does not hear you. I will call more loudly. Daughter Melibea!

MELIBEA (*outside*). Señor!

PLEBERIO. Who is that walking and making noise in your bedchamber?

MELIBEA (*outside*). Señor, it is Lucrecia, who went to bring me a pitcher of water. I had a great thirst.

PLEBERIO. Go to sleep, Daughter, I thought it was something else.

LUCRECIA (*outside*). Only a little noise wakes them. They spoke with great fear.

MELIBEA (*outside*). There is no animal so meek that it is not agitated by love or fear for its children. But what would they do if they knew I had left my chamber?

SCENE 8

CALISTO. Close that door, lads. And you, Pármeno, bring up a candle.

SEMPRONIO. You must rest and sleep, Señor, the time that is left till day breaks.

CALISTO. I will, for I have great need of it. What do you think now, Pármeno, of the old woman you had so little praise for? What has been done by her hands would not have happened without her.

PÁRMENO. I did not feel your great passion, nor was I aware of Melibea's gentility and high merit, and thus I have no guilt. I did know Celestina, and her wiles. I warned you as servant to master. But now it seems she is a different woman. She has changed all her ways.

CALISTO. Greatly changed!

PÁRMENO. So much that had I not seen it I would not believe it. But as you are alive, it is true.

CALISTO. So, have you heard what passed between my dear mistress and me? What were you two doing? Were you afraid?

SEMPRONIO. Afraid, Señor? Of what? You may be sure that nothing in the world would frighten us. You have found your timorous fellows all right! We were waiting close by, primed, with weapons in hand.

CALISTO. Did you sleep at all?

SEMPRONIO. Sleep, Señor? Slumber is what *boys* do! God knows I never sat, even put my feet together. I kept looking all around, so that if I heard any alarm I would quickly leap in and do everything my strength would help me do. Pármeno, who up to this time you thought had not served you willingly, was as eager when he saw the men with the torches as a wolf on the trail of sheep. He was planning to take their weapons until he saw they were too many.

CALISTO. Do not be surprised, for it is in his nature to be bold, and even if not for me, he would do it because men like him cannot go against habit. Although a vixen may change her pelt, no inner change is ever felt. I assure you that I told my dear mistress Melibea about you two, and how safe I am with you guarding my back. Lads, I am much obliged to you. Pray God for good health, and I will reward you more fully for your good service. Go with God and find rest.

SCENE 9

PÁRMENO. Where shall we go, Sempronio? To bed to sleep or to the kitchen to break our night's fast?

SEMPRONIO. You go wherever you wish, but before day breaks I want to go to Celestina to collect my part of the chain. She is a sly old whore; I do not want to give her opportunity to contrive some wicked way to exclude us.

PÁRMENO. You speak well; I had forgotten about that. Let us go there, and if she is planning something, we will give her the fright of her life. Friendship has no worth where money is concerned.

SCENE 10

SEMPRONIO. Psst, psst! Softly; she sleeps near this little window! (*Knocks*) Señora Celestina, open the door.

CELESTINA. Who is that knocking?

SEMPRONIO. Open up, it is your sons.

CELESTINA. I have no sons who come at such an hour.

SEMPRONIO. Open for Pármeno and Sempronio; we have come to break bread with you.

CELESTINA. What pranksters you are! Come in, come in! Why did you come at such an hour, is it already dawning? What have you done? What happened to you? Did Calisto give up or is he still hoping? How was he?

SEMPRONIO. How, Mother? If it were not for us, his soul would be wandering about seeking eternal rest. If he could count up the figure of what he owes us for this evening his estate would not be enough to pay the debt. What is said is true, that life and person are more valuable than anything.

CELESTINA. Jesú. Were you in that much difficulty? God a'mercy. Tell me about it.

SEMPRONIO. Look, so *much* difficulty that, 'pon my faith, my blood boils in my body when I think of it again.

CELESTINA. Calm down as God would have, and tell me.

PÁRMENO. You are asking for a long tale, and we are agitated and exhausted from the rumpus we have been through. You would do better to prepare us some food; perhaps that would calm our agitation. One thing I am certain of: I am in no mood to run into a man who wants peace. My glory now would be now to find someone on whom I could vent the anger I was left with because those who caused it fled.

CELESTINA. Strike me dead if it does not frighten me to see you so fierce! You must be playing games with me. Tell me now, Sempronio; you, by my faith. What happened to you two?

SEMPRONIO. God's blood, I come here half crazed, desperate, though with you it would be best to temper my wrath and agitation and wear a different expression from the one I showed those men. I have never been able to do much with those who can do little. All my weapons, Mother, are broken to bits: the shield without its grip; the sword, like a saw; my helmet badly dented and rolled up in my hood. I have nothing left to use when my master has need of me, and he left it agreed he would go to the garden this night. So, buy new ones? I do not command a maravedí that will bury me after this kills me!

CELESTINA. Ask for it, Son, from your master, for it was paid for and lost in his service. You know he is a person who would quickly fit you out, not one of those who say, "Come live with me but look for someone else to maintain you." He is so generous that he will compensate you for that, and even more.

SEMPRONIO. Ha! Pármeno has also lost his; at this rate, our master's riches will be exhausted on weapons. Do you want us to be so ungrateful as to ask more than what he wants to provide, which is a lot? I do not want it said of me that if you give me a span I ask for four. He gave us the hundred coins. Then he gave us the chain. A third gift like that will clean the wax out of his ears. This business is costing him a lot. Let us be content with what is reasonable; let us not lose everything by wanting more than that, for he who embraces a lot keeps very little.

CELESTINA. So the ass is amusing! Bless my bones, if we were talking about food, I would say we have all eaten too much. Are you thinking clear, Sempronio? What does your reward have to do with my salary, your bonus with my favors? Am I obliged to repair your weapons to offset your shortcomings? Well I believe—this kills me— you have seized upon a few words I said to you the other day as we were walking down the street: that everything I had was yours, that as long as I had my strength I would never fail you, and that, if God showed me good fortune with your master, you would lose nothing. For you know already, Sempronio, that such offers, such words of love, are not binding. Not everything that glisters is gold; if it were, gold would sell more cheaply. Tell me, am I in tune with your thoughts, Sempronio? You will see, even though I am old, I do know what you may be thinking. Son, in good truth, I have a worse problem, one that is driving me mad. When I came from your house, I gave that silly Elicia the chain that I brought with me so she would be merry, and now she cannot remember where she put it. All this night long neither she nor I has been able to sleep, from worry. Not for the worth of the chain, which was not all that much, but for her taking such bad care of it. And then I was struck again by bad fortune. Some people I know came by. I fear that they may have taken it, saying, "If I see you, it was just a game." So now I want to go into this a little. If your master did give me something, you must see that it is mine. I did not ask for a share of your brocade doublet, nor do I want it. We all did our part; he will give to each of us what we deserve. And if he has given me something, I have twice put my life on the line for him. I have blunted more tools in his service than you; I have used more supplies. So, my sons, you must consider that this has all cost me dearly. I provided even my knowledge, which I did not achieve in frolicking—and Pármeno's mother was good witness to that. God rest her soul! I worked for this; you two for something different. I do this as a trade, with hard work; you do it for recreation and pleasure. And that being so, you must not expect the same reward for play that I earned with suffering. But even with everything I have said, all is not lost. If my chain appears, I will give you both a pair of scarlet breeches, the finest garment a young man can have. And if not, accept my good wishes and I will say nothing about my loss. And all this in love, because you wanted me to profit from these events. And if you are not content, it will be to your harm.

SEMPRONIO. This is not the first time I have commented on how this vice of avarice reigns in the old; when poor, generous; when rich, greedy. So in acquiring, greed grows. And with avarice comes poverty, for nothing makes the miser poor but his riches. O God, how greed increases with plenty! Who heard this old woman say that she would give me all the gain from this venture if I wanted, thinking that it would be small! Now that she sees it growing she does not want to give any part, which corroborates the children's refrain that says, "Of little, little; of a lot, nothing."

PÁRMENO. She will give you what she promised or we will take it all. I told you many times who this old crone is, if only you had believed me.

CELESTINA. If you come with this excess of anger at yourselves, or your master, or about your weapons, do not take it out on me. I know where this came from. I know pretty well which foot you limp on. Not, of course, from any need you have for what you are asking, nor even your greed to have it. It is your thinking that I will have you all your lives tied and bound to Elicia and Areúsa, not wanting to look for other girls for you. That is why you make these threats about money. Why frighten me with these fears about shares? Well hush that, for the one who knew to put you in touch with those girls will find you another ten, now that there is more understanding and reason and merit on your part. And in these matters I know how to do what I promise. Tell him, Pármeno. Tell him, tell him. Do not be too shy to tell what happened when Areúsa had the pain in her belly!

SEMPRONIO. I say leave and he pulls down his breeches. I am not going where you want. Do not reply to our demands with jests. If I have anything to do with it, you will bag no more hares with that hound. So no more talk. An old dog will not come to "Here, puppy, here, puppy." Give us the two-thirds of what Calisto gave you. You do not want it to be known who you really are. Save your talk for others, old crone!

CELESTINA. Who am I, Sempronio? Did you find me in some low brothel? Hold your tongue, do not throw dirt on my gray hair, for I am an old woman as God made me, no worse than any. I live from my trade the way any official does from his: cleanly. I do not seek those who do not like me. They come to look for me at my house. They plead with me in my house. God judges whether I live well or badly. And do not think of mistreating me with your anger, for there is justice for all, equal for all. Although a woman, I will be heard, just as much as you coxcombs. Leave me in my house with my fortune, good or bad. And you, Pármeno, do you think I am your captive because you know my secrets and my past life, and the matters that fell upon me and upon that poor wretch of your mother? And when God wished it, even she treated me like this!

PÁRMENO. Do not try to choke me with these memories, else I will send you to her with other news, somewhere you can complain more freely.

CELESTINA. Elicia, Elicia! Get up out of that bed! Run, bring me my cloak, for by all God's saints, I am off to get justice, howling like a mad woman! What is this? Who are you to make such threats in my own house? You are all strength and bravery when you have a meek sheep? A hen tied on a string? A sixty-year-old woman? Get out; I've had enough of the likes of you! Go parade your wrath before someone who straps on a sword, not a fragile distaff. It is a sign of great cowardice to attack the weak, those who can do very little. Filthy flies bite only the scrawniest, skinniest oxen; bad-tempered curs save their wildest barking for penurious pilgrims. If that girl lying up there in that bed had believed me, this house would never have been left at night without a man, nor would we lie awake half the night keeping on guard, but being loyal to you we suffer this solitude. And as you see us as women, you talk and demand too much. Something which, if you were at the inn, you would not do; for as they say, "A tough adversary cools anger and fury."

SEMPRONIO. Avaricious old drab. Gullet dying of thirst for money! Will you not be content with a third part of what we earned?

CELESTINA. What third part? Go with God . . . out of my house. And tell your friend not to shout or rouse the neighborhood. Do not make me lose my mind. You do not want the business of Calisto and you to be aired in the plaza.

SEMPRONIO. Yell, shout. You will do what you promised would be done, or you yourself will be done today.

ELICIA. For God's sake, put away your sword! Hold him, Pármeno, hold him. Do not let this insane man kill her.

CELESTINA. Constable! Constable, neighbors! Constable! These ruffians are killing me in my own house!

SEMPRONIO. Ruffians you say? Just wait, Señora sorceress, for I intend to send you to hell with your credentials in your hand!

CELESTINA. Ay, he has killed me! Ay! Ay! Confession! Confession!

PÁRMENO. Do it, do it! Finish her off, now you started it; someone will hear us. Die! Die! Of enemies, one fewer!

CELESTINA. Confession!

ELICIA. O cruel enemies. You saw yourself with evil power. And for whom were you brave! My mother, my life, is dead!

SEMPRONIO. Run, run, Pármeno. A crowd of men is coming this way. Look out, here comes the constable.

PÁRMENO. Poor sinner I am! We have no way to go, they are at the door.

SEMPRONIO. We will jump out the windows. We will not die in the hands of the law.

PÁRMENO. Jump, I am following you.

ACT THIRTEEN

(Calisto, Tristán, Sosia)

PLOT

Calisto, awakened from sleep, is talking to himself. After a bit he calls Tristán and his other servants. Calisto falls back to sleep. Tristán takes his place at the door. Sosia arrives, weeping. Questioned by Tristán, Sosia tells him of the death of Sempronio and Pármeno. They go to tell the news to Calisto, who, knowing the truth, falls into lamentation.

SCENE 1

CALISTO (*alone*). O how well I have slept following that sweetest interlude, following that angelic conversation! I have had a magnificent rest; calm and repose evolve from my joy. O my fine sleep was caused either by physical activity or by the glory and pleasure of my spirit. And I am not amazed that one and the other joined together to close the padlocks of my eyes, for I labored with both body and person, and rejoiced in mind and senses this past night. It is certain that melancholy conveys thought, and much thinking impedes sleep, as in recent days with my doubting that I had the ultimate glory I now possess. O mistress and love, my Melibea! What are you thinking now? Are you sleeping or awake? Are you thinking of me or of another? Are you up or still abed? O blessed, fortunate Calisto—if it is true that it was not a dream! Did I dream it or did I not? Was it fantasy or did it in truth happen? But I was not alone; my servants were with me. They were two, and if they say it truly happened, those two are equal to the tribunal. I will have them summoned to confirm my pleasure. Lads! Tristanico! Get up here!

TRISTÁN. Señor, I am up.

CALISTO. Run, summon Sempronio and Pármeno.

TRISTÁN. I am going, Señor.

CALISTO. Your sweet sleep and repose
from this moment start,
for Melibea loves you
in her deepest heart.
May pleasure banish care
no ill be seen again,
For Melibea loves you
most among all men.

TRISTÁN. Señor, there is no servant in the house.

CALISTO. Well, open those windows, see what the hour is.

TRISTÁN. Señor, well into the day.

CALISTO. Then close them again and let me sleep until it is time for food.

SCENE 2

TRISTÁN. I will to go down to the door so my master can sleep without being interrupted; and all those who come to seek him I will turn away. O what a commotion I hear in the market! What is it? There must be a hanging, or maybe everyone arose early to run the bulls. I do not know what to make of such an outcry. But here comes Sosia, the stable boy. He will tell me what it is. The little pismire is all rumpled. He must have been brawling in some tavern, and if my master catches sight of him he will be in for two thousand lashes. Well, the boy is half mad, but a flogging will bring him around. I think he has been crying. What is it, Sosia? Why are you crying? Where have you come from?

SOSIA. O I am cursed! O what a great loss! O what dishonor to my master's house! O what a black day dawned today! O poor doomed lads!

TRISTÁN. What is it? What is all this sadness? Why are you killing yourself? What is so bad?

SOSIA. Sempronio and Pármeno . . . !

TRISTÁN. What are you saying? Sempronio and Pármeno! What *is* all this? Are you mad? Speak more clearly, you are troubling me.

SOSIA. Our companions, our brothers . . . !

TRISTÁN. Either you are drunk or you are out of your head. Or you are bringing bad news. Will you tell me what it is you are saying about those lads?

SOSIA. That they are in the plaza, beheaded!

TRISTÁN. O what foul fortune, if it is true! Are you sure you saw them or did someone tell you?

SOSIA. They were already slipping away, but one, with terrible difficulty, as he felt I was looking at him and crying, clapped his eyes on me, lifted his hands to heaven, almost like giving thanks to God or as if asking me what I felt about his dying. And then in sign of sad farewell, he lowered his head with tears in his eyes, giving me to understand that he would not see me again until the great Judgment Day.

TRISTÁN. You did not hear well; it could have been he was asking you whether Calisto was there. And since you bring such clear signs of this cruel sorrow, we must hurry and take the sad news to our master.

SCENE 3

SOSIA. Señor, Señor!

CALISTO. What is it, you idiots. Did I not tell you not to wake me?

SOSIA. Wake up, get up, for if you do not go back for your men we will suffer a great loss. Sempronio and Pármeno lie in the plaza beheaded like public culprits, with criers broadcasting their crime.

CALISTO. God help me! What is this you are telling me? I do not know if I believe such unexpected and mournful news. Did you see them?

SOSIA. I saw them.

CALISTO. Think what you are saying, for they were with me tonight.

SOSIA. Well they saw the dawn to die.

CALISTO. O my loyal servants! O my grand servitors. O my loyal secret keepers and counselors! Can such a thing be true? O dishonored Calisto! Disgrace will follow you for all your life. What will become of you, with two such servants dead? Tell me, for God's sake, Sosia. Why were they killed! What is the crier saying? Where did they take them? Which authorities did it?

SOSIA. Señor, the cruel executioner was shouting the cause of their death, saying: "Justice demands these violent murderers die!"

CALISTO. Whom had they killed so quickly? How can this be? It is not more than four hours since they bade me goodbye. What was the name of the victim?

SOSIA. It was a woman named Celestina.

CALISTO. What are you telling me?

SOSIA. What you hear.

CALISTO. Well if this is true, then you kill me; I will forgive you. For if it is Celestina, the one with the knife scar across her face, who is dead, there is more trouble than you have seen or can think of.

SOSIA. She is the one. I saw her there, lying in her house, with more than thirty stab wounds and a servant girl weeping over her.

CALISTO. O my poor lads! How did they go? Did they see you? Did they speak to you?

SOSIA. O Señor, if you had seen them your heart would burst with pain! One's brains were spilling out of his head, and he was as good as gone; the other had both arms broken and his face was mangled. Both of them were covered with blood; they had jumped from high windows to flee from the constable. So they were nearly dead when they lopped off their heads. I think they no longer felt anything.

CALISTO (*apart*). O, my honor is in question. I wish to God I were they, that I had lost my life and not my honor, and not the hope of achieving what was just begun, the thing I mourn the most. O my poor name and reputation, how you will be spread across the city, from mouth to mouth! O my most secret secrets, how publicly you will wander through plazas and markets! What will become of me? Where will I go? Shall I go there? I cannot undo the deaths. Shall I stay here? That will appear to be cowardice. What counsel shall I take? (*Aloud*) Tell me, Sosia. What was the reason they killed her?

SOSIA. Señor, her servant girl, screaming, weeping over her death, told it to all who wanted to hear, saying it was because she did not want to share with them a golden chain you gave her.

SCENE 4

CALISTO (*alone*). O day of anguish! O formidable tribulation! A day on which my riches travel from hand to hand and my name from tongue to tongue! It will all be public, all that I said to her and to them, all they knew about me, about what they were doing for me. I will not dare go out among people. O sinful lads, to suffer such a sudden calamity! O my joy, how you are dissolving! It is a very old proverb, that from great heights great falls occur. I had gained so much last night, and today I have lost so much. Rare indeed is quiet on the high seas. I had good reason to be happy, had my fortune chosen to still the stormy winds of my perdition. O Fortune, how greatly, and in so many ways, you have assaulted me. Well, though you hover over my dwelling and oppose my person, adversities must be met with equal spirit; in them is proved the strong or weak heart. There is no better test by which to judge the carats of a man's virtue and strength. Well, whatever evil and harm may befall me, I will not fail to obey the command of the woman for whom all this has taken place. More important to me than to mourn the loss of those who died is to obtain the benefit of the glory I long for. The lads were arrogant and bellicose: they were fated to pay now or some other time. It appears from the deal she had made with them that the old woman was evil and false, and that they ended by quarreling over their gains. It was divine will that she ended that way, in payment for the many adulteries engendered through her intercession. I will have Sosia and Tristanico get ready. They will travel with me down my intensely anticipated road. They will bring ladders, for the walls are high. Tomorrow I will make it known that I am returning from being away, and I will see if I can avenge these deaths. If not, I will base my innocence upon my feigned absence—or I will pretend I am mad, the better to enjoy the delectable pleasures of my love, as did that great captain Ulysses to avoid the Trojan War and revel with Penelope his wife.

ACT FOURTEEN

(Melibea, Lucrecia, Sosia, Tristán, Calisto)

PLOT

Melibea is very upset as she talks with Lucrecia about Calisto's being late, as he had vowed to come that night to visit her. He does arrive, and with him, Sosia and Tristán. After he has fulfilled his wish, all three return home. Calisto withdraws to his bedchamber and laments having been with Melibea for such a brief time. He begs Phoebus to hide his rays, so he can renew his desire.

SCENE 1

MELIBEA. The caballero we are waiting for is very late. Do you know, or conjecture, where he might be, Lucrecia?

LUCRECIA. Señora, I believe he has met up with an unavoidable impediment and that it is not in his control to be here sooner.

MELIBEA. May the angels be looking over him and may he not be in danger; then his lateness would not concern me. But I am worried. I can think of many things that could happen to him between his house and here. Who knows whether he, with his wish to arrive at the promised time, coming along in the way that such young men at such hours tend to do, may have run into the night watch, and as they did not recognize him they have taken him in, and he to defend himself has struck them, or been struck by them? Or whether barking guard dogs with their cruel teeth, those that do not know whom to attack and whom not, may have bitten him? Or what if he fell into some deep ditch along the road, or into a deep hole where he suffered harm? Poor me! What are these problems this love of mine puts before me, and these tormenting fantasies that visit me? May it not please God for any of these things to happen. Rather, let him be as he pleases without seeing me. But listen. I hear footsteps in the street, and I even think they are talking at the other side of the garden.

SCENE 2

SOSIA. Put up that ladder, Tristán. This is the best place, though it is high here.

TRISTÁN. Climb up, Señor. I will go with you, because we do not know who is inside. They are talking.

CALISTO. You stay here, idiots. I will go in alone, for that is my sweet mistress I hear.

SCENE 3

MELIBEA. No, it is your servant, your captive. It is the one who holds your life more dear than her own. O my señor, do not leap from such a height, for I will die to see it. Come down the ladder, step by step. Do not come with such haste!

CALISTO. O angelic image! O precious pearl, next to whom the whole word is ugly. O my dear mistress and my glory! I hold you in my arms, and I do not believe it. Such a whirlwind of pleasure dwells within me that I cannot feel my joy.

MELIBEA. My señor, I put myself in your hands because I wanted to do your will; may I not be the worse for being merciful rather than aloof and without mercy. Do not harm me in exchange for such brief pleasure, and in so short a time. For when bad things are done, they can sooner be reprehended than mended. Enjoy what I enjoy, which is to see you and be close to you. Do not ask for, or take, that which once taken will not be in your power to return. Take care, Señor, not to harm what all the world's treasures cannot restore.

CALISTO. Sweet mistress, I have spent my lifetime in obtaining this favor; would I, when it is given me, toss it away? You will not command me, sweet mistress, nor will I be able, to restrain my desire. Do not ask me to be so fainthearted. No one who is a man would be capable of doing such a thing, particularly not loving as much as I do. Swimming through the flames of your desire all my life, do you not want me to reach sweet port and rest from my labors?

MELIBEA. 'Pon my life! Though your tongue may speak what it wishes, deter your hands from doing as they want! Still them, my señor. Be content that I am yours. Enjoy outwardly the time-honored fruit of lovers; hold back your wish to steal the greatest gift nature has given me! It is just and proper that the good shepherd sheer his sheep, but not destroy and harm them.

CALISTO. Be content? For what, my mistress? That my passion not persist? To suffer anew? To take the game back to the beginning? Forgive, dear girl, my reprehensible and shameless hands that with their unworthiness never thought to touch even your clothing; now they rejoice in reaching your sweet body and beautiful, delicate flesh.

MELIBEA. You may leave, Lucrecia.

CALISTO. Why is that, my sweet mistress! I would rejoice that there be witness to my glory.

MELIBEA. I want none to my error. If I had thought that you would have your way with me so immoderately, I would not have entrusted my person to your cruel company.

SCENE 4

SOSIA. Tristán, do you hear everything that is happening? What is the progress of their rendezvous?

TRISTÁN. I hear so much that I judge my master to be the most fortunate man ever born. Cuds me! And that though I am just a boy, I would give as good an account of myself.

SOSIA. With such a jewel any man would find himself commanding. But let him have his bread, for it has cost him dear: two lads were lost in the sauce for these loves.

TRISTÁN. He has already forgotten them. We die serving despicable masters! Do mad things counting on their protection, and then . . . ! "Living with a count," my mother used to tell me, "do not kill the man." And our masters? You see them happy in each other's arms and their servants disgracefully beheaded.

MELIBEA (*apart, inside*). O my life, my señor! How have you wanted that I lose the title and crown of virgin for such brief delight? O Mother! Sinner! If you had knowledge of such a thing, how willingly you would welcome death, and have need to take mine by force! How you would be the cruel executioner of your own blood! How I would become the sorrowful end to your days! O my honored father, how I have stained your reputation and given cause and place to the downfall of your house! O what a traitor I am! Why did I not first look at the ruinous error that would follow his entering, the great danger that awaited?

SOSIA. I wish it were I who had been there to listen to your amazing words. All you women know the orison that comes after what cannot be stopped from happening. And that stupid Calisto is listening to it!

SCENE 5

CALISTO. Day wants to dawn. What is this? It does not seem that we have been here an hour, but the clock is striking three!

MELIBEA. Señor, God be with us. Everything is yours. Now I am your dear mistress; now you cannot deny my love; now you cannot refuse me a sight of you by day, passing by my door. At night, where you command. May you come to this secret place at the same hour, where I will always await you anticipating the joy you leave with me, and thinking of nights to come. And for the present, go with God; you will not be seen, for it is very dark, nor I heard in the house, for it has not as yet dawned.

CALISTO (*to those outside*). Lads, put up the ladder.

SOSIA (*from outside*). Señor, here it is. Come down.

MELIBEA. Lucrecia, come here, I am alone now. The señor has left. He leaves his heart with me, and he carries mine with him. Did you hear us?

LUCRECIA. No, Señora. I have been asleep.

SCENE 6

SOSIA. Tristán, we must go very quietly because the rich tend to get up at this hour; those greedy for worldly goods; the godly in temples, monasteries, and churches; lovers like our master; laborers in tilled fields; shepherds who with the dawn bring their sheep to these folds to milk, and it might be that one would hear something in passing that would smirch his honor and Melibea's.

TRISTÁN. You simple-minded stable boy! You tell me to be quiet, and then you speak out her name! You would make a great guide or officer to lead people through the land of Moors by night! In prohibiting, you allow; covering over, you reveal; assuring, you offend; promoting silence, you yell and shout; asking, you give answer. As you are so subtle and discreet, will you not tell me in what month the feast day of Santa María de Agosto falls, so we will know if there is enough hay in the house to feed an ass like you?

CALISTO. My worries and yours are not the same. Go in quietly; they will not hear us in the house. Close that door and we will rest. I want to go alone to my bedchamber. I will take off my armor myself. You two go to your beds.

SCENE 7

CALISTO (*alone*). What a wretch! How much my nature is soothed by solicitude and silence and darkness! I do not know whether the reason is that I recall my betrayal as I took my leave of the damsel I love so much before it was nearly light, or whether it is the sorrow of my dishonor. Ay! That is it. That wound is the one I feel now that passion has cooled, now that the blood is chill that yesterday boiled, now that I see the shame cast upon my house, the loss of my servants, the ruin of my patrimony, the infamy heaped upon my person following the death of my servants. What did I do? What did I not do? How was I able to suffer, for I did not show myself as a man injured, vengeful, proud, and quick to act because of the manifest injustice done me? O miserable sweetness of this so brief life! Who is so covetous of life that he does not choose to die immediately but, rather, to enjoy a year of life insulted and dishonored, staining the good name of his ancestors? Particularly as there is no certain, prescribed hour, not even a single moment. We are all debtors with no allotted time; we are always obliged to pay in the end. Why did I not even go out to look carefully for the truth of the secret cause of my manifest ruin? O brief worldly pleasure! How does your sweetness last so little and cost so much! Repentance is not as dear. How miserable I am! How do I redress such an overwhelming loss? What shall I do? What counsel shall I take? To whom shall I reveal my dishonor? Why do I conceal it from my servants and my relatives? I am being excoriated in the council, but they do not know it in my house. I want to go out, but if I do it is late to tell that I have been here, early to say I was absent. And to enlist old friends and servants, relatives and adherents, time is needed, as it is to acquire weapons and other tools of revenge. O cruel judge! How badly you have repaid me, having eaten so freely of my father's bread. I thought that with your favor I could kill a thousand men with no fear of punishment. Wicked, false oppressor of truth, depraved villain! It will be said of you, correctly, that lacking good men you were made magistrate. You will see that you and those you killed in serving my predecessors and me were companions; but when the loathsome man becomes rich he has neither relatives nor friends. Who would have thought that you would be the one to destroy me? There is, certainly, nothing that can do more harm than an unsuspected enemy. Why did you want them to say of me: "From the woods he brings what will consume him," and "I raised a crow that will peck out my eye." You are a public offender, yet you have executed men who killed in private. You know that the clandestine crime is not as heinous as the public one, and less effective, as the laws of Athens set out. They are not written in blood; instead they propose that not to sentence the malefactor is less an error than to punish the innocent. O how dangerous it is to present a just cause before an unjust judge! How much worse this excess on the part of my servants, who were not lacking in guilt. But if evil has been done, there is a tribunal in heaven and one on earth; so before God and the King you are a criminal, and to me, an eternal enemy. What was one's sin in what the other did? Why only for being his companion did you kill them both?

But, what am I saying? With whom am I speaking? Am I in my right mind? What is this, Calisto? Were you dreaming, sleeping, or are you awake? Are you up or abed? Look, you are in your bedchamber. Do you not see that your offender is not present? With whom is your argument? Come back to your senses. You know that those who are absent are never treated fairly. Listen to both sides before you pass judgment. Do you not see that to carry out the law you do not consider friendship or kin or upbringing? Do you not see that all must be equal before the law? See how Romulus, the first founder of Rome, killed his own brother because he had violated the law. Look at the Roman Torquatus, who killed his son because he overstepped the order of the tribunal. Many others did the same. Consider that if the judge were present here, his answer would be that perpetrators and accessories deserve equal punishment, even if it meant killing both for what only one committed. And if he sped up their deaths, that it was a notorious crime and not much proof was required; also they were caught in the act of killing, and one was already dead from the fall he suffered. And also you must believe that the weeping maidservant in Celestina's house gave him strong reason for haste with her sad tears, and he, in order not to create an uproar, not to defame me, not to wait till people rose and heard the crier proclaiming the great infamy following me, and as it was, after all, necessary for the official crier to call out the news of the execution and its accomplishment, ordered the lads to be executed early in the morning. All of which, if done as I believe, is cause for me to be in his debt and obliged to him for as long as I live. Not like someone brought up by my father, but like a true brother. And if the case was not that way, if he did not honor the past as he should have, then remember, Calisto, your enveloping pleasure, remember your dear mistress, your well-being. And since your life is nothing if not in her service, you do not have to be greatly concerned about the deaths of others, for no sorrow will ever equal the pleasure you have received.

O sweet mistress, my life! I never thought in my absence to offend you. It may seem I hold in little esteem the favor you have done me. I do not want to think in anger; I do not want now to be acquainted with sadness. O incomparable benefaction! O insatiable contentment! And what more could I ask of God as reward for my merits, if there be such in this life, than what I have received? Why am I not content? For there is no reason I should be ungrateful to the one who has given me such favor. I want to recognize that; I do not want to let anger destroy my good sense so that damned I fall from such lofty possession. I want no other honor, no other glory, no other riches, no other father or mother, no other kith or kin. By day I will be here in my bedchamber, by night in that sweet paradise, in that happy garden, among those gentle plants and cool verdure. O night of my repose, if you were but here again! O radiant Phoebus, make haste along your accustomed path. O delightful stars, come out before the hour of eternal order! O leaden clock, still I would see you in the blazing fire of love! For if what awaits me when you strike twelve were awaiting you, you would never be obedient to the will of the master craftsman who assembled you. And you now hidden months of winter, return with your long nights and exchange them for these wearisome days! Already it seems a year since I have known that gentle repose, that delightful comfort to my toil.

But, what is it I am demanding? What am I asking, crazed, impatient? What never was nor can be. Nature's courses do not veer and weave in disorderly fashion; there is one course for all; for all the same space for death and life, a circumscribed pattern for the secret movements of the celestial firmament, for the planets and the north star, for the waning and waxing of the monthly moon. Everything is governed by the same reins, everything prodded by the same spur: heaven, earth, sea, fire, wind, heat, cold. What does it benefit me if the iron clock strikes twelve if that hour has not been struck in heaven? For however early I get up, dawn will come no sooner.

But you, sweet imagination, you that can, come to my aid. Bring to my fantasy the angelic presence of that radiant image; carry to my ears the soft sound of her words: those palely uttered parries, that "Step back, Señor, do not come near me," that "Do not be ill-mannered" I heard from your rosy lips; that "Do not covet my perdition" that you proposed from time to time; those loving embraces between words; that letting me go and clasping me to you; that fleeing and approaching; those sugared kisses. . . . Those last words with which she bade me farewell left her lips with such pain! With such waving of arms! With so many tears resembling seeds of pearl that fell without her awareness from her clear, shining eyes!

SCENE 8

SOSIA. Tristán, what do you think about Calisto? Has he slept all this time? It is four o'clock in the afternoon and he has not called or eaten anything.

TRISTÁN. Hush, for sleep does not want to be rushed. Besides that, he is troubled on the one hand by sadness about those lads, and on the other entranced with the immeasurable pleasure he has received from his Melibea. So with two such strong, conflicting emotions you will see how they stay the weakened body they have inhabited.

SOSIA. Did you think that he greatly laments the deaths? If the girl that from this window I see walking down the street is not grieving more, she would not be wearing that color on her head.

TRISTÁN. Who is it, Brother?

SOSIA. Come over here and look before she turns the corner. See that sorrowful girl wiping the tears from her eyes? That is Elicia,

Celestina's servant and Sempronio's friend, a very pretty girl, although now the poor sinner is lost because Celestina acted as her mother and Sempronio was her principal love. And that house she is going into? A beautiful woman lives there, very fresh and charming, very loving, though near to being a whore, but anyone who had her without paying much would think himself extremely blessed. Her name is Areúsa. I know she caused poor Pármeno more than three bad nights, and I know she will not be pleased to hear of his death.

ACT FIFTEEN

(Elicia, Areúsa, Centurio)

PLOT

Areúsa is hurling insults at a ruffian named Centurio, who says goodbye to her as Elicia arrives. Elicia tells Areúsa of the deaths that have come about because of the love of Calisto and Melibea, and Areúsa and Elicia agree that Centurio should avenge the deaths of the three by making the two lovers pay. Finally Elicia tells Areúsa goodbye, not consenting to do what she asks her because she does not want to lose the pleasure of living in her own house.

SCENE 1

ELICIA. What is all that noise coming from my cousin's? If she already knows the sad news I am bringing her, I will not witness the outburst of sorrow that comes with such a message. Weep, weep, let the tears fall, for such men are not found on every corner. It pleases me that she feels it so much. Tear your hair, as I have done in my sorrow; know that to lose a good life is worse than death itself. When I see the strong emotion she is demonstrating, I love her much more than I did before!

ARE Ú SA. Get out of my house, ruffian, villain, liar, swindler; you have deceived me—idiot that I was—with your foolish offers. With your cajolery and flattery you have stripped away everything I have. I gave you, O you rogue! food, a doublet and a cloak, a sword and a shield, a pair of shirts embroidered to a marvel. I gave you weapons and a horse, I placed you with a señor whose shoes you were not worthy to lick. Now that I ask you to do one thing for me you give me a thousand excuses.

CENTURIO. Sister mine, command me to kill ten men in you service, but not to go a league on foot.

ARE Ú SA. Why did you gamble away your horse, you fig o' Spain? If it were not for me they would have hanged you already. Three times I have saved you from the law; four times rescued you from the gaming house. Why do I do it? Why am I such a fool? Why do I have faith in this coward? Why do I believe his lies? Why do I let him come through my doors? What good is there in him? Kinky hair, knife-scarred face, two public floggings, sword hand crippled, thirty whores in the brothel? Get out of here! I do not want to see you again. Do not speak to me or say you know me; if you do, by the bones of the father who begat me and the mother who bore me, I will have a thousand blows landed on those grain-grinder's shoulders of yours. As you already know, I have someone who knows how to do that, and having done the deed come out clean.

CENTURIO. Wail and carry on, you crazy girl! For if I am crossed, someone will truly weep. But I will go now, I do not know who that is coming. We do not want to be heard.

SCENE 3

ELICIA (*apart*). I want to go in, but when there are threats and insults that is not the sound of good weeping.

AREÚSA. Ay, how sad I am! Is it you, my Elicia? Jesú, Jesú! I cannot believe it. What is this? Who dressed you in sorrow? What is this mourning? You frighten me, Sister. Tell me quickly what it is, for I am numb; you are drawing the last drop of blood from my body.

ELICIA. Such overwhelming grief! How great the loss! I am showing only little of what I am feeling. My heart is blacker than my mantle, blacker than the cloth on my head. O Sister, Sister, I cannot say more. I am so hoarse I cannot squeeze my voice out of my throat.

AREÚSA. Ay, my grieving friend, you have me in suspense! Tell me. Stop pulling your hair, stop clawing your face and beating your breast. Does this frightening thing have to do with us both? Does it touch me?

ELICIA. Ay, my cousin and my love. Sempronio and Pármeno are no longer living, they are no longer in this world. Their souls are paying for their error. They are now free from this sad life.

AREÚSA. What are you saying? Do not tell me that. Hush, dear God, or I will fall dead right here.

ELICIA. There is more bad news than what you hear. Listen to this sad woman, who will tell you of further sorrows. Celestina, whom you have known so well, the one who was like a mother to me, the one who indulged me, the one who smoothed over my faults, the one whom I thought I was perhaps able to call an equal, the one who made me known through all the city and its environs, that woman is now giving an accounting of her works. Before my eyes I saw them drive their knives into her a thousand times; they killed her in my lap.

AREÚSA. O tribulation! O dolorous news, deserving of mortal weeping! O swift come such disasters! O irrecoverable loss! How has Fortune turned her wheel so quickly? Who killed them? How did they die? I am stunned, numb, like someone who hears something impossible. It has not been a week since I saw them alive, and now we are saying, "God forgive them." Tell me, my friend. How did such a cruel and disastrous thing occur?

ELICIA. You will know. You have already heard, Sister, of the affair of Calisto and that demented Melibea. You will know how, with Sempronio's intercession, Celestina had taken on the task of acting as go-between, expecting to be well paid for her work. She put such diligence and care into the project that with only the second dousing she struck water. Well, as Calisto quickly saw that a good result had issued from what he never expected to have, he gave my poor aunt, in addition to other things, a chain of gold. And as that metal is of such value, the more we drink of it the greater our thirst becomes, an unholy greed. When she saw herself so rich, she held onto her prize and did not want to share it with Sempronio and Pármeno, though they had an agreement among them that they would divide what Calisto gave them. Well, as they came back one morning, very weary after accompanying their master all night, irate over some dispute, I do not know what, they asked Celestina for their share of the chain to alleviate their problems. She started by denying that they had an agreement or promise, arguing that all the reward was hers, and even letting other little things slip out. As is said, "When old procuresses squabble . . ." So they were enraged; for one thing because they had need, which is far stronger than love, and for another, the great wrath and weariness that look for a quarrel. And not the least, the loss of their greatest hope. They did not know what to do. They argued for a long time. Finally, finding her so avaricious, so persistent in her refusal, they drew their swords and ran her through a thousand times.

AREÚSA. O most unfortunate of women! And is this how her old age should end? And what do you tell me of them? What happened to them?

ELICIA. They, as they had committed the crime and needed to flee from the constable who by chance was passing by, leapt from the windows, and were nearly dead when they were taken and without further delay beheaded.

AREÚSA. O Pármeno, my love! What pain your death brings me! I mourn the great love begun for so short a time, for it was not to last. But, as now this terrible evil has been done, as now misfortune has already struck, and as now tears cannot buy or restore their lives, do not exhaust yourself so, you will blind yourself with that weeping. For I believe that you have little advantage over me in emotion, and you will see with what patience I get through it.

ELICIA. Ay, I am furious! Ay, wretch that I am, I am losing my mind! Ay, I find no one who feels as I do! There is no one who loses what I lose. O how much better and more honest my tears would be for another's pain rather than my own! Where will I go, for I lose a mother, a protector, and shelter; I lose a friend, and one so close I never missed a husband. O wise, honored, and respected Celestina, how many of my flaws you covered with your knowing ways! You labored, I frolicked; you buzzed around the house like a bee, I destroyed the hive, for I knew no other thing. O my well-being and earthly pleasure; while we had you we did not value you, and you never let yourself be known until we lost you. O Calisto and Melibea, how many deaths you have caused! May your love come to a bad end, and your sweet pleasure be turned to a foul taste. May your glory be converted to weeping, your rest become labor. May the ambrosial grasses in which you take your stolen pleasures change into serpents, your songs to weeping; may the shady trees of the orchard become dry and parched before your eyes, their fragrant flowers faded to black.

AREÚSA. Hush, Sister, as God would have. Silence your laments, restrain your tears, wipe your eyes, come back to your life. For when one door closes Fortune often opens another, and though this day is cruel, it will remedy itself. And many things that cannot be remedied can be avenged, and though this has little remedy, the vengeance is at hand.

ELICIA. On whom can we take revenge? For I grieve for her and for her killers. I am no less disturbed by the punishment the guilty received than I am by the crime they perpetrated. What do you suggest be done? For it all falls on me. O how I wish I were with them and not left to weep for them. And what is the deepest pain for me is that despite everything that has happened, that vile man, so uncaring, will continue his visits to his dung heap of a Melibea, reveling every night; she must be very proud to see blood spilled in her service.

AREÚSA. If that is true, on whom may we better take revenge, following the adage that he who had the meal should pay. Let me deal with it. I will follow their trail, when and how often they are seen, where and at what hour, and if I do not make their love curdle then I am not the daughter of the old seller of sweets you knew so well. And if I put it on the one you saw me quarreling with when you came in, then he should turn out to be as good an executioner of Calisto as Sempronio was of Celestina. And how happy he will be that I asked him to do something in my service, for he was very sad that I treated him badly! He will see the heavens open around him if I speak with him and order him about. Therefore, Sister, tell me from whom I can learn how things are going and I will have Centurio set a snare that will have Melibea weeping as much as she is now rejoicing.

ELICIA. I, my friend, know another of Pármeno's companions, a stable boy named Sosia, who goes with Calisto every night. I will work on him, get all the secret out of him, and he will be a good path toward what you tell me.

AREÚSA. But let me have that pleasure: you send this Sosia here to me. I will delight and flatter him, over and over, until I leave nothing in his body of what was done and to be done. Later he and his master will vomit up every pleasure they have eaten. And you, Elicia, my friend, do not grieve. Send your clothing and belongings to my house, and come to keep me company, for you will be very alone and sadness is friend to solitude. With a new love you will forget the old. A newborn son compensates for the loss of three who are dead; with a new successor happy memories and past pleasures will be lost. Of every loaf of bread I have, you will have half. I am more saddened by your sorrow than I am by those who caused it for you. True it is that the loss of what one has is more painful than the pleasure that comes from hope for something new, even though it is assured. But what has happened cannot be mended, and the dead cannot be revived, so as is said, "May they die and we live." Leave the living to my care, for I will give them as bitter a syrup to sip as they have given you. Ay, Cousin, Cousin, how well I know, when I am enraged, to weave these schemes, though I am but a girl! And may God avenge the dead, because Centurio will take vengeance on Calisto for me.

ELICIA. Look, I believe that even if you call on the one who does what you command, it will not have the effect you want; the penalty for those who died because they discovered the secret will frighten the living into keeping it. I am grateful for what you said about my coming to your house. And may God shelter you and make you happy in all your needs, for you demonstrate that kinship and sisterhood are not just wind, but of benefit in times of adversity. But as much as I would like to do that in order to enjoy your sweet company, it cannot be because of the harm it could do me. The reason does not need to be told; for I am speaking with someone who understands. There, Sister, I am known; there I am one of the parish. That house will never lose the name of Celestina, may God be with her. Girls who knew her well and acquaintances all come there, and relatives of the girls she brought up. That is where plans are laid, from which I will still draw some benefit. And also those few friends I have left do not know me in another dwelling. You know already how difficult it is to leave what is familiar, and changing habit is much like dying; a rolling stone gathers no moss. There I want to be, if for no other reason than the rent is paid for the year, and that should not be wasted. So that although each of these things is not enough in itself, all of them together work to my benefit. Now it seems to me that it is time for me to go. I take with me the charge of what we talked about. God be with you, I am on my way.

ACT SIXTEEN

(Pleberio, Alisa, Lucrecia, Melibea)

PLOT

Pleberio and Alisa believe that their daughter Melibea has con-served her virginity—though, according to what seems to have passed, that is far from true—and they are discussing marriage for their daughter. The words Melibea hears from her parents give her great pain, so she sends Lucrecia to be the cause for them to cease talking on that subject.

SCENE 1

PLEBERIO. Alisa, dear woman, time, it appears to me, is, as is said, slipping through our fingers. The days are racing by like water down the river. There is nothing as fleet in passing as life. Death follows and circles round us; we are its close neighbors, and we tend to follow its banner, as nature decrees. This we see very clearly if we look at our equals, our brothers and kin around us. All of them are being eaten by the earth, all are in their eternal dwellings. And as we are uncertain as to when we will be called, seeing such certain signs we must make what amends we can and prepare to take up our pilgrim's sacks to make that obligatory journey; we do not want to be surprised or startled by the cruel voice of death. Let us have time to set our souls in order, for it is better to foresee than to be foreseen. Let us give our earthly goods to our sweet successor, provide our only daughter with the husband our status demands, so that we may leave this world refreshed and free of sorrow. So with great diligence we must now put these thoughts into effort, and what other times was begun will in this case be execution. Our daughter must not, because of our negligence, be left in the hands of guardians, for she will better be in her own house than in ours. We must remove her from the talk of common gossips, for there is no virtue so perfect that it does not find vituperation and slander. There is nothing that better preserves a clean reputation in a virgin than early marriage. Is there any in all the city who would shun kinship with us? Who, one would like to know, would not find himself happy to take such a jewel into his company, one so fully endowed with the four principals demanded in a marriage: the first, discretion, honesty, and virginity; the second, beauty; the third, high birth and family; and last, wealth. Nature endowed our daughter with all these. And anything asked of us as dowry will easily be satisfied.

ALISA. God keep her, my señor Pleberio, so that we see our wishes fulfilled in our lifetimes. First, I think there will be no equal to our daughter; in accord with your virtue and noble blood there will not be many who deserve her. But as this is the role of fathers, and far from the woman's role, it will be as you decide, and I will be happy, and our daughter will obey, in keeping with her chaste living and her honest and humble life.

LUCRECIA (*apart*). If only you knew everything, you would be shattered! But, ay! the best is lost! Such bad times for your old age! Calisto has taken the best. There is no one to restore maidenheads now that Celestina is dead. You awoke too late! You should have risen earlier!

LUCRECIA. Listen, listen, Mistress Melibea!

MELIBEA. What are you doing hiding there, silly?

LUCRECIA. Come over here, Mistress; you will hear your parents' haste to arrange your marriage.

MELIBEA. Gods a'mercy, hush, they will hear you. Let them talk, let them rave on. That is all they have done or thought about for a month. It seems that their hearts have told them of the great love I have for Calisto, and everything that for a month has been happening between us. I do not know if they have felt something, I do not know what troubles them more greatly just now. But I set them this task in vain, for it is long after the warning bell has rung. Who is he who will take away my glory? Who to separate me from my pleasures? Calisto is my soul, my life, my señor, he is the one in whom I place all my hopes. I know from him that I am not deceived. As he loves me, in what other way can I repay him? All the debts in the world receive compensation of some kind; love accepts only love as payment. Thinking of him makes me happy, seeing him gives me pleasure, hearing him I am in glory. Let him do with me and command me at his will. If he wants to cross the sea, I will go with him; if he circles the world he will take me with him; if he wants to sell me in the land of enemies, I will not resist his wish. My parents must let me be joyful with him if they want to be joyful with me. Let them dwell no more on such illusions, on the idea of marriage; it is better to be a good mistress than a bad wife. Let me enjoy my happy youth if they want to enjoy their weary old age; if not, they will soon have prepared my perdition and their burial. I have no regret but the time I lost not having pleasure of him, of not knowing him after I came to know myself. I do not want a husband, I do not want to sully the bonds of marriage, have another man treading upon a husband's footsteps, like many did I found in the ancient books I have read, women more prudent than I, higher in estate and lineage. Some were held as goddesses in the heathen world, like Venus, mother of Aeneas and of Cupid, the god of love, who though married broke the promises of her marriage vow. Others, aflame with greater passion, committed nefarious and incestuous errors, like Myrrha with her father, Semiramis with her son, Canace with her brother, and also that violated Tamar, daughter of King David. Others even more monstrously crossed over the laws of nature, like Pasiphae, wife of King Minos, with the bull. But queens they were, and grand señoras, and compared to their guilt mine could pass without vituperation. I had just cause to love: I was courted and beseeched, captivated by Calisto's high merit, urged by such an astute mentor as Celestina, and was paid perilous visits before yielding wholly to his love. And now, it is a month, as you have seen, that there has not been a night that our garden wall has not been scaled as if it were a fortress, and many times in vain, though he has not told me of suffering and toil. His servants are dead because of me, his fortune is being drained as he feigns absence from the city; he spends every day closed in his house with hope of seeing me at night. Away, away with ingratitude, away with flattery and deceit with such a true lover. I do not want a husband, I do not want a father or relatives! Without Calisto, I have no life, and because he takes pleasure of me, I am happy.

LUCRECIA. Hush, Mistress, listen, they are still discussing you.

PLEBERIO (*apart*). Well, what do you think, Wife? Shall we have a talk with our daughter? Shall we tell her about all those asking for her hand so it come of her will, so she says which will please her? For in this matter the laws give freedom to men and women, though under paternal authority, to choose.

ALISA (*apart*). What are you saying? Why are you wasting time? Who is to go to our Melibea with such momentous news without frightening her? Tell me, how! And do you think she knows what men are, whether they marry, or what it is to marry? Or that from the union of husband and wife children are procreated? Do you think that her guileless virginity will of itself incite her to a faint desire for what she does not know and has never understood? Do you think that she knows to err even in her thoughts? Do not believe that, my señor, for whether of high estate or low, whether ugly or of noble semblance, the one we order her to take will be her pleasure, and it will all be for the good. For I know well what I have instilled in my sheltered daughter.

MELIBEA. Lucrecia, Lucrecia, run quickly. Go in the back door of that chamber and interrupt their talking, interrupt their praises with some sort of made up message if you do not want me to go in and start yelling like a madwoman, as I am very angry at their mistaken idea that I am ignorant.

LUCRECIA. I am going, Mistress.

ACT SEVENTEEN

(Elicia, Areúsa, Sosia)

Elicia, lacking Penelope's chastity, decides to say farewell to the sorrow and mourning caused by the deaths of her friends, praising the counsel of Areúsa in this matter; she goes to the house of Areúsa, where she sees Sosia. Areúsa, with beguiling and deceptive words, draws from him the secret between Calisto and Melibea.

SCENE 1

ELICIA (*alone*). This mourning is not good for me. Few come to my house. Few pass by in my street. I no longer see the dawn musicians, no longer hear the songs of my friends, now there are no knife fights or rowdy night noises because of me; and what makes me saddest of all is that neither coins nor gifts come through my door. The guilt for all this is mine, for if I had taken the counsel of the one who loves me dearly, of that true sister, when the other day I took her the news of this sad business that has brought me such hardship, I would not find myself alone in these four walls, so repulsive that no one comes to see me any longer. The Devil makes me mourn someone I cannot be sure would have mourned me were I the one dead! She spoke the truth when she said, "Never, Sister, have or show more pain for the bad fortune or death of another than he would for you." If I were dead, Sempronio would celebrate, so why, silly girl that I am, do I grieve that he was beheaded? And what if he had killed me—he was crazy, and so quick to react—the way he did that old woman who was my mother? I want to follow Areúsa's counsel in everything, for she knows more of the world than I do, and see her often and get advice about how to live. O what gentle association, what pleasant and sweet conversation. Not for nothing is it said that one day with a discreet man is worth a lifetime with fools and simpletons. I want, then, to set apart the mourning, leave sadness behind, bid farewell to the tears that have been so easy to come. But as crying is the first task we perform in being born, it does not surprise me how easy it is to begin, and how difficult to abandon. But that is why we have good sense, for looking loss in the eye, for seeing that finery makes a woman beautiful, even if she is not; adornment makes the old woman young, the young woman a girl. Rouge and white paints are none other than a sticky trap in which to entangle men. Well, then, my mirror and my kohl, for I have damaged these eyes; get my white headdress, my embroidered gorgets, my clothes for being happy. I want to mix a rinse for this hair that is losing its gold lights, and when all this is done, I will stay at home and count my hens, and I will make my bed, because cleanliness brightens the heart. I will sweep my door and sprinkle the street, so those who pass by will see that sorrow has been exiled. But first I want to visit my cousin, to ask her if Sosia has been there, and what she has said or done with him, for I have not seen him since I told him how much Areúsa wanted to talk with him. Pray God that she is alone, for she is always surrounded by gallants, like a tavern filled with winos. The door is closed. There is probably no man with her. I will knock. (*She knocks.*)

A R E Ú S A . Who is there?

E L I C I A . Open my friend, it is Elicia.

A R E Ú S A . Come in, Sister. May God see what pleasure you give me in coming as you have, with your black habit of sadness gone. Now we will be merry together, now I will visit you, we will see each other in my house and in yours. Perhaps for both of us Celestina's death was for the best, for already I feel that times have improved over what they were. That is why it is said that the dead open the eyes of the living, some with riches, others with freedom, as with you.

E L I C I A . Someone is knocking at your door. That gives us only a little time to talk, and I wanted to ask you if Sosia had come here.

A R E Ú S A . No he has not come; we will talk later. What a racket they are making! I want to open, for it has to be either a madman or a favorite knocking.

S O S I A . Open for me, Señora. I am Sosia, Calisto's servant.

A R E Ú S A . By all the saints, it is the wolf in sheep's clothing. Hide, Sister, behind that drapery, and you will see how I fill him with wind and flattery, and he will think when he leaves that he is the only one for me. And with honeyed words I will draw from his craw all he or anyone else knows, as smoothly as he curries dust from the horses.

SCENE 3

A R E Ú S A . Is it my Sosia, my secret friend? The one I am so fond of without his knowing? The one I want to know because of his good reputation? The one so loyal to his master? The one who is such a good friend to his companions? I want to embrace you, my love, for now that I see you I believe there are more virtues in you than they have told me. Come in, come in. Let us go in and sit down, for it pleases me to look at you, you remind me somehow of that unfortunate Pármeno. And this is why the day is so bright, because you have come to see me. Tell me, friend Sosia, had you heard of me before you came?

SOSIA. Señora, the word of your gentility, of your graces and wisdom, flies so high around the city that it must not surprise you too greatly that you are better known by others than you know them, for no one speaks of beautiful girls who does not first think of you.

ELICIA (*apart*). Hopeless whoreson, how much better you speak! We have seen you take your horses to water, riding bareback, with your bare legs sticking out of your smock, and now we see you dressed out in trousers and cloak; you have grown wings and a tongue.

AREÚSA. Your words would make me blush if anyone were here with us to hear how you are jesting with me; but as all men bring with them these prepared phrases, these deceitful words of praise, ready for us girls and made precisely for your purposes, I will not let you alarm me. And I must assure you, Sosia, that you have no need of them. Without your praise I love you, and without your having to win me anew, you have won me. There are two reasons why I sent a message asking you to come see me, which, if I detect further flattery or deceit in you, I will not tell you, though they be to your benefit.

SOSIA. My dear señora, God does not want me to deceive you. I came feeling confident that you plan to do me a great favor, and are now doing. I did not feel worthy to remove your shoes. Guide my tongue, answer your questions for me, I will take them as valid and firm.

AREÚSA. My dear love, you know how much I loved Pármeno, and how they say, "Who deeply loves Beltrán loves all that is his." I found all his friends to be pleasant, and his good service to his master as rewarding to me as it was to him. Wherever he saw harm coming to Calisto, he fended it off. Well, as this is how things are, I decided I would have you know the love I have for you, and how happy you and your visits will always make me. In this you will lose nothing; rather, if I have anything to do with it, you will benefit. Another, the second reason is that ever since I set eyes on you, and because of my love, I have wanted to advise you to guard yourself against danger and, more important, not to reveal your secret to anyone—you have seen what harm came to Pármeno and Sempronio because of what Celestina knew—and I would not want to see you die the same unfulfilled death as your companion. I have wept enough over one. You need to know that a person came to me and told me that you had told him about the love between Calisto and Melibea, and how he had won her, and how you accompanied him every night, and many other things that I would not know how to relate. You see, my friend, not keeping a secret is a natural trait of women; well, not all of them, but those of low estate, and also children. You see that great harm can come to you, and this is why God gave you two ears and only one tongue, so you can see and hear double what you speak. And you see that you cannot trust your friend to keep secret what you told him when you consider that you do not know if you can keep it yourself. When you have to go with your master Calisto to the house of that señora, make no noise; do not let the earth hear you, for others have told me that you go every night yelling like a pleasure-crazed madman.

SOSIA. O how uninformed and unstrung are the people who bring you such tales. Whoever told you that he had heard it from my lips does not speak the truth. Others, who see me in the moonlight when I take my horses to water, happy and enjoying myself, singing songs to forget my labor and banish anger—and all this before ten— were wrong to suspect anything; suspicion they make a certainty, and they affirm what was only conjecture. Calisto is not so stupid that he would go at that hour for such imprudent business without waiting for people to be abed and resting in their first sweet sleep. Even less would he go every night, for that endeavor will not tolerate daily visitation. And if you want to see more clearly their falseness, Señora—as is said, it is easier to catch a liar than a man who is lame—in one month we have gone only eight times, and they who say every night are naught but gossipmongers.

AREÚSA. Well 'pon my life, my love, in order for me to catch them up in the snare of their false testimony, you must leave in my memory the days you have planned to go out, and if they are mistaken in the day I will be sure your secret is safe, and certain of their malicious lies. Because if their message is not true, you will not be in danger, or I alarmed regarding your life. I have hope of enjoying myself with you for a long time.

SOSIA. Señora, you need not put off testing the witnesses. His visit in the garden is set for tonight when the clock strikes twelve. Tomorrow you can ask what they know, and if anyone gives you the right signs, they can cut off my hair like a criminal.

AREÚSA. And what part of the garden, my soul, so I can contradict them better if they are in error, or hesitate?

SOSIA. Along the street of the fat vicar, behind his house.

ELICIA (apart). Stop now, Don Rags'nTatters! No more is needed! Cursed be he who entrusts himself to the hands of a muleteer like him! Time to silence the clapper in that bell!

AREÚSA. Brother Sosia, what we have discussed is enough for me to recognize your innocence and the evil of your adversaries. Now go with God, for I am engaged with another matter and have spent a lot of time with you.

ELICIA (apart). How wise you are! A deserved dispatching, as the ass merits who let out his secret so quickly!

s o s i a . Gracious and gentle señora, forgive me if I have irritated you with my stay. As long as you enjoy my service, you will never find one who in serving you will so freely risk his life. May the angels be with you.

a r e ú s a . God guide you . . . Now be off, muleteer! God's mercy, you leave with such conceit! So take this treat for your eyes, you pimply rogue, and forgive that I turn my back on the person I am speaking to! Sister, come out. What do you think of how I sent him away? I know how to treat men like him, that is how asses leave my hands, beaten like this one; madmen, chased away; the prudent, frightened; the devout, agitated; and the chaste, inflamed. Well, Cousin, watch and learn, for this is a different art from Celestina's. She thought I was a stupid girl, because that is how I wanted it. And now with our meeting here we learned all we wanted to know, and we must go to the house of that other man, the one with the face of a man on the gallows, the one I insulted and threw out of my house in front of you. You will act as if you want to make us friends, and that you begged me to go see him.

ACT EIGHTEEN

(Elicia, Centurio, Areúsa)

PLOT

Elicia decides that she will follow Areúsa's scheme and pretend to renew the friendship between Areúsa and Centurio, and they go to Centurio's house, where they ask him to wreak vengeance on Calisto and Melibea for the deaths of their friends, which he promises to do. But as it is natural for such men not to do what they promise, he does not do what he said he would, as is seen in the progress of the story.

SCENE 1

ELICIA (*apart*). Is anyone here?

CENTURIO. Boy! Run see who dares enter without knocking at the door. No, come back, come back, I have seen who it is. Do not cover yourself with that cloak, my fine Areúsa; you cannot hide now, for when I saw Elicia come in first, I knew that she would not be bringing bad company or news that would disturb me, but that you girls came to give me pleasure.

AREÚSA. Let us not, 'pon my life, go in any farther, for the blackguard is already feeling superior, thinking I come to plead with him. I would enjoy much more the sight of others of his sort than the one we have here. Let us leave, God willing, for I am dying just at the sight of his ugly face. Does it seem to you, Sister, that you bring me for a good purpose, or that it is reasonable to come at vespers and go in to see a coxcomb like this one here?

ELICIA. Come back, for my sake, do not go; if you do, you will leave half your cloak in my hands.

CENTURIO. Hold her! God's bones, Señora, hold her. Do not let her go.

ELICIA. I am amazed, Cousin, by your good sense. What man is there so insane and beyond reasoning that he is not proud to be visited, especially by women? Come over here, Señor Centurio, for by my soul I will have her embrace you, and I will be responsible for it.

AREÚSA. I would rather see him in the hands of the law or dead in the hands of his enemies, than for me to give him that pleasure. He has had his last contact with me for as long as he lives! And for what reason must I tolerate what he spews at me, or even have to see this enemy? I plead with him the other day to go a little distance to do something that was life or death for me, and he said no.

CENTURIO. Order me, my respected señora, to do something I know to do, something in the line of what I do. Give me a challenge of three at one time, and if more come, I would, because of your love, not flee. Kill a man; cut off an arm or a leg; slash the face of a woman who thinks she is as good as you. Things like this will be done before they are ordered. But do not ask me to travel down the road or to give you money, for you know that money does not last in my hands; you can turn me over three times and a coin will never fall out. No one gives what he does not have. I live, as you see, in a house in which a pestle could roll through without bumping into anything. My jewels consist of two cudgels and a sleep mat, a broken jug, a spit without a point. The bed I sleep on sits on the bosses of bucklers, with a pile of ripped and twisted mail for a mattress and a bagful of dice for a pillow. I would like to offer you a light collation but I have nothing to pawn except this tattered cloak on my back.

ELICIA. I like it as it is, your words please me greatly. Like a saint he is obedient, he speaks to you like an angel; he makes good sense. What more would you ask of him? 'Pon my life, speak to him and soften your anger, for he willingly offers you his person.

CENTURIO. Offer, you say, Señora? I swear to you by all the holy martyrs, from A to Z, my arm trembles from anticipating what I intend to do for her. I constantly think of ways to keep her happy, but never succeed. Just last night I dreamed that I took up weapons and a challenge in her service; it was from four men she knows very well, and I killed one. And of the others who fled, the one who was in best shape dropped his left arm at my feet. But I will do much better awake, in daylight, if someone merely touches your slipper.

AREÚSA. Well, I hold you to it, we have come in good hour. I forgive you, on the condition that you take vengeance on a caballero named Calisto, who has angered me and my cousin.

CENTURIO. A pox on the condition! Tell me whether he has had confession.

AREÚSA. You do not have to be priest of his soul.

CENTURIO. Well, so be it. We will send him to dine in hell without confessing.

AREÚSA. Just listen, do not interrupt. You will take him tonight.

CENTURIO. Say no more, I know the end. I know all about his love, and those who because of him are dead, and how it touched you two, where he goes, and at what hour, and with whom. But tell me how many will be with him?

AREÚSA. Two lads.

CENTURIO. Easy prey. That would be little bait for my sword. There is much better elsewhere tonight. I am already committed.

AREÚSA. That is just an excuse not to do it. Throw that bone to a different dog, such hesitation is not for me. I want to see whether saying and doing eat together at your table.

CENTURIO. If my sword told you what it has done we would have no time left to talk. What but it has filled the most cemeteries? What enriches the surgeons of this land? What provides continuous employment for armorers? What destroys the finest mail? What demolishes Barcelona bucklers? What cuts through a Calutayud helmet but my sword? And it slices Almazen casques as if they were melons. Twenty years now it has provided me food. Because of it I am feared by men and loved by women . . . except you. Because of it they named my grandfather Centurio, and my father was named Centurio, and I am well-named Centurio.

ELICIA. Well, what did your sword do that earned that name for your grandfather? Tell me, was it by chance because he was captain of a hundred men?

CENTURIO. No, but he was panderer for a hundred women.

AREÚSA. We need no talk of ancestors and ancient deeds. If you choose to do what I tell you, without the delay, decide, for we want to go.

CENTURIO. I want the night to make you happy more than you want to see yourself avenged. So that everything be done as you want it, choose what death you want me to inflict. I can show you a list on which there are seven hundred and seventy kinds of deaths; you will see which most pleases you.

ELICIA. Areúsa, for my sake do not put this task in the hands of such a fierce man. It would better be left undone and not scandalize the city, for that would do us more harm than what has already happened.

AREÚSA. Hush, Sister. Tell us one that would not make much noise.

CENTURIO. The ones I use these days, the ones I do best, are floggings with my sword, on the back, leaving no blood, or a pummeling with the hilt, or a crafty drubbing across the chest, which I leave punctured like a sieve, or a reverse slashing, or a mortal thrust. Or I just cudgel my victim to give my sword a rest.

ELICIA. Do not, please, go further; so flog him, so he be punished and not killed.

CENTURIO. I swear by the holy body of the litany, it is no more in my right arm to give a flogging without killing than it is for the sun to stop circling the heavens.

AREÚSA. Sister, let us not make piteous complaint. Let him do whatever he wishes, kill him whatever way he would like. May Melibea weep as you have done, Sister. Let us leave it to him. Centurio, give a good account of what we entrusted to you. We will be happy with any death. See that he does not escape without some payment for his error.

CENTURIO. God forgive him, if somehow he gets away from me. I am left grateful, my señora, that something, though small, has presented itself by which you may realize what I know to do for your love.

AREÚSA. May God give you a good right hand on your sword, and I commend you to him, for we are going.

CENTURIO. And may he guide you and give you more patience with yours.

SCENE 2

CENTURIO (*alone*). So there they go, two whores crammed with ideas! Now I must think how I can avoid what I promised but have them think I put spirited diligence into doing what I said I would do, not negligence, so as not to get myself in danger. I could pass myself off as being ill, but what will that get me? They will repeat their demand when I get well. And if I tell them that I was there, and that I ran them off, they will ask for signs of who they were, and how many, and in what place I overcame them, and what clothing they were wearing, and I will not know how to answer. O I am lost! For what advice may I take that will act for my safety and their demand? I will send for Traso the Lame, and for his two companions, and tell them that because I am busy tonight with a different matter they must rattle their swords in an aggressive way and frighten off some wastrels who are my responsibility to take care of. For all this is easy going, and it is not to do them harm, but make them flee and then go home to bed.

ACT NINETEEN

(Sosia, Tristán, Calisto, Melibea, Lucrecia)

PLOT

Calisto, with Sosia and Tristán, goes to the garden of Pleberio to visit Melibea, who is waiting, and, with her, Lucrecia. Sosia tells what happened with Areúsa. When Calisto is in the garden with Melibea, Traso and others come at Centurio's bidding to do what he promised Areúsa and Elicia. Sosia goes to meet them. Calisto, from the garden where he is with Melibea, hears the racket they are making and tries to go over the wall, an action that leads to bringing an end to his days, because that is the reward given to his sort, and why lovers must know not to love.

SCENE 1

SOSIA. Be very quiet so we are not heard as we go from here to Pleberio's garden. I will tell you, Brother Tristán, what happened between Areúsa and me today, for I am the happiest man in the world. You will learn that because of the good things she had heard about me she was a prisoner of my love, and had sent Elicia to me, begging me to visit her. And leaving apart the other questions of good counsel we discussed, she showed herself to be as much mine as she had for some time been Pármeno's. She begged me to visit her constantly, and told me she planned to enjoy my love for a long time. But I swear to you, by the dangerous road we are traveling, Brother, that two or three times I was just at the point of throwing myself on her, but I was stopped by shame at seeing her so beautiful and adorned and myself in my old mouse-eaten cloak. As she moved about she loosed a scent of musk; I stank of the dung in my boots. She had hands like the snow, and when from time to time she pulled off a glove it seemed that orange blossom spilled through the house. So for this reason, and also because she had a little something to do, I held my daring in check for another day. And also because on the first visit not all things are easily treated, and the more communication there is, the better the relationship you build.

TRISTÁN. Sosia, my friend, another more mature and experienced brain, not mine, would be needed to give you counsel in this matter, but with what I can suggest at my tender age and average intellect, I will tell you. This woman is a common whore, as you yourself have told me; what happened to you with her you must believe was not lacking in deceit. Her offers to you were false, though I do not know for what purpose. If to love you for your distinction how many more has she tossed aside; if for being rich, she knows very well that you have nothing more than the dust that clings to you from your curry comb; if for being a man from a noble family, she already knows that you are named Sosia, and that your father was named Sosia, born and brought up on a farm breaking clods of dirt with a hoe, something you are more prepared to do than be a lover. Look, Sosia, and remember well that she might like to draw from you some bit about the secret of this road we are traveling so that with what she learns she could stir up Calisto and Pleberio . . . all out of envy of Melibea's pleasure. Where envy sets in, it is an incurable illness, a guest that exhausts the innkeeper; instead of reward it always takes pleasure from another's ill fortune. And if this is the case, how that evil female wants to deceive you, using Melibea's high name and basking in a reflected glow! With her poisonous vice she would sell her soul to sate her appetite, send houses into turmoil to satisfy her perverse will. O procuring woman! How white the bread in which she wrapped the dog poison she ground for you! She would sell her body to provoke contention. Hear me, and if you believe this is how it is, turn the tables and hand her back a trick of your own, one I will tell you, for he who deceives the deceiver . . . You know what I mean. For if the vixen is clever, how much more he who takes her. Counter her evil plans, scale the walls of her vile castle when she feels most secure, and later you will sing in your stable, "The bay thinks one way but the one who saddles it another."

SOSIA. O Tristán, how wise you are! You have told me more than I would have expected from your age. You have raised a shrewd suspicion, one I believe is true. But, because we have already reached the garden and our master is coming this way, let us leave this subject, which is very long, for another day.

SCENE 2

CALISTO (*outside the garden*). Here, lads, put up the ladder, and quietly, for I think I can hear my sweet mistress. I will climb to the top of the wall, and once there listen to see if I hear, as she thinks me absent, some good sign of her love for me.

MELIBEA. Sing more, Lucrecia. It makes me happy to listen while my señor is on his way here. Sing very low, here amid all this greenery, so those passing by will not hear us.

LUCRECIA (*singing*). O I would be gardener
of these ambrosial flowers,

picking them as we are parted
in the early morning hours!

The iris and lily blossoms
are bedecked in new color,
releasing new fragrances
when he enters, as their favor.

MELIBEA. O how sweet it is to hear you! I am dissolving with pleasure. I beg you, do not stop.

LUCRECIA (*singing*). Happy sings the fountain clear
to her whose thirst is unfulfilled;
but when she spies her lover's face
her happiness is sweeter still.
For though the night is deep and dark
her eyes will take him in,
and when she sees him clear the wall,
her embraces he will win!

Leaps of boundless pleasure come
when wolves the lambs discover;
and kids seeking the maternal teat;
and Melibea, with her lover.

Ne'er was a man more desired
by a woman who found him dear,
nor a garden as well known,
nor a night so fresh and clear.

MELIBEA. What you say, friend Lucrecia, takes form before me; it seems I see it all with my eyes. Continue, you do it so melodiously, and I will sing with you.

LUCRECIA AND MELIBEA (*singing*). Tall, sweet shady trees
bow down to admire
the beautiful, vivacious eyes

of the one you so desire.
O beauteous north and morning stars
shining in the sky so deep,
will you not awaken him
if my happiness lies asleep?

MELIBEA. Now you listen, for I want to sing alone.
(*Singing*) Mockingbirds and nightingales,
that sweetly greet the day,
take a message to my love
that I grieve with this delay.

The midnight hour has come and passed,
and he is not here.
Tell me, does he have another love
that he holds dear?

SCENE 3

CALISTO. I am conquered by the sweetness of your soft songs. I can suffer no longer your sorrowful waiting. O my sweet mistress and my life! What woman born could obscure your supreme perfection? O memorable melody! O pleasureful moments! O my heart! And could you not have suffered longer without interrupting your delight and fulfilling the desires of us both?

MELIBEA. O delicious betrayal! O sweet alarm! Is that the señor of my soul? Is it he? I cannot believe it. Where were you, my blazing sun? Where did you have your bright rays hidden? Were you listening long? Why did you allow me to cast senseless words upon the air in my hoarse swan voice? Everything in this garden rejoices at your arrival. Look how clearly the moon shows herself to us; see how the clouds are fleeing. Hear the water flowing from this little fountain, how much softer its murmur through the cool grasses. Listen to the tall cypresses, how their branches, swayed by the breeze, rub and kiss one another. See their quiet shadows, how dark they are, and joined together to conceal our delight. Lucrecia, what are you doing, my friend? Have you gone mad with pleasure? Leave him to me, do not take him apart as you remove his weapons, do not belabor his limbs with your tight embraces as you take his clothes from him. Let me enjoy what is mine; do not purloin my pleasure.

CALISTO. Well, my dearest mistress, my glory, if you value my life do not cease your soft singing. Do not let my presence that makes you happy be worse than my absence, which exhausts you.

MELIBEA. How do you want me to sing, my love? How shall I sing, when it was my desire for you that ruled my melody and made my song resound? For with your arrival my longing disappeared, my voice lost it sweetness. And since you, my señor, are the exemplar of courtesy and good breeding, how do you command my tongue to speak but not your roving hands to remain quiet. Why do you not forget their artful tricks? Order them to be at rest and leave their irritating ways and unsupportable manners. Look, my angel, just having you quiet beside me is agreeable to me, but your roughness annoying. Your honorable games give me pleasure, your dishonorable hands exhaust me when they surpass what is reasonable. Leave my clothing in place, and if you wish to see if my outer gown is of silk or cotton, why do you touch my shift? You know it is of linen. We can frolic and play in a thousand different ways that I will show you, but do not hurt and mistreat me as you are wont to do. What benefit is it to you to damage my clothing?

CALISTO. Mistress mine, he who wishes to eat the bird must first pluck off the feathers.

LUCRECIA (apart). May I die of buboes if I listen any longer. This is life? Here am I burning with jealousy, and she being elusive in order to be begged! Ah, yes, the sounds are quieting, there is no need for me to step between them to establish peace. But I could do the same if his idiot servants would talk to me someday, but they wait until I have to go and seek them.

MELIBEA. O my señor, would you like for me to send Lucrecia to bring a small collation?

CALISTO. There is no collation for me but to have your body and your beauty in my power. Eating and drinking is sold everywhere; it can be had at any time, and anyone can have it. But as for what is not to be bought, what there is no equal to on all the earth, is what I have in this garden, so how can you order me to let a moment pass without pleasure?

LUCRECIA (*apart*). Now my head hurts from listening, but not theirs from talking, not their arms from touching, or their mouths from kissing. Ah, good. They are quiet at last. Three is the charm.

CALISTO. I would wish, my dearest mistress, that the dawn would never come, considering the glory and repose my senses receive with the noble touch of your delicate limbs.

MELIBEA. Señor, it is I who have pleasure, I who benefit; it is I to whom your visits do incomparable favor.

SOSIA (*apart, outside*). Aha, there, scoundrels, rogues! Did you come to frighten those who do not fear you? Well I swear that if you stay I will see you leave in the manner you deserve.

SCENE 4

CALISTO. Beloved señora, that is Sosia shouting. Let me go to his aid. I do not want him killed, for he has only a young page with him. Quickly, give me my cloak, it is beneath you.

MELIBEA. O what a turn of fortune! Do not go there without your cuirass; arm yourself again.

CALISTO. Señora, what cloak and sword and heart cannot do will not be done by cuirass and helmet and cowardice.

SOSIA (*apart, outside*). So you are back? Wait for me, you may have come for wool but . . .

CALISTO. Let me go, my dear heart, for the ladder is up.

MELIBEA. How wretched I am. Why do you go so abruptly and with such haste, unarmed, to put yourself among those you do not know? Lucrecia, come quickly, Calisto has heard noises. Let us throw his weapons over the wall, they are still here.

TRISTÁN (*outside*). Hold, Señor. Do not come down, they are gone. It was only Traso the Lame and other ruffians who were yelling as they went by. Now Sosia is coming back. Hold. Hold tight, Señor; put your hands on the ladder.

SCENE 5

CALISTO. O help me, blessed Mary! I am dead! Confession!

TRISTÁN. Come quickly, Sosia, for our poor master has fallen from the ladder and is not speaking or moving!

SOSIA. Señor! Señor. He doesn't answer! He is as dead as my grandfather! O disaster!

SCENE 6

LUCRECIA. Listen, listen! What terrible accident is this!

MELIBEA. What is this I hear, I am in such distress!

TRISTÁN (*outside*). O my señor, my well-being! O my señor and our devastated honor! O sad death, without confession! Sosia, pick up those brains from the stones and put them with the head of our wretched master. O day of bad augury! O violent end!

MELIBEA. O how disconsolate I am! What is this? What can be as horrible as what I am hearing? Lucrecia, help me climb this wall. I will look upon my sorrow. If not, I will bring down my father's house with my screams. My life, my pleasure, all gone up in smoke! My happiness lost! My glory consumed!

LUCRECIA. Tristán, what are you saying, my love? What is this copious weeping?

TRISTÁN (*outside*). I am weeping for my bad fortune, I am weeping for my many sorrows! My señor Calisto fell from the ladder and is dead. His head is split into three pieces. He perished without confession. Tell his sad new friend to wait no longer for her heart-rending love. You, Sosia, take up the feet. Though he died here in this place, we will carry the body of our beloved master somewhere he will not suffer detriment to his honor. Weeping will accompany us, and loneliness; desolation will follow us; sadness will visit us; we shall be clad in mourning and sackcloth.

MELIBEA. O the saddest of all the sad! Pleasure so late achieved, pain so quickly come!

LUCRECIA. Señora, do not claw your face or tear your hair. One moment pleasure, the next sadness! What planet was it that so abruptly changed its influence? How little strength is this? Get up, for God's sake. Do not be found by your father in this suspicious place; you will be heard. Señora, Señora, can you not hear me? Do not swoon, I ask of God. Be strong and bear your pain, for you were daring in your pleasure.

MELIBEA. Do you hear what those lads are saying? Do you hear their sad songs? They are bearing away my entire life, hear their prayers and responses! They are taking away my happiness! This is not the time for me to go on living. Why did I not take more pleasure from pleasure? Why did I value so lightly the glory I held in my hands? O mortal ingrates, you will never know your blessings until they are taken from you.

LUCRECIA. Be lively, get up! There will be greater trouble in your father's finding you in the garden than you had in the pleasure of your lover's arriving, or your grief in seeing him dead. We will go back to your bedchamber, you will get into the bed. I will call your father and we will feign a different malady, for this is not something that can be concealed.

ACT TWENTY

(Pleberio, Lucrecia, Melibea)

PLOT

Lucrecia knocks at the door of Pleberio's bedchamber. Pleberio asks what she wants. Lucrecia asks him to hurry and come see his daughter, Melibea. Pleberio gets up, goes to Melibea's chamber. He consoles her, asking what her ailment is. Melibea feigns it is her heart. Melibea sends her father to bring her musical instruments. She and Lucrecia climb up into a tower. Melibea sends Lucrecia away and closes the door after her. Her father comes to the foot of the tower. Melibea reveals to him everything that has passed. Then she throws herself from the tower.

SCENE 1

PLEBERIO. What do you want, Lucrecia? What has you in such a hurry? What are you asking with such urgency and flurry? What has happened to my daughter? What can be so calamitous that you do not give me time to dress, or even to get out of bed?

LUCRECIA. Señor, you must hurry if you want to see your daughter alive; for I do not even know her illness it is so grave, or even her any longer, her face is so distorted.

PLEBERIO. Let us go quickly; you go ahead of me; go in and draw back that portiere and open the window wide, so I can see her face. What is it, my daughter? What is your pain? What is so different? Why so little strength? Look at me, I am your father. Talk to me, tell me the cause of this shattering pain. What do you have? What do you feel? What do you want? Say something; look at me; tell me the reason for your pain so it may be quickly remedied. I am in my last years and you do not want to send me to the grave with all this. You know that you are my only blessing. Open those happy eyes and look at me.

MELIBEA. Ay, the pain!

PLEBERIO. What pain can it be that equals mine at seeing you? Your mother swooned on hearing of your illness. She could not come to you she was so disturbed. Be strong, invigorate your heart, gather yourself so that you can come with me and visit her. Tell me, my soul, the reason for this feeling.

MELIBEA. My remedy is dead!

PLEBERIO. Daughter, my beloved child and love of an aged father, do not let the cruel torment of this illness, this suffering, make you despair, for weak hearts come to know pain. If you will tell me your malady, it will be remedied; you will not lack for medicines, or physicians, or servants to bring back your health; you will have herbs and stones and sorcerer's spells, and the secret substances deep in the bodies of animals. But do not fatigue me more, do not torment me, do not make me lose my senses: tell me what you are feeling.

MELIBEA. A mortal wound in the middle of my heart that will not let me speak! It is not like other ills; my heart must be taken out to be cured, for the illness lies in its most secret part.

PLEBERIO. You have too soon taken on the feelings of age. Youth tends to be pleasure and joy, the enemy of problems. Get up from your bed. Let us go to enjoy the cool air of the river; you will be happy with your mother; your pain will ease. To turn away from pleasure is the very worst you can do to allay your affliction.

MELIBEA. We will go where you say. Let us, Father, go to the highest roof and from there enjoy the delightful view of the ships; with luck my anguish will be lessened somewhat.

PLEBERIO. We will go up, and Lucrecia with us.

MELIBEA. But, if it please you, Father, send for some stringed instrument that may help me to tolerate my pain, either strumming or singing, so though the modulation in one part may be troubling, that will be mollified by the sweet sounds and happy harmony in another.

PLEBERIO. That, my daughter, will immediately be done. I go to tend to it.

MELIBEA. Lucrecia, my friend, it is very high here. Now it sorrows me to leave my father's company. Go down to him and tell him to stop at the foot of this tower, that I want to tell him I forgot something I want him to tell my mother.

LUCRECIA. I am going, Señora.

SCENE 2

MELIBEA. I am in every way left alone; the manner of my death is well prepared. I feel some relief from knowing that I and my beloved, my lover Calisto, will soon be together. I will close the door so that no one can come to deter my death. Let no one impede my departure, let no one block the road I will travel, very soon, to visit on this day the one who visited me the past night. Everything has been done to my will. I will have time to tell Pleberio, my dear father, the reason for my already crafted end. I do an injustice to his gray hairs, great offense to his age, I send his way great fatigue with my error, I leave him in great loneliness. And though my dying may shorten my beloved parents' days, who can doubt that there have been others much crueler to theirs? Prusias, king of Bythnia, for no reason, not suffering pain as I am, killed his father; Ptolemy, king of Egypt, his father and mother and brothers and wife in order to take his pleasure of a concubine; Orestes, his mother Clytemnestra. The cruel emperor Nero had his mother, Agrippina, killed, simply for pleasure. These deserve their guilt, these are true parricides, but not I, who with my suffering, with my death, purge the guilt that might fall to me for their sorrow. There were many others more cruel who killed sons and brothers, compared to whom my error will not seem as grave. Philip, king of Macedonia; Herod, king of Judea; Constantine, Roman emperor; Laodice, queen of Cappadocia; and Medea, the necromancer. They all killed their beloved children and lovers for no reason, they themselves remaining safe. Finally, I think of the great cruelty of Phrates, king of the Parthians who, so that there would be no successor to follow him, killed Orodes, his aged father, and his only son and thirty brothers and sisters. These were crimes worthy of culpable culpability; to protect themselves from danger they killed their elders and descendants and brothers. It is true that although all this is so, I should not have done the evil they did; but that is not in my hands. You, my God, who are witness to what I am saying, you see how little strength I have, you see how my freedom is imprisoned, my feelings captive to a love for the dead caballero so powerful that it overpowers that which I have for my living parents.

PLEBERIO. My daughter, Melibea, what are you doing alone? What is it you want to tell me? Do you want me to come up there?

MELIBEA. My father, do not struggle or make an effort to come up where I am, for that would interfere with what I want to tell you. Soon now you will feel sadness at the death of your only daughter. My end has come, my rest and your suffering has come, my relief and your pain, my accompanied hour and your time of solitude. There will be no need, my honorable father, for instruments to ease my pain, only bells to entomb my body. If you listen to me without tears, you will hear the desperate reason for my imperative and happy departure. Do not interrupt it with weeping or words, for if you do you will more regret not knowing why I am killing myself than you are sorrowful to see me dead. Do not ask me or offer as response more than what I want to tell you willingly, because when the heart is laden with torment the ears are closed to counsel, and in such a time fruitful words, instead of calming, inflame ferment. Hear, my venerable father, my last words, and if, as I hope, you accept them you will not blame me for my error. You can clearly see and hear the sad and painful mourning felt throughout the city. You can hear the clamor of bells, people shouting, dogs howling, the breaking of weapons in tribute. I was cause of all this. On this day I cloaked in mourning and sackcloth most of the city's caballeros; I left many servants without a master, I stole away rations and alms for the poor and humble. I was the reason the dead have the company of the most perfect man born in grace; I took from the living the exemplar of nobility, of gallant inspiration, of finery and tapestry, of speech, bearing, courtesy, and virtue. I was the reason the earth will eternally embrace the most noble body and freshest youth the world has created in our age. And because you will be dismayed by the news of my unaccustomed crimes, I want to clarify for you more fully what happened. For many days, Father mine, a caballero, one you knew well, Calisto by name, suffered for love of me. You also knew his parents and his noble heritage. His virtues and goodness were manifest to all. So great was the torment of his love, and so little the opportunity in which he could speak to me, that he revealed his passion to an astute and wise woman named Celestina. She came to me on his behalf, and she drew my secret love from my breast. I related to her what I kept concealed from my beloved mother. In some way she won my will, and she fashioned a plan by which his desire and mine could be effected. If he loved me greatly, he did not live deceived. She designed the design for the sweet and ill-starred execution of his wishes. Vanquished by his love, I let him into your house. With ladders he overcame the walls of your garden, just as he overcame my resistance. I lost my virginity. From that pleasureful error of love we took joy for nearly a month. This past night he came as was accustomed, and as he was preparing to take leave, and as was disposed and ordered by mutable Fortune, following her disorderly custom, the walls were high, the night dark, the ladder flimsy, the servants he brought not skilled in that manner of serving, and as he was descending hastily to investigate the noise his servants were raising in the street, in that great rush he did not see the rungs well. He put his foot between them and fell, and with that woeful fall the deepest recesses of his brain were scattered across rocks and walls. The Furies cut their threads; they cut short his life without confession, they cut short my hope, they cut short my glory, they cut short my accompaniment. So, how cruel it would be, Father, if as he died falling I would fall into a lifetime of sorrow! His death invites mine, invites me and compels it to be soon, without hesitation, shows me that it must be by falling, in order to follow him in every way. Let it not be said of me, "Dead and gone, not remembered long . . ." Thus I shall content him in death, as I had little time to do in life. O my love Calisto, wait for me, I am coming! Hold up. If you wait for me, do not reproach the delay I create by giving this last account to my aged father, for I owe him much more.

O my most beloved father! I beg of you, if you have in this past and painful life had love for me, see that we are buried together, together have our obsequies! Some words of consolation I would offer you before my welcome end, gathered from those ancient books that you, to enliven my mind, ordered me to read; except that now, with my memory so perturbed by grief, I have lost them, and also because I see your unconcealed tears running down your wrinkled face. Carry my message to my dear and much loved mother; may she learn from you in detail the sad reason for my death. I am very grateful that I do not see her here before me! Accept, venerated father, the gifts of your age; for with long days long sadness is suffered. Accept the compensation for your senectitude and there receive your beloved daughter! I carry great sorrow with me, greater than yours, much greater than my aged mother's. May God be with you and with her. To Him I offer my soul. Guard this body that will fall before you from public view.

ACT TWENTY-ONE

(Alisa, Pleberio)

PLOT

Pleberio returns to his bedchamber weeping uncontrollably. His wife, Alisa, asks him the cause for such sudden grief. He tells her of the death of their daughter, Melibea, showing her the torn and bruised body and, with tears and moans and sobs, all concludes.

ONLY SCENE

ALISA. What is this, my señor Pleberio? Why these loud cries and lamentations? I was senseless from the grief that struck me when I heard you say our daughter was feeling pain. Now, hearing your wails, your loud voice, your unaccustomed plaints, your tears and anguish, it penetrated my inner being in such a way, it pierced my heart in such a way, that my perturbed senses were revived and the previously heard grief went through me like a spear. One sorrow evoked another, one sad feeling another. Tell me the cause for your laments. Why do you curse your honorable years? Why do you seek death? Why do you pull out your snow-white hairs? Why do you wound your honorable face? Is Melibea beset by some trouble? For God's sake, tell me, because if she is in pain I do not want to live.

PLEBERIO. Ay, ay, noble wife! Our joy is in the tomb! Our well-being is lost! We will not want to live! And because sorrow unknown gives greater pain, all at once without thinking, so that you go sooner to the tomb, so that I do not weep alone the mournful loss that bears upon us both, look there and see the one to whom you gave birth, the one I engendered, become a torn and bruised body. I heard the cause from her, and I have learned more from her grieving servant. Join me in weeping over the wound of our last years.

O, you who come to my sorrow, O friends and caballeros, help me feel my pain! O my daughter and my life! It will be cruelty for me to live longer than you; my sixty years are more worthy of burial than your twenty. The order of dying was upset by the sadness that afflicted you. O my white hairs, grown to know anguish, the earth would better have possessed you than these blond hairs I see before me! Harsh days abound, too many to live. I shall reproach death, accuse her of delay, of leaving me to live alone after you. May my life be taken since your so pleasing company has been taken from me. O my wife! Rise up from embracing her, and if any life remains in you, spend it with me in sad mourning, in affliction and sighing. And if it happens that your spirit rests with hers, if you have already left this life of pain, why would you wish that I bear this alone? In this you women have the advantage over men, for a terrible sorrow can take you from this world without your knowing, or at least you swoon, which is part of rest.

O a father's hard heart! How do you not break with grief, now that you are left without your beloved heir? For whom did I erect towers? For whom did I acquire honors? For whom did I plant arbors? For whom did I build ships? O cruel earth! How do you sustain my weight? Where will my disconsolate old age find shelter?

O fickle Fortune, agent and steward of earthly goods! Why did you not execute your cruel wrath, your restless waves, on he who is subject to you? Why did you not destroy my patrimony? Why did you not burn my dwelling? Why did you not lay waste to my vast lands? You should have left me the flowering plant over whom you had no power, and had you, tempestuous Fortune, given me a sad youth and merry old age, you would not have perverted order. Far better to suffer your deceits and deception at a strong and robust age, rather than at the end of my days.

O life of suffering, with the company of misery! O world! O world! Many have had much to say of you; many have eagerly dedicated themselves to your properties; they have compared you to various things they have heard, but I, from sad experience, will tell it. I, as one who did not prosper in the purchases and sales I made at your deceitful fair, as one who has until now kept silent your duplicity in order not to inflame your ire with my hatred, lest you wither the flower that today you cast out from your power. For now I will go without fear, as one who has nothing to lose, as one to whom your company is already vexatious, as a poor pilgrim, who without fear of cruel highwaymen makes his way singing in a loud voice. I thought, in my most tender years, that you and your deeds were governed by some form of order; now, having seen the pro and con of your prosperity, you seem to me a labyrinth of errors, a fearsome desert, a den of wild beasts, a game of men who dance the ring-around-the-rosy, a mud-filled lake, a region filled with thorns, a high mountain, a stony field, a meadow of serpents, a flowering orchard without fruit, a fountain of cares, a river of tears, a sea of miseries, labor without benefit, sweet poison, vain hope, false happiness, true grief. You entice us, false world, with your dish of delights, and with the tastiest bite you reveal the hook. We cannot flee from it, for it has already captured our wills. You promise much, you fulfill nothing; you cast us away from you so we cannot ask you to keep your vain promises. We run through the meadows of your deliciously vile vices, carefree, unbridled; you show us the snare when it is too late to turn back. Many left you with fear of being impetuously left behind; they will consider themselves fortunate when they see the reward you have bestowed on this sorrowful old man as payment for such long service. You put out our eyes and then anoint our heads with your consolation. You do evil to all, so that no sad person finds himself alone in adversity, and you say it is relief to the wretched, like me, to have companions in pain. Ah, disconsolate and old, how alone I am!

I was sad not to find a companion, an equal with a sorrow similar to mine, however much I sort through my exhausted memory, through the present and the past. For if the rigor and patience of Emilius Paulius should come to console me, he who with the loss of two sons within a week said that his courage worked to console the Roman people and not the people him, it does not satisfy me, for he was left with two other sons given in adoption. What companion would that Pericles, the Athenian captain, be to me in my sorrow, or the stalwart Xenophon, for their losses were of sons absent from their countries. It was not difficult for one of them to maintain a serene countenance and smooth brow, or for the other to reply to the messenger who brought the sad news of his son's death that he would not receive any penalty, for he himself felt no sorrow. For all this is very different from my suffering. And even less, evil-saturated world, can you say that Anaxagoras and I had a similar loss, that we are equal in our feeling, and that I should respond to my beloved daughter's death as he did the death of his only son, saying, "As I was mortal, I knew the one I engendered had to die," because my Melibea killed herself by her own choice, before my eyes, with a great fatigue of troubling love, and the other was killed in legitimate battle. O incomparable loss! O aggrieved old man! For however much I seek consolation, the less reason I find to be consoled. Though David, the prophet and king, wept over his son when he was ill, and on his death he did not, saying that it was near madness to weep over what could not be recovered, he was left with many others with whom to heal his wound. And I do not weep saddened that she is dead, but at the monstrous cause of her dying. Now with you, my unhappy daughter, I shall lose the fears and trepidations that have frightened me every day; only your death allows me to feel secure.

What shall I do when I go into your bedchamber and find it empty? What shall I do if you do not answer when I call? Who will be able to fill the great absence you leave with me? No one has lost what I have today, although I am reminded of something similar in the fierce animosity of Lambas de Auria, duke of Genoa, who with his own arms threw his wounded son from his ship into the sea. Because all these are deaths that, though they take life, are done for the sake of honor. But who forced my daughter to die but the prodigious force of love? So, obsequious world, what remedy do you offer my exhausted years? How can you command me to continue on earth knowing your deceits, the bonds, chains, nets with which you entrap our weak wills? Where do you put my daughter? Who will be my companion in my companionless dwelling? Who will be my solace in my declining years?

O love, love! I did not think that you had the strength or power to kill your subjects! I was wounded by you in my youth. I walked over your red hot coals. Why did you release me only to take revenge for my flight in my old age? I thought you had freed me from your bonds when I reached forty, when I was content with my conjugal companion, when I saw myself with the fruit you today cut from me. I did not think that you took vengeance on the children to repay the parents. Nor did I know whether you wounded with iron or burned with fire. You leave clothing intact and wound the heart. You make men love the ugly and it seems beautiful to them. Who gave you such power? Who gave you the name that is so unfitting? If you were Love, you would love your servants; if you loved them you would not give them pain: if they lived in happiness, they would not kill themselves as my beloved daughter has. How did they end, your servants and your agents? The duplicitous procuress Celestina died at the hands of the most faithful companions she had ever found in your venomous service. They died beheaded, Calisto from a fall, and my sad daughter chose the same death in order to follow him. You were the cause of all these things. You were given a sweet name but you work bitter deeds. You do not give out equal rewards: iniquitous is the law that is not equal for all. The sound of your name makes us happy, but serving you brings pain. Fortunate are those you did not know, and those with whom you had no dealings! "God," others called you, I do not know by what error of their senses. What god kills those he created? *You* kill those who follow you. Enemy of all reason! To those who serve you least you give the best gifts, until you have them in your dance of death. Enemy to friends, friend to enemies, why do you rule without order or harmony? They paint you blind, poor, and youthful; they put a bow in your hand that you aim and release haphazardly. Blinder still are your agents, who never feel or see the unsavory guerdon you give to those who serve you. Your fire is a lightning bolt that gives no signal of where it will strike. The wood your flames consume are the souls and lives of human creatures, so many that I scarcely know where to begin to name them; not only Christians but Gentiles and Jews, and all in payment of good services. What can you tell me of that Macias of our time, of whose sad end you were the cause? What did Paris do for you? Or Helen? What did Hypermnestra do? Or Aegisthus? Everyone knows that. And Sappho, Ariadne, Leander? What payment did you give them? Even David and Solomon you did not want to leave without pain. Samson paid what he deserved for your friendship, for having trusted a woman in whom you forced him to put his faith. And many others I will not mention, because I have enough to recount of my own pain.

I complain about the world because in it I was created, because had it not given me life I would not have engendered Melibea; had she not been born, she would not have loved; had she not loved, my querulous and disconsolate life would have run its course in my last years. O my good companion! O my battered and bruised daughter! Why did you not want me to stay your death? Why did you not take pity on your dearly loved mother? Why did you show yourself to be so cruel with your aged father? Why did you leave me when it is I who should have left you? Why did you leave me in such pain? Why did you leave me sad and alone *in hac lachrimarum valle?*

BIBLIOGRAPHY

Auerbach, Erich. *Mimesis: The Representation of Reality in Western Literature.* Introduction by Edward W. Said. Princeton: Princeton University Press, 2003.

Bataillon, Marcel. *'La Célestine' selon Fernando de Rojas.* Paris: Didier, 1961.

Bloom, Harold. *The Western Canon: The Books and Schools of the Ages.* New York: Harcourt and Brace, 1994.

Derrida, Jacques. *Dissemination.* Translated by Barbara Johnson. Chicago: University of Chicago Press, 1981 [1972].

Deyermond, A. D. *The Petrarchan Sources of "La Celestina."* Oxford: Oxford University Press, 1961.

Dunn, Peter N. *Fernando de Rojas.* Boston: Twayne, 1975.

Elliott, J. H. *Imperial Spain 1469–1716.* New York: Penguin, 2002.

Gilman, Stephen. *The Art of "La Celestina."* Madison: University of Wisconsin Press, 1956.

——. *The Spain of Fernando de Rojas: The Intellectual and Social Landscape of 'La Celestina.'* Princeton: Princeton University Press, 1972.

González Echevarría, Roberto. *Celestina's Brood: Continuities of the Baroque in Spanish and Latin American Literature.* Durham, NC: Duke University Press, 1993.

——. *Love and the Law in Cervantes.* New Haven: Yale University Press, 2005.

Green, Otis H. "The *Celestina* and the Inquisition." *Hispanic Review* 15 (1947): 211–16.

———. "Fernando de Rojas, converso and hidalgo." *Hispanic Review* 15 (1947): 384–87.

Herrero, Javier. "Renaissance Poverty and Lazarillo's Family: The Birth of the Picaresque." *Publications of the Modern Language Association of America* 94 (1979): 876–86.

Hinrichs, William H. "The Invention of the Sequel: Imaginative Expansion in Early Modern Spain." Ph.D. diss., Yale University, 2009.

Michael, Ian, and David G. Pattison. *Context, Meaning and Reception of 'Celestina': A Fifth Centenary Symposium.* Oxford: Carfax, Taylor and Francis/University of Glasgow, 2000.

Severin, Dorothy. *Memory in "La Celestina."* London: Támesis Books, 1970.